S0-BIZ-457

Hasan lifted the magic rod that commanded the jinn, and struck it upon the earth. Thunder roared, the ground shook and cracked, sulphurous billows of smoke roiled, and a hideous ifrit appeared. It resembled a huge, grotesquely muscular man, with two descending tusks and mighty wings.

"Dahnash bin Faktash reporting, O master of—" the creature boomed . . . then it did a double-take. "Oh, *brother!* Not *you* again!"

Hasan smiled. This was his ifrit, alright. "Jinn," Hasan said, "I order you to carry us back to Baghdad!"

Dahnash sighed. "Null program, mortal. Matter of Demonical Precedent, bin-Bishr vs. al-Khawwas, Pleistocene period."

Hasan blinked. "Then how do we escape from the dread Empire of Wak?"

"Oh, the usual—a seven-year journey on foot, enduring terrible perils and hardships and horrors and such, through frightful wastes and demon-haunted mountains without number . . ."

"Can you at least get us some horses?" Hasan groaned.

The ifrit smiled. "*That* I can handle, mortal." And Dahnash did smite the ground with his foot and dropped into the gulf that opened under him. "*Classy exit, no?*" his voice said as the ground closed.

PIERS ANTHONY

HASAN

Look for all these Tor books by Piers Anthony

ANTHOLOGY
THE E.S.P. WORM (with Robert E. Margroff)
GHOST (hardcover)
HASAN
PRETENDER (with Frances Hall)
PROSTHO PLUS
RACE AGAINST TIME
THE RING (with Robert E. Margroff)
SHADE OF THE TREE
STEPPE

PIERS ANTHONY

HASAN

A TOM DOHERTY ASSOCIATES BOOK

This is a work of fiction. All the characters and events portrayed in this book are fictional, and any resemblance to real people or incidents is purely coincidental.

HASAN

Copyright © 1969 by Ultimate Publishing Co., Inc.
Additional material copyright © 1986 by Piers Anthony Jacob

All rights reserved, including the right to reproduce this book or portions thereof in any form.

Reprinted by arrangement with The Borgo Press

First Tor printing : January 1986
Second printing: February 1987

A TOR Book

Published by Tom Doherty Associates, Inc.
49 West 24 Street
New York, N.Y. 10010

Cover art by Don Maitz
Map by George Barr

ISBN: 0-812-53131-0
CAN. ED.: 0-812-53132-9

Printed in the United States of America

0 9 8 7 6 5 4 3 2

*For Richard Delap, Ted White, and
Robert Reginald who believed in* Hasan
*before the mundanes did, and without whom
this novel might never have been published.*

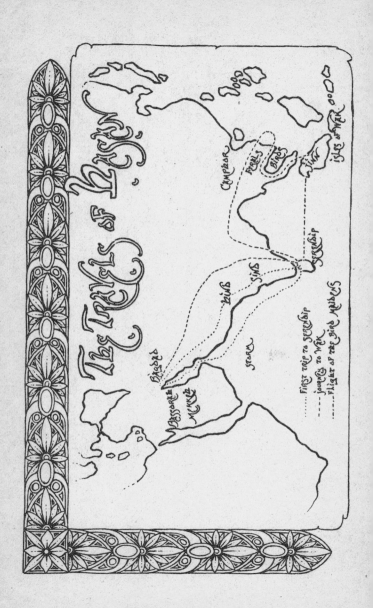

The Travels of Jaimal

.... First trip to Serendib
━━━━━━ Journey to War
━·━·━· Flight of the Bird Maidens

Chapter 1. Persian

"Gold!—from copper?" Hasan's loose headcloth fluttered with his impolite laughter.

The white-bearded Persian nodded gravely. He was dressed in a handsome robe and wore sturdy sandals: a man of moderate wealth. He looked remarkably pious under his tall white turban—but Persians were in bad repute in Bassorah.

Hasan had seen the man move slowly down the street, investigating the crowded stalls on either side. This was the metalworkers' section of the city, and there were splendid displays of copper, silver and gold, all intricately wrought. Many were far more spectacular than Hasan's own—yet the Persian had paused longest here, exclaiming to himself and shaking his head.

Hasan soon concluded there was little prospect for a sale, for otherwise the customer would have demeaned the merchandise in an effort to reduce its price. He pretended to read an old book, fretfully waiting for the intruder to move on and leave the space clear for some legitimate client.

Why did he linger so? Could he be a bandit from the marshes to the north, hiding from the Caliph's justice amidst the towering reeds? Impossible; yet—

At the hour of the mid-afternoon prayer the shops cleared of customers, but the Persian remained. Hasan did not trust him. All True Believers went to prayer-call promptly. There was something furtive in the way the man's eyes shifted about, though his voice was cultured and persuasive enough.

"Young man, you are a most talented craftsman. Your father trained you well."

"I have no father," Hasan replied shortly, trying to maintain his prejudice in the face of such flattery.

The Persian became unctuous. "Ah, the good man has

1

joined Allah—may His name be praised. And I—I have no son." Hasan grew uncomfortable under the man's intense scrutiny. "Yet I could hardly ask for a finer son than you. Your locks are as long and black as the mane of a fine stallion. Your body is straight and strong. If I had a son like you, I would weigh him down with wealth beyond tabulation."

"Wealth?" Hasan said, too quickly.

"Provided he didn't object to a little innocent alchemy, in a good cause."

"Alchemy!" This was forbidden in Bassorah.

"How else is an honest merchant to convert common copper, or even brass, into an equal weight—of gold?" The Persian's eye was fixed upon Hasan's, challenging him to protest.

And Hasan had laughed—but not for long. "If you can do such a thing—change copper to gold—why are you shopping here? You could be rich in a single day."

The Persian shook his head in seeming sadness. "And what are riches, to one who has no son?" An artful tear coursed down one wrinkled cheek, "I have no wife, no concubine, for how am I to trust a woman, and I an alchemist? Many men have begged me to instruct them in my secret art, and I have refused them all. But love of you has gotten hold upon my heart, for you are the fairest lad in all the city, and if you will consent to become my adopted son I will teach you this skill. You will toil no more with hammer and anvil; you will sweat no more in the heat of the charcoal and fire. No, not one more day!"

The old man was beginning to make sense. "Teach me now," Hasan said, maintaining his guard, for he suspected a swindle in spite of his desire to be convinced.

"Tomorrow," the Persian said. "I will bring my preparations here early in the morning, and you must make ready some copper. I do not ask you to believe until you see this for yourself, my son." With that he departed, leaving Hasan both doubtful and wildly excited.

Gold! Could it be?

He was too disturbed to finish the day patiently in his stall. He closed up shop and tramped blindly out of the city, his head spinning. Gold! Key to rich living. He would dine on candied locusts and choice Persian stew. He would sip sweet sherbet from the colored glass of Sidon. He would garb himself in a robe of embroidered damask, and sleep under a sheet of finest oriental silk. Choice slave-girls would fan away the biting flies while he dispensed largesse to groveling beggars and needy holy men and thus store up great favor with Allah.

He looked up to see the dry mud flats, cut by shallow irrigation ditches, that stretched from the two great rivers toward the foul marshes. The People of the Reeds dwelt in floating huts, not so far away, neighbors of unclean pigs. They sat with their vicious dogs around fires of buffalo dung. Hasan knew little of them for civilized men were not welcome in the reedy swamps. There had been occasional skirmishes . . .

He turned back to face the city. Gold! The cultivated fields became rosy in the glow of dusk, the hot sands saffron. Clustered date-palms beckoned in a momentary gust of wind, and swarms of sea-fowl dotted the sky, calling him to his destiny.

The sun sank, and Hasan quickly spread out his prayer-mat, and kneeled with his face to the distant west of Mekkeh. He prostrated himself ritually and called upon Allah for blessing. Gold!

His old, careworn mother was cynical. Hasan sat bare-footed on a cushion of the divan, leaned against the plastered wall, and smacked his lips on stale bread and sour camel's milk while she harangued him about the business of the day. She was adept at prying and wheedling information that didn't concern her, he thought, as were all women whom time had deprived of physical charm. She had the story from him almost as he entered the run-down dwelling.

"Hasan, don't pay attention to such superstitions. Beware especially of Persians, and never do anything they urge upon you. They are nothing but infidels and sharpers, and if this man pretends to alchemy you can be sure it is only to steal the money of an honest man.''

''But we are poor, Mother,'' Hasan pointed out rudely, half lost in his dreams of wealth. The good house, now suffering from lack of repair, was all that remained of their original fortune. ''How could he covet the little bit of gold I have in the shop, when he has the power to manufacture as much as he wants, from copper?''

She looked at him despairingly. ''How can you trust the word of a stranger—a Persian!—who makes such a ridiculous promise? Have you forgotten already the leeches and loafers who promised you their undying friendship—until the wealth your father left was exhausted catering to their expensive tastes? And where are these friends now? Where would *you* be now, were it not for the kindness of your father's friend, the goldsmith, who took you in and taught you his trade?''

''But I am tired of this trade,'' Hasan said defensively. ''I thought all goldsmiths were rich, but—''

''But, but!'' she exclaimed. ''My son, Bassorah is a wealthy city, for this is where the long sea meets the richest farmland east of Egypt. The traders come here in great number, and the boatsmen and camel-drivers and farmers. But you can't expect to make your fortune as a goldsmith without working for it. All day you sit idly in your shop and read books about the adventures of liars like that Sindbad of the Sea, instead of calling out to passing merchants who might pay you well for your effort. No wonder you sell nothing!''

''I'm sure this Persian is honest,'' Hasan argued uncertainly. ''He wears a turban of pure white muslin, in the best manner of the True Believer. And he wants to adopt me as his son!''

He ignored her look of reproach and retired, but sleep was slow in coming. Gold!

*   *   *

Hasan woke at dawn, performed the morning ablution, and rushed to his shop without speaking to his mother. Anxiously he cast about for copper; this was a detail he'd almost forgotten. It would not be wise to use a finished utensil, because if anything were to go wrong the loss would be awkward, particularly when his mother learned of it. Ah—there was a broken platter that would have to be melted down anyway. It was copper, or at least good brass, and it should do well enough.

Before long the Persian appeared. Hasan jumped up. "Welcome, O noble Uncle! Let me kiss your venerable hands."

The Persian restrained him. "We must do this business quickly, before the neighboring smiths arrive, or everyone will know the secret. Have you heated your furnace?"

"O yes, Uncle!"

"Set up the crucible and apply your bellows."

Hasan hastened to comply, forgetting in his eagerness yesterday's promise of freedom from such labors. The fire blazed up hotly, until it seemed the crucible itself would melt.

"Where is your copper?"

"Here, Uncle!"

"Take your shears and cut it into small pieces and melt them down promptly."

Hasan was amazed at the businesslike air of the man who yesterday had waxed so sentimental. He followed the terse instructions, sweating profusely under his tunic from the unaccustomed heat and effort. The metal became a thick liquid as he wrestled mightily with the bellows.

The Persian inspected it approvingly. He removed his turban, reached inside, and brought out a folded wad of paper. A few ounces of yellow powder were inside. "Stand back, boy," he said, "but don't let up for a moment on the bellows."

Hasan pumped until he thought he would expire, while still trying valiantly to observe every detail of the magic.

The old man held the paper above the crucible. "In the

name of Jabir ibn-Hayyan, the father of alchemy, and by
virtue of this catalyst he created and bequeathed to me in
dire secrecy, let this base metal be converted forthwith to
purest gold!'' He shook in some of the bright powder.

It seemed to Hasan that the pot bubbled angrily and that
an ominous glow suffused the room. This was evil magic,
and the Persian had not invoked the name of Allah. . . .

''Hold!'' and Hasan relaxed gratefully. He wiped his
smarting eyes and peeked into the crucible.

Gold.

''Test it,'' said the Persian, smiling. ''You will find it
to be of rare quality.''

Hasan quenched it and manhandled the still hot mass out
of the pot and rubbed it with a file. It was genuine. He
leaned against the counter for support, dazed by the reality. Gold! The magician had not been lying.

The Persian gave him no rest. ''Quickly, son, hammer it
into an ingot before the merchants come.''

Hasan bent hastily to the task, while the Persian watched
with an inscrutable expression. ''Are you married?''

''No, sir!'' The ingot was almost shaped.

''Very good,'' the old man said to himself, with another appraising glance at Hasan. ''Now carry this gold to
the market and sell it quickly. Don't waste time haggling
over the price; as soon as you have a good offer, take the
money, go home without a word to anyone, and put it
away where no one will see it. We don't want the people
to interrogate you about the origin of this gold.''

Hasan agreed, although he regretted being denied an
immediate spending spree. His mother would insist that he
put most of the money back into the goldsmith business,
and he would get little pleasure from it. Of course, if she
saw the ingot, she might not let him sell it at all, since
many fine utensils could be fashioned from it.

He picked up the ingot, which weighed several pounds,
wrapped it in a fold of his tunic, and rushed to the richest
business section of Bassorah.

The assembled businessmen were amazed at the size and

quality of the ingot. Bidding was rapid. "A thousand dinars," a fat purple-cloaked moneychanger offered. Hasan turned his back disdainfully. "Twelve hundred," another said, barely concealing his eagerness to possess such refined gold. Hasan yawned. "Fifteen hundred," a green-pantalooned merchant said.

Hasan studied the last bidder calmly. "Allah open on you another door," he said, in a time-honored convention that indicated too low a bid. That is, Allah would have to open the door to merchandise at such a price, for Hasan certainly wouldn't.

The first moneychanger squinted, catching on to the fact that this young man was not entirely innocent about the value of his merchandise. "Eighteen hundred dinars—no more," he said.

"Allah open—" Hasan said, then remembered the Persian's warning. "This fine gold is a gift at such a price—but I am weary of carrying it. Take it for two thousand dinars."

In such manner he completed the richest transaction of his life.

"Look at this, Mother!" he cried as he burst into the house with the hefty purse of coin. "My father the Persian has shown me how to make gold from a broken platter, and I sold it for half a year's income, and I'm going to be rich!"

The old woman shook her head lugubriously, despite the proof displayed before her. Hasan had forgotten his resolve to hide the news from her. "No good will come of this. It is devil's money." And she blessed herself, saying "There is no majesty and there is no might, except in Allah, the Glorious, the Great!"

"I must take more metal to the shop," Hasan said, paying no attention to her words. He picked up a large metal mortar, a pot once used for crushing onions, garlic and corn cakes. Heedless of his mother's expostulations, he carried it out the door.

The Persian was still sitting in the shop, relaxing in its

shade with his turban in his lap. His hair was almost as white as the headpiece. "What are you doing with that thing?" he demanded.

"I'm going to put it on the fire and turn it into gold," Hasan said.

"Have the jinn taken your wits?" the Persian exclaimed, choking. "The surest way to arouse suspicion would be to appear in the market twice in a day with mysterious ingots of perfect gold. The merchants would be certain you had stolen them, and this would cost us both our lives."

Hasan was chagrined. "I hadn't thought of that."

"If I am to teach you this craft—and there is more to it than mere sprinkling of powder—you will have to promise to practice it no more than once a year. That will easily bring enough income to maintain you."

"I agree, O my lord!" Hasan said, anxious to master the process. So long as no limit was set upon the amount converted in that annual session. . . .

He placed the crucible over the furnace and heaped more charcoal on the fire.

"Now what are you up to?"

"How am I to learn this craft if we don't go through the steps again?"

"There is no majesty and no might save in Allah!" exclaimed the Persian, laughing at the youth's audacity. "You have the singlemindedness of a thirsty camel, lad. But you hardly demonstrate the wit required for this noble craft. Do you expect to learn such an art in the middle of the street? With all the grasping shoppers and beggars looking on? Don't you know what they do to proven alchemists?"

"But—"

"If you really want to master this mystery immediately, come to my house, where there will be privacy."

"Let's go!" Hasan replied immediately, closing up his shop.

But as he followed the Persian, he began to reflect upon his mother's warning. Such men did have a bad reputation.

How could he be certain this was not some elaborate trick to lure him into slavery, perhaps in the uncharted marshland? Handsome young artisans were valuable, and few questions were asked if their tongues were cut out. Did he really know this stranger well enough to trust himself to his house? His feet dragged, and finally he stopped in confusion.

The Persian turned to see him lagging. "Are you having foolish second thoughts *now*, my son? Here I am, trying to do you the greatest favor of the age because of the love I have in my heart for you—while you hang back, accusing me of bad intent!"

Hasan felt quite guilty, but his doubt remained. The man was leading the way out of the city, and it was hard not to suspect pork in the cookpot.

"Ah, the folly of youth!" the Persian expostulated. "Well, boy, if you're afraid to come to my house, I must go to yours. I can teach you there just as easily, so long as you provide the materials."

Hasan brightened. "You can?"

"Show me the way, son."

Hasan's mother was not delighted. "You brought the idolator *here*? I will not share the roof with him!"

"But this way he is proving his good faith. What harm could he do at my house?"

"What harm could a cobra do in your house? A swordtusked boar? You—"

"He's standing outside our door right now."

"No! He is nothing but a ghoul, an evil influence. I will not remain while he sets foot in this house!"

"But he is teaching me to make gold out of—"

"He is making mush out of your brains. I'll stay at my cousin's house until he is gone." She was already busy setting the house in order, however, lest the unwelcome guest find anything to criticize. At length she finished her preparations and left by the back way, so as not even to see the Persian, and Hasan was free to invite the guest inside. Then he had to run to the market to buy food, while the Persian waited some more.

Hasan spread his best circular cloth on the floor, in the corner near the two divans, and arranged the meal. He set up a stool supporting a large brass tray, upon which were several copper dishes. Around these were round, flat cakes of bread, some cut limes, and small wooden spoons. He had hired a servant-boy for the meal, who now brought large napkins and a basin and ewer filled with water to each of them. They rinsed their mouths and washed their right hands ceremoniously as they sat cross-legged on the two divans. It would never do to eat with an unclean hand.

"In the name of Allah, the Compassionate, the Merciful," Hasan said, serving himself first in accordance with the ritual. This showed that the food he offered his guest was wholesome. He drew a dish of mutton toward him, stewed with assorted vegetables and with apricots, and removed a morsel with the aid of a piece of bread.

The Persian did likewise. For a moment it looked as though he was about to touch the food with his left hand, and Hasan marveled at this. All True Believers knew that the left hand was unclean. It was unthinkable that the hand that cleaned the privates should ever touch the face . . . yet the visitor had almost—

He was imagining things. Even in Persia, they were not that slovenly. He should abolish such unnatural suspicions.

Hasan drank some cool water from a porous earthen bottle. "Praise be to Allah," he said—but did not mention that it had been many weeks since Allah had blessed him with a repast like this.

"May your drink produce pleasure," the Persian replied, also following the ritual. But his gaze was calculating.

"Now there is the fellowship of bread and salt between us," Hasan exclaimed as they ate. "What loyal servant of Allah would violate that?"

"What, indeed," the guest replied dryly.

They finished the meal, and the Persian leaned back, belched politely, but did not wash his hand again. "What did you bring for dessert?"

Hasan stammered in confusion. He had forgotten this detail.

"No trouble, my son. You just run down to the market again and fetch us something suitable, some sweetmeats." He closed his eyes comfortably, anticipating no refusal.

Hasan rose hastily and dashed off, forgetting to send the servant, and returned shortly with an armful of pastries. The Persian eyed the monstrous amount the young man had brought home in his enthusiasm and shook his head with mock perplexity. "O my son—the likes of you delight the likes of me. Nowhere, in all Bassorah, could I have found a *more* appropriate subject for my purposes!" He hardly bothered to conceal the sneer, but Hasan in his naivete flushed with pleasure.

After they had eaten their fill and washed hands and face again, the Persian stretched lazily and uttered the magic words. "O Hasan, fetch the gear."

Hasan shot out of the house like a colt let out to fresh green pasture in the spring. He ran to his shop and carried all the apparatus he could sustain back to the house, once more panting and sweating with the exertion he hoped to be relieved of so soon.

The Persian withdrew from his turban a package of some weight. "My son, this wrapping contains three pounds of the elixir I demonstrated this morning, and each ounce of it will transform a pound of copper into the finest gold. When this is gone, I will make up another batch for you."

Hasan trembled as he took the package and stared at the glittering yellow powder. "What do you call this?" he inquired. "How is it made?"

The Persian laughed far more than the innocent questions deserved.

"Must you know everything at once, boy? There will be time for that later. The manufacture of this elixir is quite complicated; for now you should be satisfied to keep quiet and master its proper application." Hasan did not notice the increasingly overbearing tone or the poor breeding the laughter betrayed. Gold dazzled his mind's eye. He found a brass platter and cut it up and threw the pieces into the melting pot. He blew up the fire until the metal melted, then shook in a little powder and stirred the mixture vigorously. He was so intent on what he was doing that he never thought to call upon Allah for blessing.

Nevertheless, the molten potful steamed up, shimmered, and took on the golden hue. "It worked!" Hasan shouted. "I did it! I made gold!"

He removed his crucible from the heat and fumbled with the tongs as the golden lump cooled. He did not see the Persian break open one of the surplus pastries, shake in a little powder of a different complexion and seal it up again. He did not overhear the exuberant chuckle.

"You have done very well, my son," the Persian said. "You seem to have a natural talent for what I have in mind, and I am most pleased with your performance. Did I mention that I have a daughter, who is as lovely a girl as anyone has ever seen?"

Hasan pulled his eye momentarily away from the glistening mass of gold. "Sir, I thought you were unmarried. How can you have a daughter?"

The Persian paused, but corrected himself quickly. "You are astute, my boy. True, I have no wife *now*. I had one, a very discerning and gracious and obedient woman of singular beauty, but she died five years ago and I have brought my daughter up and educated her myself. Since you are to be my adopted son, it seems appropriate that I marry her to you."

Things began to fall into place for Hasan. A marriageable daughter; an offer of unlimited gold. The full commitment was coming to light.

"Well, I hadn't planned to—"

"I assure you, she is no less beautiful than yourself, a fitting match. Her face is like the full moon, her hair darker than the night, her cheeks rosy as—"

"Shouldn't I see her first?" Hasan asked cautiously, disturbed by the manner the Persian seemed to be reading his face.

"Her posture is like a slim bamboo among plants; her eyes are as large and dark as those of a delicate young deer."

"Yes, but—"

"Her two breasts are like fresh round pomegranates; her buttocks are like wind-smoothed hillocks of sand . . . and she is just fourteen years of age!"

"Done!" cried Hasan, carried away by this vision. After all, there was always the gold, in case the damsel fell short of the description.

"Congratulations! Let's celebrate with another sweet-meat," the Persian said, pressing the one he held on Hasan.

The young man bit into it automatically, careless of all ceremony, thinking of gold and hillocks of sand. Once more he forgot to praise Allah before taking food.

A vacant expression came over his face. He reeled and collapsed, unconscious.

"O dog of an Arab!" the Persian exalted. "O carrion of the gallows! How many months have I searched for as handsome an innocent as you. Yet how near you came to slipping my net. But now I have you! If an elephant smelled that bhang I fed you, he would sleep from year to year."

Nevertheless, he took the precaution of binding Hasan hand and foot, gagging him, and packing him into a great chest, which he locked. Then he gathered together all the money from the sale of the first ingot of gold, and every-thing else of value in the house including the second ingot, and packed it all into another chest. Before long he had summoned a porter from the market and assigned him the second trunk, instructing him not to drop it. He dallied only long enough to scribble a message on the wall, and departed in haste.

A rented ship, provisioned and crewed, was waiting for him in a special harbor outside the city, in the direction he had attempted to lead Hasan earlier. He paid off the porter, loaded the merchandise on board, and set sail immediately with a fair wind.

What a welcome awaited Hasan's mother when she came home that evening! The door was open, the rooms ransacked, and her cherished son was gone. All that remained were cryptic words printed crudely on one wall, near a half-eaten bit of sweetbread.

The spirit came and wakened one from bed;
But when he woke, he found the spirit fled!

Chapter 2. Voyage

Vinegar and acrid powder choked Hasan, and he came to his senses coughing and sneezing violently. The world seemed to be swaying and tilting in crazy combinations, now one way and now another, so that he could hardly orient himself. He felt sick.

A black ifrit stood before him. "So the Arab pig opens his eyes!" a harsh voice said near his ear. Hasan recognized the voice of the Persian, despite the change in tone. Was he a demon?

His eyes cleared slowly, and he saw that what he faced was not an infernal creature, but a grinning Negro slave, a eunuch. Beyond the slave was a short wooden deck, and beyond that—

He was aboard a ship! He could see the lapping waves, the distant shoreline. No wonder he had reeled to the steady rocking of the floor. He was sitting on one of the great chests his mother had saved, and beside him sat the Persian. How had such a thing come about?

"There is no majesty and there is no might, except in Allah, the Glorious, the Great!" he swore. "We belong to Allah and to Him we shall return."

"Don't prate your ridiculous faith aboard this ship!" the Persian snapped. 'You are in my power now, you incredible simpleton."

Hasan began to understand. He had eaten a pastry this man had handed him—and suddenly found himself among strangers and far from home. He had been drugged! But why?

"O my father," he said quietly, "what have you done? Didn't we eat bread and salt together, so that neither could betray the other?"

The Persian stared at him. "Do you expect me to be bound by your superstitions? Your life means nothing to me, and your friendship less. I have slain nine hundred and ninety-nine whelps like you, and you shall surely be the thousandth." His expression was so serious that Hasan could not doubt that he meant what he said. All of it had been a trick after all, to lure him into this situation. His mother's warning had been valid, and his own early suspicions justified.

He shifted his hands and found them tied behind him. His feet were free, but he was helpless. Yet obviously they weren't going to kill him right away; the ship must have a destination, and a far one, or it would not have been employed at all. Was he to be a sacrifice? He had heard of such things, at least in the far reaches of the world where the jinn-folk lived. He should be safe for a few days, at least.

Hasan was frightened, but not nearly as much as he thought he ought to be. Perhaps the drug the Persian had given him still affected his senses. Still, he had always longed for adventure and never had the means to undertake it. Now it had come upon him unawares, and though the shaft of fate was painful, it was not wholly repulsive. The Persian might be bluffing, testing him, trying out his mettle; if not there were a thousand things that might happen before the sentence was carried out. Well, perhaps a hundred, or at least ten. . . .

"Who are you?" he asked the Persian. "What do you want with me?"

The man studied him as if annoyed that there had been no screaming or begging. "I am Bahram the Guebre, the foremost magician of Persia. I will use you to obtain the essential ingredient for my elixir of gold, and you will not survive that use."

"Why don't you kill me now, Bahram?" Hasan was astonished at his own temerity; he had never imagined that he could contemplate death so calmly.

"Don't be impatient, lad; you have three months to live yet; maybe more. I would have killed you before now, if more important considerations didn't restrain this pleasure."

"Do you expect me to live three months without eating?" Hasan asked him. "How good a magician are you?"

The Persian refused to take offense at the tone. "Untie his hands and give him some water," he directed his slave.

The eunuch came forward cheerfully. He was big and wore bright red pantaloons; evidently he had once been muscular, but now was running to fat. His eyes were sleepy, but his hands, as he reached around Hasan to undo the cord, were clever and gentle. "Now tread lightly, Arab," he murmured into Hasan's ear as he worked.

Hasan stretched his arms. His wrists were chafed and stiff where the rope had bound them, but were after all serviceable. He accepted the jug the slave offered. As he drank, his eyes ran over the ship.

It appeared to be a fair-sized merchant ship, built for the open sea. There were no oars—if merchanters carried oarsmen, there would be little space for cargo—and he could see the tall center mast reaching up into the single square sail. She might be as much as forty-five feet from stem to stern—but old. Even though he was no Sindbad, he could sense the wallow and see the age of the calking in the worn deck. This tub would not be worth much in a storm.

Hasan finished his drink and returned the bottle to the eunuch. "Praise be to Allah," he said, and launched himself from the chest.

And sprawled on the deck. The slave had neatly tripped him. He was neither as sleepy nor as stupid as he looked, that eunuch.

"Tie the ingrate up again," Bahram said. "We won't give him another chance to betray our trust."

"Betray your trust!" Hasan exploded. "Why you dog, dog-fathered, grandson of a dog! How can you act other than as a dog? *Trust!*"

Bahram stood up. "By the virtue of the Heat and the Light of the Fire I worship, do not tempt me to violence, boy!"

"What temptation remains for the uncircumcised cur who foully betrays bread and salt?"

"Silence!" the Persian roared. His hand swung round to deal Hasan a blow that sent him crashing to the deck. This time, with his hands bound, he struck face down. He felt his teeth digging into the dirty planking as he passed out.

His trial was not over. Sea water dashed in his face brought him spluttering to his senses a second time. He knew that only a moment had passed. His nose stung fearfully in the salt and he could taste the blood running over his bruised lips. His front teeth felt as though they had been driven back into his head; angry tears trickled down his cheeks.

The eunuch propped him up and mopped away some of the mess. "You have more to lose than a few drops of blood, Arab," he murmured, his voice so soft that Hasan knew the magician was not intended to overhear. "Appease his fancies; it won't hurt Allah, the All-knowing."

Hasan nodded, not certain whether this was a genuine condolence or another trap. Certainly he would not again insult the Persian to his face. Not while he was bound, anyway.

"Make a Fire!" Bahram said, and two young boys, white servants, appeared with a brazier. They filled it with charcoal and tinder and struck sparks into it, and soon a hot flame crept up through the chunks. Hasan wondered what would happen if such a stove were to be overturned on the deck. No—the wood had just been soaked down, and would not ignite.

"What is the purpose of that?" Hasan inquired, discovering that his fall had not affected his power of speech, despite the discomfort of teeth and nose.

"This is the Fire, my Lady of Light and Sparkles! She is the goddess I worship, not your foul bread-and-salt Allah. See how bright She is! How fair!" Indeed, as the magician looked into the flame his expression was rapt, and he stood tall and bold.

Hasan was disgusted, but he held his peace. How could he ever have been fooled by such a creature?

Bahram turned to him, his eyes burning fanatically. "O Hasan—this is my Beloved! Worship Her as I do, and I swear to you I will give you half my wealth and marry you to my maiden daughter. Worship the Fire, and I will set you free and find some other sacrifice." He waited expectantly.

Hasan forgot his recent resolution.

"Woe to you!" he cried out angrily. "You are a criminal who prays to a vanishing element instead of to the True God, the King of the Omnipotent, the Creator of Night and Day. How can you desert the God of the Prophets Moses, Jesus, and the great Mohammed? This is not worship you practice—it is nothing but calamity!"

Bahram stiffened. "O dog of the Arabs, are you refusing to worship with me?"

"I will never turn my face away from Allah!"

The man's eyes smoldered like the coals of the brazier, but he did not strike Hasan again. He faced the fire, dropped to his knees, and prostrated himself before it ritually. "O Sacred Fire, I will punish this infidel for his blasphemy!"

He stood up and spoke to the eunuch. "Cast him on the deck on his face!" The slave obeyed, muttering dolefully into Hasan's ear.

"I told you. I told, Arab. You didn't have to renounce Allah in your heart. 'Appease his fancies,' I said, 'It won't hurt your god,' I said. But you—" Then Hasan hit the deck, more gently this time, and the remaining advice was lost.

"Strip him down," Bahram directed. Hasan felt the eunuch's careful black hands pulling away his tunic, leaving him bare from neck to calf.

"I don't like this any better than you do," the slave muttered as he worked, untying and retying the bindings. "Next time, keep your mouth shut, eh?"

"Take your elephant-hide whip and beat him!" the
Persian said. And the eunuch dutifully laid on with the
stiff knotted thongs.

Hasan had determined to maintain silence during the
beating, and refuse the magician the satisfaction of his
screams, but a cry of agony tore free at the first blow.
Hasan had never before experienced such pain. His entire
back flamed up with the savage rasp of the rough leather.
The second blow fell and he screamed again; the very skin
seemed to be wrenched from his body. A third blow, this
time across the posteriors—and now he felt the blood
running down from the cuts of the lash.

A fourth blow: "Allah!" he screamed. "Protect me!"
But there was no protection. A fifth blow; he wrenched up
his head and implored the Almighty in the name of Mohammed, the Chosen Prophet—but there was no succor.

A sixth blow. He thought he would faint with the pain,
the terrible destruction of his body . . . but he could not
faint. Now the tears rolled down his face like the dripping
sea water, and in the humiliation and agony he said what
he could no longer avoid saying.

"In the name of the Fire: mercy!"

The seventh blow did not fall.

"Raise him up," the Persian said gently. "We shall be
eating now."

The slave clothed him again and set him on the chest,
and the servant-boys brought wine and boiled rice and set
them before him. But Hasan was ashamed of himself—
though he had never renounced Allah in spirit—and did
penance by fasting. He refused to eat the lowly rice or sip
the forbidden beverage.

"You'll eat when you get hungry, boy," Bahram said
wisely. "If not today, tomorrow." Hasan knew he was
right.

Hasan was kept tied at all times except for meals. He
never had a chance to look around the ship, or to talk with
the crewmen, though he saw half a dozen of them in the
course of their normal duties. It was evident that they

feared and disliked the magician, but would not interfere. Undoubtedly they had been hired for such voyages before, or were under regular contract with Bahram, and had learned to ignore the cries and appeals of helpless captives.

Each day the ship coursed south along the Persian shore, farther away from Bassorah and civilization. Each night it hove to in some natural harbor for safety from the demons of night and water. Some days the winds were adverse, and the ship was unable to make significant progress; Hasan blessed Allah for such weather. On other days the winds were fair, and Hasan watched the shore parade by, its rocks and beaches and inlets ever less familiar, in growing despair.

The days became weeks, the weeks months, or so it seemed to one who had no accurate way to reckon time. Hasan also bemoaned the fact that he was unable to perform the required ablutions and prayers. First, the Persian would have beaten him again if he had attempted any obvious homage to Allah, and he did not feel strong enough to undergo such pain the prescribed five times each day. Second, he could be certain of neither the precise time of day nor the direction of the Holy City, which he had to face during prayer. Third, he had no water with which to cleanse himself before prayer. Fourth, he was constantly bound, and could not accomplish the motions and gestures of the normal ritual. He felt unclean and defiled, but there was nothing he could do, and after a time he ceased to worry about it unduly. Allah was all-powerful and all-knowing; if it was His will that his servant be unable to pray properly, who was Hasan to protest?

The shoreline became mountainous, then leveled off into a steady jungle. Great rivers carried their rich sediment into the sea. At times the shore on the opposite side had been visible, but now, crane his head around as he might, Hasan could see nothing but a blue expanse of sea. He heard the crewmen talking, and knew that the ship was approaching the magical land of Hind. This must be their destination, and the number of his days was dwindling.

"Praise be to Allah," he said to himself fervently. "May he send a wind to dash this vessel away from that shore!"

This time it seemed that his informal prayer was to be answered. In the afternoon a sudden blackness came upon the sky, and the sea grew dark and wild. A strong wind sprang up so quickly that it caught the sail before the crewmen could furl it and blasted the ship away precipitously from land. She rocked and pitched sickeningly and her old timbers creaked; Hasan himself, who had much more to gain than to lose, began to fear for his life. A sailor screamed as the boat yawed and pitched him into the whipping sea; before his friends could help him he was gone. They brought the sail down, somehow, but it was already torn. It would be many days before they could make it serviceable again.

Still the wind rose, screaming through the ancient rigging and smashing sheets of water over the tired deck. Now the rain was marching over the ocean, a nebulous army, and the dark of the storm was closing down upon them. Men ran wildly and uselessly about as planking tore loose from the deck and upended into the liquid melee. There was little they could do now except hold on and pray.

Hasan, still bound, was helpless—but he seemed to be in no more trouble than the others. They all were prisoners for the time being.

Suddenly the stout captain worked his way to the space where Hasan lay and the dampened Persian clung with his two boys and the eunuch. "By Allah!" the captain swore, "this is all because of that fair youth you are mistreating. Let him go, and the wrath of God will abate."

"Mind your own business!" Bahram screamed at him. "This youth is mine, and I will not tolerate any interference. Go secure the ship; that's the only way you can save us all."

The captain made as if to release Hasan himself, but the eunuch, at a sign from Bahram, interposed. The captain withdrew, grumbling.

For a moment the sea calmed. Then there was a scream of fear. Hasan looked out over the water where a crewman pointed and beheld a monstrous and terrifying shape. It was an enormous funnel, tiny where it touched the water, but whirling up into a black cloud as big as the sky. High-pitched thunder came from it, a sustained scream like that of a savage sandstorm.

"A marid!" the captain exclaimed, naming the most powerful of the tribes of jinn. "Now we are lost indeed!"

Every person watched, fascinated, as that awful creature waltzed across the ocean, now leaning toward the ship, now artfully retreating. In a moment it would tire of its game and descend upon the ship and tear it apart and smash the fragments, wood, cloth and bone, into the hungry wake.

"Kill the magician!" the captain cried. "He is responsible for this. Appease that marid!"

The crewmen rushed upon Bahram in a body. The Persian drove them back temporarily with threats and demonaic gestures, for they were all afraid of him still, and the big eunuch got between them again. Three men bore him down; a knife flashed, the ship rocked, and suddenly the slave was crawling across the deck, bleeding from a gut wound. Once more the ship pitched, and he rolled over the edge of the deck and disappeared.

The two young servants screamed and tried to escape. They too were caught and sacrificed. Only the Persian himself remained, as the crewmen gathered to bring down the last of the supernatural's grievances. As they delayed, in a larger swell of the sea that forced them all to cling frantically to the tenuous woodwork, Bahram somehow made his way to Hasan and cut his ties.

"It was a mistake, my son," he shouted through the gale. "I do not mean to sacrifice you. Come, I will dress you in fine raiment and take you back to your native land. We are friends!"

The marid lifted its tail into itself and whirled back into the clouds. It had spared the ship. The wind eased and the

waves subsided. "You see!" Bahram harangued the crewmen. "There is no quarrel between me and Allah; none
between me and this fair lad. The marid was only passing
by, and you chose to interpret this as divine intent. You
are attacking us for nothing!" And he put his arm around
Hasan and kissed him on the cheek.

The captain hesitated. "Is this true, O man of Bassorah?"

Hasan was too confused by the storm and the abrupt
change in his situation to answer immediately. "Of course
it's true!" shouted the Persian, instilling belief by the
power of his voice. "The marid has gone and Allah has made
the water quiet. What other evidence do you need?"

Still the captain hesitated, fingering his knife. He was
not, in the clutch, a timid man, and he did not change his
mind easily. "I want an answer of the boy, the one you
have tied and beaten."

Hasan gathered his wits. Certainly he could never trust
the Persian again, and would be foolish to throw away this
chance to eliminate him permanently. One word would do
it—

He opened his mouth, but Bahram spoke first, directly
and compellingly. "O my son, in the name of Allah,
forgive me for the evil I have done you and do not seek
revenge. Let me prove to you how sure a friend I can be. I
repent my cruelty to you, and wish only to make amends."

Hasan had thought he hated this man, but there was
something so touching and persuasive about the magician's
present appeal that he knew he could not go through with
it.

"You see," Bahram shouted immediately to the crew,
"*he* does not wish my end. Forget the matter and go about
your business!" And the captain, an honest but uncertain
man, in the face of Hasan's silence, obeyed.

Things were considerably more pleasant after that. Hasan
was provided with good clothing and permitted to perform
his ablutions in the prescribed manner. Several members
of the crew joined him every day. Bahram said no more

about fire worship, though he did not honor Allah either. Everyone was friendly now and Hasan learned many things about the structure and handling of a ship.

Several days were required to repair the sail and the other damaged sections of the ship. Hasan was anxious to commence the journey home, but somehow, in those idle days, he found himself agreeing to Bahram's proposal that they proceed to the original destination.

"O my son, surely you don't believe that I ever intended you evil? I was only testing you in order to be certain that you were indeed a devout servant of Allah and a fit match for my lovely daughter. Only in the heat of the fire can the surest sword be tempered. And you have vindicated yourself gloriously! How can you give up the marvelous adventures that await you, now that you have proven your right to them? Do you want them to laugh in Bassorah and say 'Hasan journeyed three months, but changed his mind in sight of adventure'?"

"What adventure is this?" Hasan asked cautiously.

"O my son, we are bound for the Mountain of Clouds, the most magnificent mountain in the world, upon whose summit are the ingredients for the elixir that makes gold. You want to make more elixir, don't you?"

"Yes, but—"

"I knew you would agree. I knew you had the heart of an adventurer. Oh, it is a place of rare enchantment and beauty, the like of which few men are privileged to see. You will find it fascinating, this mountain in Serendip."

Hasan look up from the restless waves. "Serendip? You mean the island Sindbad visited?"

"Who?"

"Sindbad the Seaman. He's famous in Bassorah. He—"

Bahram smiled indulgently. "Believe me, Hasan, his name will never be known beyond your city. A common seaman!"

Thus Hasan discovered one day that he had agreed to go on, although he remained leery of the Persian's friendly words. The ship set sail once more for the fabled land

Hasan had read about, that nothing now could keep him from: Serendip. Perhaps, on his return, he would pay a call on the seaman. . . .

More weeks passed. They left behind the marvelous country of Hind, where monstrous elephants were said to roam wild, and bore south along a mountainous coast. Finally the land curved again, and they faced the rising sun; then at last the ship bore north. It was as though they had circled the world and were ascending its far side. Then they cut east again, directly out to sea—and new land came into view. Serendip at last!

The green surf broke against shallow islands under the water and sent white breakers foaming onto the beach. Familiar palm trees came up to the shore here and there, but the rest of the scenery was strange. The sands were not white, but colored—pebbles of white and yellow and sky-blue and black and every other hue, intermixed with un-usual rocks. And in the shallow waters were remarkable fishes, no less colorful than the stones, and even stranger marine formations. Bahram had been right: this was a land of adventure!

"O my son," the Persian said, "Make ready, for this is the place we desire. We must go ashore."

Hasan was delighted at the news. He wanted nothing better than to run along that bright beach and to explore the magic landscape beyond. This was a far cry from Bassorah! He could see already that the earth was not brown, but red, as though the blood of a god had colored it. He no longer regretted his decision to continue the voyage.

But he had uneasy second thoughts when he observed Bahram making arrangements with the captain, who was to remain behind with the ship and safeguard the goods aboard. He had thought, somehow, that the entire party was coming along, and did not relish the solitary company of the magician. Yet of course the ship could not be deserted . . . and the land excursion should not take long.

He made up a pack of supplies, and was ready, physi-

cally and emotionally, when the time came to jump into
the shallow waves and wade ashore.

The adventure had begun!

Chapter 3. Mountain of Clouds

They left the beach and marched inland, east, until the
ship and the sea itself were out of sight. After a few miles
Bahram called a halt, set down his pack, and took out a
kind of kettledrum fashioned of copper and a silken strap.
Hasan marveled at the man's possession of such a useless
object, here in the wilderness, but said nothing. The Persian
was full of surprises.

Bahram set up his drum and began beating it regularly
with the strap, so that it made a rhythmical music. Hasan
stared. Had the man come this far merely to hear himself
play? Allah did not approve of music—but this was ridiculous! Or was the man contemplating some kind of sinister
spell, of which this was but the prelude? Hasan once more
regretted his actions; he should never have come ashore,
away from the friendly captain and crew. He was without
protection now.

"Something bothering you, my son?" Bahram inquired.

"I—"

The beat was never faltered. "By the truth of the Fire and
the Light," Bahram said, "you have nothing to fear from me.
If I hadn't needed you to accomplish this exploit, I would
never have brought you ashore. I tell you that the adventure
we have had is as nothing compared to what lies ahead. But
if you would rather give up and return. . . ."

"No sir," Hasan said quickly, irked at his own timidity.
He was free, wasn't he? If the Persian intended foul
dealings, Hasan could always outrun him, couldn't he?

The monotonous beat continued for half an hour. A
cloud of dust appeared across the plain. Was it an attack?

"Don't alarm so easily, boy," Bahram said, amused. "Rejoice—for that cloud is what we have been waiting for."

Hasan, only moderately reassured, watched as the dust swelled and advanced, coming directly toward them. After a while he was able to make out the shapes of three dromedaries, sleek and riderless, and he laughed to think of his fears about the jinn.

The animals came right up to the magician, who put away the drum and caught hold of the leading one. "Hang our supplies on this beast," he grunted. "We'll ride the other two."

This was unexpected. Hasan had assumed that their destination was within walking distance of the ship. The use of these camels meant a much longer trip. But he lacked the courage to protest now; he mounted, and soon they were riding in style across the countryside.

As they moved inland the palms became scattered and in time disappeared entirely. The plain dried out, although it was hardly hot by the standards of Arabia. The camels picked up speed as the ground increased in firmness; but as the hours passed Hasan grew bored. His attention expanded to embrace the landscape, and he began to realize what exotic marvels he had hitherto shut out in his concern for his own affairs.

There were clumps of trees, like little islands or oases, scattered throughout the plain, and occasional boulders hundreds of feet high, and many strange plants and bushes between them. Hasan had never seen such masses of sheer stone, for there was nothing of the kind in all Bassorah or the lands about it. Meandering ditches contained stagnant water, which in turn contained fat and lazy crocodiles three times the length of a man, which at least he could recognize. A number of rats scuttled out of the way, and once he saw a python, longer than a crocodile, which quickly disappeared in the brush. Undoubtedly much more animal life existed, but it kept out of sight.

They were still on the plain as the sun sank. Hasan was afraid to inquire how much farther they were to journey, for he might not like the answer. Bahram rode stolidly ahead, making no conversation; he might have been asleep, from his appearance, but when Hasan guided his mount to one side the magician quickly turned his head to cover him.

They halted beside a great mangrove tree growing near a muddy river. Branches spread out in every direction, and new shoots, or perhaps new trees, sprouted from the main body to make a wonderland forest by itself. They ate from the supplies the third camel carried and spread out blankets amidst the tangled jungle of roots for the night. Hasan performed his evening prayers, facing toward the setting sun, while Bahram gazed on contemptuously.

Hasan lay on his back and stared at the sky. The land was dark, but the sky was deep blue, merging into quiet flame shot with brilliant streamers of gold. A lone hawk seemed to hang motionless far above, and the piping of the frogs grew loud. The sky flushed slowly red, clouds became dark, and finally the day was gone.

The scene and sounds were not unlike those of the land around Bassorah. He found them novel because he had never before slept in the wilderness, so close to it all.

Hasan did not drift quietly to sleep. He rolled about in his blanket, as swarms of mosquitoes attacked, and slapped at the pricks of biting crawlers. He still did not entirely trust Bahram, and peered through the darkness to see whether the wrapped shape of the magician had moved. Hard roots appeared under his body where none had seemed to be when he lay down, and he fidgeted constantly in a fruitless effort to find a really comfortable bed.

The raucous screeching of birds woke him at daybreak. A flock of peafowl were scratching nearby—beautiful birds with elaborately colorful tails, but the ugliest voices imaginable. (Hasan did not know the name of the creatures of Serendip at this point, but later he was to become so thoroughly familiar with them that it seemed he had never been in ignorance.) A closer motion caught his eye, and he froze in terror as he recognized a deadly cobra sliding between him and the Persian. But the snake paid him no particular attention; it was neither bold nor timid, and after

a while Hasan saw that it did not possess a hood. It was
merely a snake resembling the cobra, and was probably as
harmless as such creatures cared to get. It disappeared into
an especially thick tangle of roots, somewhat to his relief.
In a moment he heard the dying screech of a small rat, and
understood the business of the snake.

Hasan stretched—and discovered something hanging from
his arm. It was a leech—a legless thing an inch long,
fastened to his flesh by means of a large sucker. He
yanked it off instinctively—and the creature, already partly
gorged on his blood, left its teeth in his body. The bite
itself had been painless, but now there was an angry,
smarting wound. He was nauseated.

After the morning ablution—Hasan disliked using the
slimy water of the river, but there was nothing else—they
ate and remounted the camels. Another long day's journey
commenced.

This continued for several days. The forests gradually
became thicker and richer and animal life increased. Hasan
actually saw elephants browsing in the distance, and nearer
at hand were hares and pig-like creatures. There were
many insects, both flying and crawling; they had to detour
at one point around a marching column of warrior ants,
complete with sentinels and scouts, and Hasan was stung
horrendously by a hornet once. The pain and swelling
were terrible; he was sure that anyone who blundered into
a colony of such insects would be lucky to escape with his
life.

By day they had to struggle through the thickening
growths and entangling vines of the forest, scratched and
sweltering. Thorn bushes ran their cables from the branches
of larger trees and stretched across the animal trails; several times it was necessary to backtrack, yielding to the
impregnable branches.

In the evenings swarms of flying insects appeared, followed by crows and rarer birds, and bats of all sizes filled
the air. At night the crawling insects took over, horrible in
the flickering firelight. Some were actually harmless, like

the six-inch millipede Bahram picked up carelessly and
tossed away; but others were deadly, like the foot-long
dark-purple scorpion that, figuratively, picked up the Persian
and tossed *him* away. Hasan learned very quickly which
creatures to fear, and when to choke back laughter, by
observing Bahram's reactions.

Morning again, and Hasan was amazed at the profusion
of spider webs sparkling in the dew. They covered every
tree and bush and were strung from rock to rock and across
the pathways.

This was a strange kingdom, but its appeal gained on
Hasan as he adapted to its rigueurs. Never had he seen such
proliferation of plant-life, so many unusual animals. Hordes
of chattering monkeys swung through the trees and paced
the travelers for hours at a time. Hasan threw a stone at
one, and after that was constantly pelted with fruit. The
monkeys swung closer and closer, daring him to make
another hostile move, but he had learned his lesson.

Seven days passed, and in all that time the one animal
he discovered conspicuously missing was the camel. Could
the three trained beasts they rode be the only ones of their
type on the island? Were they, the most ordinary living
things he had encountered here, apart from the palms and
mosquitoes, actually of magical derivation? If the commonplace were magical and the extraordinary natural, what
might he anticipate at the end of this journey?

During the seventh day they encountered the mountains.
Progress slowed, as the animals toiled up gradual but
wearying slopes, or were led through rough terrain. The
vegetation became jungle-thick, and many more birds,
animals and insects appeared. The leeches, here in the
hills, were twice the size of the few he had met on the
plain, and infested the foliage; he was glad he was able to
ride most of the time. The mountains were beautiful, and
frequently they were refreshed with rain.

As they passed through a long gorge, Hasan looked up
to spy the first evidence of man in this strange land: high
on the tallest mountain in the east was a beautiful green

dome, and beside it an emerald structure flashing in the sun. "O Uncle," he exclaimed, "what is that on the mountain?"

"A palace," Bahram said, but he did not sound pleased.

"Are we going to spend the night there? Is that our destination?" Hasan longed for the comforts of civilization.

Bahram grew angry, for no reason Hasan could fathom. "Don't be foolish, boy. Don't even mention that foul place to me, understand? It is the abode of jinn, ghouls and devils. An enemy of mine lurks there."

"An enemy? What did he do to you?"

"I said I didn't want to talk about it!" Bahram shouted, red with rage. And talk he did not; they rode for the rest of the day in silence.

Hasan was sorry to leave the palace behind. Even from this distance it was the most beautiful structure he had ever seen, scintillating like a jewel set in the mountain, and its aura of enchantment fascinated him. Could ghouls and devils really create such loveliness? Once this mission had been accomplished, he intended to visit that palace, regardless. . . .

They fared on through hills, forests and fields of increasing splendor. The weather changed abruptly; massive clouds loomed above, sprewing lightning and thunder and bringing a deluge upon their heads. This was a new and frightening phenomenon to Hasan. Rains were rare in Arabia, and more seemed to fall here in a single hour than in a year at home. Though it did not last long, its wasteful force was shocking. Hasan and Bahram could not talk at all, even by shouting, in the torrential wash of liquid. Flash floods filled the gullies and valleys; trees were undermined by the seething currents, and some were uprooted.

Suddenly the heavens brightened and the sun came out as though it had never departed, warm and friendly, and the steaming jungle smiled as though it had enjoyed its purge.

The mosquitoes thinned and vanished as elevation increased, but the leeches were worse. Animals were everywhere—deer, monkeys, bear, anteaters, and even prickly porcupines inhabited the massed trees. By day and night, Hasan could hear the sounds of the struggle in the wilderness, as the ceaseless competition for existence drew startlingly near. Beautiful mats of flowers covered the fields, oblivious to that struggle, and orchids bloomed wherever the sun pierced the forest foliage.

The trail curved until they faced directly west, and finally north again. Hasan knew they were near the end of the long trek. He became uneasy.

Bahram pulled up at the crest of a low hill. "O Hasan, what do you see now?"

Hasan stared ahead. "I see a monstrous wall of cloud from east to west."

"That is neither cloud nor mist," Bahram said, "but one vast mountain that splits the clouds and reaches above them. There will be sunshine on the top while there is a raging storm below. And that is what we came for."

"A mountain?" Now he remembered the Mountain of Clouds.

"A mountain. What I require is on its summit, and I cannot complete my task without your help."

Hasan's alarm flared up. In just what manner did the magician intend to use him? "By the right of what you worship, tell me what you have in mind!" His eye was on the surrounding jungle. He would not risk that leech-infested wilderness on foot unless he had to; but if the Persian—

Bahram looked at him as though reading his thought. "My son," he said with deceptive gentleness, "you know that it is through the practice of alchemy that I am able to transform copper into gold. The manufacture of the essential powder requires many exotic ingredients; but the rarest of them all is derived from a herb that is found only at the top of that mountain, and nowhere else in all the world. I propose to send you up there to fetch it for me; and when we have it, I will show you the secret of this craft which you are so interested in learning. Surely you understand this?''

''O, of course, Uncle,'' Hasan agreed, not certain what it was he was supposed to understand, but compelled by the hypnotic eye and tone of the older man. He was afraid; he despaired of ever returning home to Bassorah, yet he could not discover any pretext to beg off this project now. Everything was so reasonable when the magician spoke. . . .

They moved nearer to the foot of the mountain, which was farther away than Hasan had supposed, and larger. He could hear the booming of a swollen river cascading a few hundred or a few thousand feet to the side, and rolling thunder echoed from cliff to cliff. Sheer sheets of rock, impossible to climb, fronted the mountain. Hasan looked at these and became faint. He was not an athlete, and would surely die if he were to attempt so precipitous an ascent.

Bahram observed his fright and came over to reassure him. ''O my son, I can understand your concern about this matter, but I assure you that everything will work out exactly as I planned.'' He kissed the young man's cheek. ''Bear me no ill will for the manner in which we began this voyage, for I will make up for that by guarding you carefully on your trip up the mountain. You will not have to risk your life in an impossible climb; I have a special method to get you safely to the top. Once you are there, follow my instructions and do not play me false, and you and I shall share appropriately in the profit.''

''To hear is to obey,'' said Hasan, hardly reassured.

Bahram opened a bag and removed a small handmill and some wheat. He ground the grain and kneaded three round cakes from the flour; then he made a fire and baked the hard bread. He sprinkled the cakes with some strong-smelling herbs, so that their odor was not at all appetizing. Hasan watched with worried curiosity. Who was supposed to eat this mess?

The camels had drifted off. The Persian summoned

them with his drum and took hold of the one Hasan had ridden. He drew his knife and slit the animal's throat.

Hasan had seen animals slaughtered before, of course, but this was unexpected. His camel had been in good health, they were not in need of the meat, and Bahram had not pointed its head toward Mekkeh while it bled to death, in the manner prescribed for anything killed for food.

He watched, disgruntled, as the magician followed up the pointless slaughter by slicing open the animal's stomach and disemboweling it. He severed the head, legs, and tail and scraped the inside clean until hardly more than an empty shell remained.

"Now attend," he said to Hasan, wiping the blood off his hands. "I want you to lie down inside this skin, and I will sew it up again so it looks like an entire carcass. Then I'll withdraw a certain distance, leaving you here, and after a while the roc will come and carry you to the top of the mountain, thinking this to be its meal. Take this knife with you, and when you feel the bird land, slit open the skin and come out. The bird will take fright, for it is very shy in spite of its size, and will fly away. Then walk to the edge of the cliff and call to me, and I will give you further instructions."

Hasan had misgivings and a thousand questions about this procedure. There seemed to be many important things unexplained. For instance—

"You want to make the elixir, don't you, boy?"

"Yes, but—"

"You don't want to climb that cliff yourself, do you, boy?"

"No, but—"

"You're not afraid of a little blood, are you?"

"Of course not!" But he was sick as he looked at the gutted camel.

"Can you suggest any better way to get there?"

Hasan was silent. The air-route alarmed him for many reasons, but the towering mountain-face was worse. How had he gotten himself committed to this? Why was the magician able to manage him so easily?

Bahram's piercing eye was upon him. He tried once more to protest, but his mind was a whirl of voiceless doubt. He gritted his teeth and climbed into the camel.

The carcass was still warm, the blood still sticky. Hasan controlled his rebellious stomach with difficulty. Bahram handed him a leathern bottle full of water—"You'll be up there a few hours, gathering the herb"—and placed the three redolent cakes beside him, as though appetizers for the main portion which was himself, the entree for a feast of ghouls. "These are to attract the roc, and draw it to you from a distance."

Then he brought forth an enormous needle, threaded it with a strong gut line, and sewed Hasan up.

Hasan heard the man's feet retreating and knew he was on his own at last. He clutched the knife, thankful that at least he had the ability to cut himself free if he lost his nerve. The stench of the cakes mixed with that of the seeping blood and his own profuse sweat and stale breath to form a palpable mist. Every breath festooned his lungs with new nausea.

He couldn't stand it any longer! He aimed the blade, flexed his wrist . . . and relaxed again, unable to proclaim the cowardice he felt. His heart beat loudly in his ears; he counted the beats, seeking distraction. He grew faint from the suffocating miasma—then realized with hysteric amusement at his stupidity that all he had to do was put his lips to the sewn portion of the hide and suck fresh air in through the holes.

He did this, heedless of the cracking blood that peeled off to smear his lips, and found blessed relief. But this only freed his awareness for other problems. The temperature, instead of declining, rose steadily as the sun beat down outside and his own body added heat to the cramped cavity. He slipped and slid in the jelly formed by his sweat and the juices of the camel meat, and a kind of delirium clouded his senses. What if there were leeches outside, big ones, and a monster leech came, four, five inches long, and fastened itself upon his exposed lips? Or a great blue scorpion.

How many hours had passed? It had been midday when he entered this prison. It would be cool when night came, and it certainly hadn't cooled yet. Probably he had lain here less than an hour—but what an hour! How much more would he have to endure? Would the roc ever come? Did he really want it to? What if it picked him up, changed its mind and dropped him?

As though this cheering thought were the signal, a powerful beating of the air began, sending a cooling draft past his face. It was too late to change his mind. The big bird was coming!

He tried to peer out through the sutures, but he could see nothing but the bloody ground. The carcass rocked with a final blast of wind. There was a thud! as of something heavy landing, and surprisingly innocent clucking. A bird, even a big one, was still a bird.

The ground vibrated as the thing hopped toward him. There was a sudden, severe jar. It was pecking at the meat, testing it for edibility. Suppose it tried to feed right here? What if its sharp bill accidentally cut through the cord, so that the stitches unraveled and let the carcass fall open in mid-air? Why had he ever allowed himself to be subjected to this?

The carcass shook and the upper wall depressed against him heavily. The bird was on top of it, crushing him! A giant thorn, a hooked spear poked through the wall inches from his face. It was a talon of horrifying size. Six inches long, an inch thick at the base . . . and what he saw was only the tip of it, since the rest was outside a fair thickness of gristle. This bird was timid?

The monstrous beat of wind began again, a hurricane of air smashing the ground. Dust swirled into his breathing-hole. The roc was taking off! The carcass jolted and tilted crazily, sliding him helplessly back and forth as it bumped over the ground. Then it was airborne, riding smoothly in the grip of the mighty claws.

Hasan contemplated the one visible nail. Was it really

strong enough to bear his weight? Suddenly it seemed thin
and slight.

Up and up: he felt the circling ascent. If only the
position allowed him to *see!* But that would probably
terrify him; he was better off as it was, merely deathly
afraid. If the bird didn't grow forgetful and carelessly let
go—!

The flight seemed interminable, yet Hasan had hardly
become accustomed to it before it was over. There was a
tooth-rattling bump! as the claw retracted and released its
load. The carcass rolled over and over, bringing him vi-
sions of an uncontrolled drop over the precipice, before
coming safely to rest. He grasped his knife and sliced the
binding immediately. The roc might not be timid—but he
could hardly afford to let it feed while he remained inside
the morsel.

There was another blast of air and a ponderous wing-
thunder as he struggled to emerge. A shadow passed over
him. Was it attacking?

No. The bird was taking flight. It certainly was shy! By
the time he had freed himself and was able to look around,
it was gone.

He had seen no more of it than a single claw.

The air on the mountaintop was bright and heavenly
cool. Hasan was caked with noxious grime, but he forgot
this in a moment as he took deep breaths and looked
around.

The summit was level and grassy, with a few trees down
a little on the northern slope. To the south, the direction
from which he had come, the cliffs dropped off alarm-
ingly; he could see the sky come down to the mountain's
edge and go below. The view was astonishing, particularly
to one who had spent his life in lowlands: a vast panorama
of forested mountains, extending most of the way around
him, diminishing into plains with irregular patches of grass-
land and jungle, and finally the sea, a bright blue band on
the horizon.

He had thought the day was cloudy (though the heat of the sun upon the carcass could not have been his imagination), but up here it plainly was not. The clouds existed beauteously, but were only fluffs decorating the larger view.

"Glory be to Allah, the Merciful, the Mighty!" he exclaimed, absorbed in a magnificence that was fit for nothing less than worship.

Belatedly he remembered his purpose here. He walked to the edge, looked down upon the forest-carpeted folds and tucks of the earth far, far below his feet and reeled back, horrified at the immense height. Now indeed he was thankful he hadn't witnessed this journey to the peak!

He got down on hands and knees and advanced again, finally spreading himself out flat and crawling the last few feet. He poked his head over, clutching at the dirt with tense fingers, and looked down dizzily.

If he had not stood in awe of the power of Allah before, this spectacle would have made him a convert.

"Bahram!" he called, afraid that he might by the effort of shouting blow himself off the cliff, so tenuous did his contact with the ground seem. "Baah-raam!"

A few seconds later there was an answering call, and he located the Persian, a tiny figure dancing about and waving his turban excitedly in the air.

"What now?" Hasan yelled.

"Move over to your left a hundred paces and tell me what you see," Bahram called back, pointing ineffectually.

Hasan backed off until he felt safe enough to stand, counted off his paces, and looked around. He saw grass, bushes, flowers, and a number of disinteresting sticks of weathered wood. There was also a rounded white object the size of a bowl. He picked it up, turned it over . . . and found himself looking into the square eye-sockets of a human skull.

He dropped it immediately, then chided himself for his foolishness. The man had long been dead; the skull was bleached and clean. It was sad that he had not been properly buried, but perhaps he had been an infidel. He looked more carefully and saw other bones of the body spread about.

Did the rocs prey on men after all? They might, if the man were already dead. In any event, the ants and other insects would pick the skeleton clean soon enough. Since he saw no sign of broken or crushed bones, that had probably been the case here.

But why had the man—he assumed it was a man, since it would hardly be polite to look upon the naked bones of a woman—why had this man died up here in the first place?

Something uncomfortable was gnawing at his mind. A man had come here, perhaps by the same route he had employed himself. That man had died. What could have killed him? Hasan had seen nothing deadly here, and he was armed with the knife. What had he missed?

He put the unpleasant train of thought from his mind. It had been an accident, assuredly. He crawled back to the edge of the mountain and put his head over. "All I see are bones and sticks of wood," he called to the Persian.

"Good," Bahram replied. "That is the herb we seek. The wood. Gather it into six bundles, tie them with the thong I used to bind you into the camel, and throw them down to me."

"Wouldn't it be easier to bring the wood with me when I come down myself?"

Bahram grew angry. "Do as I say, boy, and don't ask foolish questions!"

Hasan's doubt continued, but he shook it off and lost himself in action. As he picked up the pieces of wood he encountered several more skeletons; some comparatively new, like the first, and some so old they were rotting away. His sense of foreboding grew. One dead man might represent an accident . . . but six, eight? How had they come here, and what macabre fate had stalked them all?

He pulled the cord loose and cut it into suitable lengths to bind the bundles of wood. It was strange—the wood looked ordinary, and he could not fathom why it should be

important. But he did not question the magician's professional competence: he had seen his own copper transformed into gold. Perhaps the art lay in recognizing the
magic properties of materials that appeared nondescript to
the layman.

He brought the bundles to the edge. "Where do you
want them?" he called. He noticed that the sun was low in
the sky; he had, as foretold, been up here several hours.

"Fling them out toward me as far as you can," Bahram
called back. He was not standing at the very base of the
mountain, and in any event, several of the rock faces were
slanted, so that the wood was likely to be snagged unless
heaved far out.

Hasan stepped back, stood up, and swung the first
bundle over the edge. He immediately fell prone and
crawled to the edge to observe its progress. It had been a
good throw—the wood sailed far out, then dropped gracefully down. It still crashed into the lower faces, but slid
across them harmlessly and came to rest in the forest at the
base. The magician would have to bestir himself to fetch
the wood, but at least it was accessible.

"That's good," Bahram agreed. "Try to place the others near it." Hasan obliged, and was pleased to see three
of the remaining bundles land practically on top of the first
and another fall near it. The last went wide when his foot
slipped, and crashed far to the side.

Dusk was falling—or rather, he saw now from the
clarity of his elevation, rising; for the gullies and valleys
were already dark, while the mountains and sky were
light. "How do I get down?" he called, not wishing to be
trapped the night with the skeletons.

Laughter came up from the shadows. "Down? Isn't it
obvious?"

"Would I have to ask, if it were?" Hasan replied
irritably.

"Oh, I have known some handsome lads, but none quite
so foolish as you!" Bahram said. "Why, you jump down,
boy!"

"But I would be dashed to pieces against the rocks!"

"Abide on the mountain, then, if you do not trust your god to bear you up. You're in good company!" And he laughed again, harshly, and spoke no more.

Hasan finally understood the reason for the skeletons. Bahram had boasted that he had slain a thousand youths—counting Hasan himself—and while that figure was probably exaggerated, he had certainly been responsible for a goodly number. One lad had been delivered here each year or so, just as he had been, and all had been rewarded in the same manner. Rather than perish in quick suicide, all these on the mountain had chosen to starve. Probably there were more bones, broken ones, at the foot of the mountain, representing those who had chosen the other method.

Why hadn't he questioned the Persian before undertaking the flight with the roc? Surely he should have secured his escape before stranding himself. "There is no majesty and there is no might, except in Allah!" he said fervently, and knew himself to be the fool Bahram had claimed. He had had ample evidence of the magician's nature, yet had listened to the artful words and shut his mind to the implications. He had refused to believe that a man could be inherently evil, even a Persian. He was, as had also been pointed out, in good company.

Darkness came upon the Mountain of Clouds in magnificent array, and the day was over. Hasan sat amid bones and sobbed, certain that his day was over, too.

He was hungry in the morning. He felt better, though he knew his situation to be as desperate as before. He found himself in a bed of grass that he did not at first remember fashioning, and miraculously free of leeches.

He went to the stinking camel-hide and took out the bottle of water and the cakes. He no longer noticed the smell of them, and gulped them down rapidly.

Sunrise was magnificent. As he watched, a giant cone of darkness lay over the world to the west, the shadow of the mountain. As the sun rose this cone shortened, clocking the dawn like the sundial of Allah. The landscape in every direction was preternatually clear, and Hasan felt glad to be alive, even for a little while.

He used some of his precious water to wash himself, so that he might be clean for his morning prayer. Allah's will would be accomplished, whatever a lone Believer might do—but a True Believer was more likely to have a beneficent fate mapped out than was a person of timorous faith. The moment Hasan neglected his homage to Allah, he would be confessing the insincerity of his worship, and therefore would know himself to deserve nothing.

He rose after the prayer and looked at the view again. Suddenly a glint caught his eye. It was to the northwest, a bright green flash in the darker green of the jungle and brush. The palace! The one Bahram hated, because it was the residence of enemies, of jinn and ghouls.

Surely, if the residents were antagonistic to the Persian, they were friends of Hasan! Even ghouls!

But he did not really believe that ghouls were there, for they were ugly creatures who had no appreciation of beauty. Their place was the crypt, not the palace. Surely persons of nobility dwelt therein. If only he could reach it. . . .

He walked north, toward the trees he had seen before. If that slope were forested, he should be able to navigate it.

His hopes were short-lived. There was forest, but too much of it. It was a tropical jungle far denser than any they had encountered below. The trees were very large and were covered with the sword-sharp thorn vines that he knew from experience he could cut through only very tediously. There was a dense undergrowth of fern and bamboo, also intertwined with the horrible thorny vines. He might hack his way through that jungle with his little knife at the rate of a thousand paces a day. It might take ten days to reach the foot of the mountain.

Hasan had no food and very little water. There were probably fruits in the forest, but he did not know which ones were edible and which were poisonous. Bahram had gathered the berries of a certain plant, informing him that the seeds contained the most deadly poison known to man.

The magician had also spoken of vines that produced the nefarious bhang, the intoxicant that Hasan himself had fallen victim to at the beginning of this venture. How could he risk eating such things now?

There was animal life; he could hear it moving deep within the mass of foliage. The animals should be safe to eat—except that they were most likely to eat him first. He would have scant power to defend himself amidst the stinging brambles.

And what, finally, when he slept? Even at the edge he could see the monstrous leeches, some three inches long. They would suck him dry before the night was over.

No, there was no escape this way. Had there been a navigable trail, Bahram would never have gone to the trouble to fetch innocent boys from faraway Arabian cities. The one-way route of the roc was the only approach.

Hasan returned disconsolately to the cliffs and looked out again. If only there was some way down! Some—

There was the briefest glint from a projecting section of the cliff. Was it a mere jewel in the rock—or something more significant? He ran to that section, threw himself flat, and put his head over.

It was metal! There was a chain fastened to a spike embedded in the rock at the top, with little stirrups every three feet. Someone—Allah only knew how long ago, or for what purpose—must have made regular trips to this summit, using the chain. Probably the first journey had been made through the jungle, laboriously forced; or perhaps the roc had somehow been harnessed. After that, the shorter, more dramatic route up the face of the cliff was open.

But why hadn't any of the other youths Bahram snared taken this descent? Hasan had the answer immediately: only through a lucky chance, a single glance in this direction when the sun happened to be in position to reflect a glint off the chain—only this way had he located it at all or even suspected its existence. If someone had told him it was there, it still would have taken him many hours to find it, checking every dangerous foot of the cliff, for the lay of the rock hid it from view.

He could sympathize with the lads before him who had instinctively shied away from the terrifying brink. Those youths had been like him; beautiful, probably pampered, naive. They were hardly fit to cope with this savage dilemma. The logic of Bahram's selection was becoming more plain. A more rustic youth, or one native to mountain country might have solved the problem readily.

Hasan had not been wiser or braver. He had been lucky. Or—Allah had woven a different skein for his life. . . .

He wasted no more time. He drank the last of his water so that he would not have to carry it, performed an automatic prayer of thanks, and took hold of the chain. If it were no longer strong enough to sustain his weight, he was doomed anyway, so it was pointless to worry about that.

"Praise be to Allah!" he shouted again, and put his foot into the first stirrup.

The chain held. Hasan climbed down as rapidly as he dared, stopping to rest when his arms grew fatigued. He reached the foot of the chain, which was only a fraction of the total distance down, and found a narrow ledge. Grasping the dangling chain with one hand, he explored the ledge, and came upon another spike and chain leading down.

He descended to a second ledge and then a third. He was hardly aware of time, but the sun changed position considerably as he maneuvered down interminable stages. Near the bottom of the mountain he landed on a ledge, looked for the following chain with bleary eyes and rock-chafed hands, and found only the broken spike that had anchored it. There was no final connection.

It was early afternoon. Suddenly the sky grew dark. A storm was coming up! Hasan searched for shelter, but there was none on this narrow ledge between vertical cliffs. He was far too tired to climb back up to a more secure level before the storm struck. He could not jump; though he was near the end, the remaining distance was suddenly appalling.

He sat down and huddled as tightly as he could against the wall, hoping that the rain would not dislodge him. After the tempest, perhaps he could sever a length of chain from above and hitch it to the lower spike. Would his knife prove strong enough to pry it loose? Meanwhile, he had to keep his position.

The rain dropped upon him. It blasted against the stone, and the howling winds slapped sheets of it about to hiss off the wall and sting his exposed face and hands unmercifully. His propped feet began to slide against an abruptly slippery surface; desperately he fumbled for a toehold, a fingerhold, anything to anchor him just a little more securely. After several minutes of this, in a momentary pause of the torrent, he realized that he should have clung to the chain itself. He jumped to reach it.

The wind, like a pouncing jinni, caught him the moment there was space between his body and the mountain. Too quickly for fear, he was teetering on the edge; then he was falling.

"Allah!" he cried, and tried to recite the funeral prayer, to remember the Koran: but these were hopeless tasks in such straits. He struck—

Water. Spluttering, he struggled upward. He had not been trained as a swimmer, but he did know the rudiments. He coughed and choked, but survived. The rain was pouring down again, but, as much by feel and fortune as by sight, he grabbed hold of strong vines and crawled ashore.

When the storm had abated he looked about and understood the miracle that had saved him. He had fallen into a flash flood formed by the water running off the mountain; already the channel was clearing, leaving a rank empty ditch.

Hasan prostrated himself and gave due thanks to Allah; then he wended his way around the mountain towards the palace of the ghouls.

Chapter 4. Rose

Two young women, unveiled and fair as moons, sat in

the vestibule of the palace, letting the refreshing breeze
ruffle their jeweled tresses while they matched wits over a
game of chess. Their dress, though elegant, was informal,
since they were alone. While they played they chattered
merrily about inconsequentials.

The younger girl, though less developed than her companion, might easily have been the inspiration for the
Persian's description of his daughter. She heard something
and looked up alertly.

Hasan stood at the entrance, weary, bloody and bedraggled. He lurched forward and staggered into the vestibule,
reaching for a column to lean against.

His eyes met those of the girl. "Allah!" she exclaimed,
astonished but hardly frightened.

The older girl immediately fastened her veil, but the
pretty junior was more impulsive. "By Allah, here is a son
of Adam!" she sang out joyfully.

Hasan stared at her, too tired to do more than admire her
beauty. He had been braced for the foulest of demons and
had reconciled himself to begging aid from the most loath-
some of enchanted creatures; but these creatures were
lovely and this enchantment delightful. Embarrassed, he
tried to put away his drawn knife, to brush back the
mud-matted hair over his forehead.

"Why, this must be the fair youth that Bahram the
Magician brought here this year!" the young girl said,
appraising the ragged shape and battered countenance before her with no awareness of incongruity.

Hasan's strength evaporated in the face of this welcome.
He threw himself to the floor in supplication. "O my
ladies, yes, by Allah, I am that unhappy fool. I am faint
and in pain, and I beg your compassion, for I cannot drag
myself any farther."

"O yes!" the girl cried, jumping up. "We will help you."

"Rose! Your veil!" the other reminded her, shocked.
"Don't disgrace yourself."

"Damn the veil! This poor man needs our help," Rose
replied hotly. "He's already seen my face." But she

paused, aware that nice girls never showed their features indiscriminately. She began to raise her veil, then brightened with a fresh idea.

She skipped over to Hasan and put her slender arm around his soggy shoulders. "Bear witness, O my sister, that I hereby adopt this man as my brother, by the covenant of Allah, and I will die if he dies and live as he lives, and his joy shall be my joy and his grief my grief, so long as I shall live!"

The older sister looked askance at this sheer impetuosity, but shrugged her shoulders in resignation. The deed was done, after all.

"Now I don't have to cover my face from him, do I?" Rose demanded.

"No, sister."

"And neither do you, because you're my sister and he's my brother and that makes him your brother too. Take off your veil."

The other girl sighed and removed her veil. Rose still wasn't satisfied. "Well, come on, sister—aren't you going to embrace your long-lost brother? Aren't you glad to see him?"

"He's *not* my long-lost—"

"But you haven't seen him in at least a year, have you now?"

"Please," Hasan said stupidly, still kneeling on the floor. "I really didn't mean to—"

"Be quiet, brother," Rose said severely.

Reluctantly, and with extreme distress, the shapely older sister knelt and put her arms around Hasan.

"And kiss him, too," Rose directed.

She kissed him lightly on the cheek, while Hasan flushed magnificently. Rose then followed her sister's example, putting considerably more enthusiasm into it, and was satisfied. "But brother," she exclaimed as an afterthought, "you're in terrible condition. Come, I'll yank off those sopping rags and dress you in fitting raiment. What's your name?"

And she led him away, hardly paying attention to his reply, while her sister sat down and rolled her eyes at the chesscloth.

An hour later Hasan, garbed in a brilliant yellow silken robe that had been tailored for a king, was in the midst of a sumptuous repast. His pain and fatigue had vanished in the glow of the attention he received from the two lovely maidens.

"Tell us the story of your life," Rose implored him. "It's been so long since we've had a live, handsome son of Adam to—"

"Rose!" her sister said, alarmed.

"—to listen to," she finished contritely.

"O merciful and radiant damsels," Hasan began formally, "my story is uninteresting. But I am anxious to know how you came to be here, in this marvelous palace in the wilderness, and why two such beautiful girls should choose to live alone like this. And what was your quarrel with Bahram the magician?"

Rose held up her hand, an impertinent but attractive pout on her face. "We asked you first!"

The older sister intervened diplomatically. "Since Bahram brought you here, it might be simplest if you explained your association with him. Then we'll know how to fill in our side of the story."

"Yes—tell us about Bahram, the dog!"

Hasan looked at the young women again, impressed by the fine contours of the one and the flashing animation of the other. This was the stuff his dreams were fashioned from, and it was hard to believe the girls were not phantasms of the jinn, sent to lead him to disaster. But he could not resist their gentle importunings, and soon launched into his story. Rose interrupted prettily with appropriate exclamations as he described his travails with the magician.

"Did you ask him about this palace?" she demanded.

"I did; but he wouldn't talk about it. He said it belonged to ghouls and devils."

Both girls jumped to their feet. "Ghouls and devils!" they exclaimed together, outraged.

"Yes." Hasan suspected that Bahram had been speaking metaphorically, but it didn't seem worthwhile to point this out.

"By Allah!" cried Rose. "I will slay him with my own hands!"

"But how can you do such a thing when you are just a girl and he is a crafty magician?" This was a deliberately leading question.

"I'm *not* just a girl," she said. "I'm a princess." Nevertheless, she quieted.

"We are not untrained in weapons," the older sister said, "and we know how to deal with this man, magician or not."

Hasan did not like the sound of this. Bahram, at least, had taught him not to be naive. There had been so many indications of the Persian's intent, if only he had been able to read them properly at the time. How could he be sure that these maidens were not after all demons in disguise? If they could actually kill the magician—

"You promised to tell me your story," he reminded them. If they were of the jinn, he was already in their power. Their tale might clarify things. Certainly he could gain nothing by acting rashly without information.

"O yes, brother!" Rose said, impulsively kissing him. Suddenly his doubts seemed foolish. No demon could be that interesting! Of course, he was technically her brother, which curtailed the romantic implications somewhat . . . perhaps fortunately. He had no serious complaint.

"Know, O my brother," Rose began portentously, "that we are the daughters of a mighty king of the jinn—"

"Rose!" The older sister was indignant.

Hasan also reacted, but for a different reason.

"All *right!* I only wanted to make it sound more impressive. I mean, what's so exciting about an ordinary mortal king? They say there is jinn blood in our—"

"I'd much rather be brother to a mortal damsel," Hasan said. Under the circumstances, tact was natural.

"You would?" Rose murmured, suddenly shy. "Oh. Well, our father is the king of the mightiest kingdom in Sind. Almighty Allah blessed him with seven daughters by one wife—"

"Seven! You mean . . . ?"

Rose pouted again. "How can I tell our story if you keep interrupting? Of course there are seven of us. Everybody knows that."

Hasan apologized.

"Anyway, he had seven daughters, and he was very proud of us, even if he did need a son. But then he got so proud it was folly. He was so jealous and stiff-necked—"

"Rose!"

"—that he would not give any of us in marriage to any man at all. And he summoned his wazirs and said to them, 'Can you tell me of any place untrodden by the tread of men and jinn and abounding in trees and fruits and rills?' And they said, 'What wilt thou therewith, O King of the Ages?' and he said, 'I desire there to lodge my seven lovely daughters.' And they said, 'O King, the place for them is the castle near the Mountain of Clouds, which was built by an ifrit of the rebellious jinn who revolted from the covenant of our lord Solomon, on whom be peace! Since his destruction none hath dwelt there, nor man nor jinni, for it is cut off from the rest of the world and none may win to it. And the castle is girt about with trees and fruits and rills, and the water running round it is sweeter than honey and colder than snow; none who is afflicted with leprosy or illness drinketh thereof but he is healed forthright.' When our father heard this he joyed with great joy and brought us here with an escort of troops and left us with everything we need.

"When he wants to visit us he beats a kettle-drum, and all his hosts present themselves before him, and he comes here with his retinue. But when he wants us to visit him, he commands the enchanters to fetch us, so that he may enjoy our company, and afterwards he sends us back here. And that's it."

Hasan was amazed. "But surely he wouldn't prevent you from marrying all your lives!"

"You don't know daddy! We've been here four years, all the time hoping for a son of Adam to keep us company—and praised be He who brought you to us! So be of good cheer and keep your eyes cool and clear, because we've got you now!"

"But where are your five sisters?"

"They're out hunting in the forest, where there are wild beasts beyond number."

"I know," Hasan said, remembering the long days of travel.

"Well, why did you ask, brother?"

Hasan did not see through her teasing. "I meant, I know there are animals, because I saw them. And insects! And the most remarkable birds."

Again the two girls reacted. "Which birds are these?" the older sister inquired.

"Why the roc, of course. I told you how it—"

They laughed as though relieved. Hasan was mystified, but attributed it to the vagaries of feminine nature. What bird could be more remarkable than the roc?

The afternoon passed in a moment amidst inconsequential dialogue. Suddenly there was the blast of a horn outside.

"They're back!" Rose cried. "Come, Hasan—you have to meet our sisters. *Your* sisters." She hauled him after her as she dashed with unladylike haste out of the palace.

Five heavily veiled warrior maidens stood before the main gate, the gutted carcass of a deer beside them. The late afternoon sunlight glinted on their metallic armor.

"Come *on*, brother! You take all day."

The leading amazon lifted her bow as soon as she recognized Hasan as a stranger. The deadly hunting arrow followed his progress unwaveringly.

"Sister! Wait!" Rose cried breathlessly. "Don't shoot him. He's my brother!"

The leader frowned under her veil. She was a hefty,

muscular woman, handsome rather than beautiful. This was evidently the oldest sister. "We have no brother," she said, increasing the tension on the bowstring, much to Hasan's alarm.

"I adopted him," Rose said. "He escaped from Bahram, the evil magician, and now he's ours. A son of Adam!"

Magic words! The women behind the leader jostled each other. Hasan could see that they ranged from sleek to voluptuous. They studied him as eagerly.

The arrow lowered. "Put him in the stable for the night. I'll question him tomorrow." The women picked up the carcass and marched on into the palace.

"See, she likes you," Rose said.

Hasan was amazed when he presented himself for the formal interview the following day. The eldest sister sat on an ornate couch, dressed in bright red pantaloons and a matching shawl. Her hair hung almost to her waist in jeweled splendor, and her eyes above the copious veil were dark and enormous. She wore a headdress like a small gold crown, and looked every inch the queen she was. He had misjudged her badly, in her rough armor.

"Tell me your story," she said abruptly. "All of it." The manner, at any rate, had not changed.

Hasan went over it again. The queen's interruptions, unlike Rose's, were intelligent and to the point. Exactly how had Bahram produced gold? How many months had the voyage on the sea lasted? Why had he come to the palace? Did he understand the obligations and restraints implicit in formal Brotherhood?

Hasan, realizing that his stay at the palace and quite possibly his life as well depended upon his answers, replied with complete candor. There was now no doubt in his mind that the seven princesses were what they professed to be; the jinn would never have needed to question him like this. But the queen did not relent. She rapped out her queries with a severity that belied the luxuriousness of her softly garbed body.

"Do you realize," she said, watching him narrowly, "that no man is permitted here except our father the King? Do you desire to stay with us, even though you know you will be horribly executed if he ever learns of your presence?"

Hasan had not known. Of course that would be the case. Why had the King isolated his lovely daughters here, if not to deny them the company of all men and thus prevent their marriage? How terrible would be his wrath if he caught a male intruder!

"There are settlements on the island," the queen said. "The natives are not of the True Faith, but traders do pass every year or so. We can provide you with money to buy your passage home. In this manner you will be safe."

Now Hasan thought about Bassorah, and his dull life there as a marginally successful goldsmith. The adventures would be over, the attractive sisters of the palace forever parted from him. He had thought only of returning home, until now—but the opportunity to do so brought serious second thoughts. At Bassorah he would look out upon bleak plains during the hot season, interminable swamps during the wet season, his dreams behind him. At all times there would be the great rivers and the ocean—and when the ships from far ports came in he would remember that he had visited paradise . . . and given it up because he lacked the courage to remain.

Tears came to his eyes as he felt the immensity, the weight of that tedium descend upon him. What use was life at all to a man alone and unloved and unable to accomplish anything that had not been better accomplished by others before him? Surely death was better than this, if it was an honorable demise for the sake of true comradeship. For the sake of Rose and her charming sisters.

"How is a man to desert his sisters?" he asked her. "The will of Allah, the Compassionate, the Merciful, shall prevail. If you would have me stay, I shall stay."

The queen removed her veil. "Welcome, brother," she said—and at that signal the room was filled with excited, unveiled girls.

They had been hiding behind the curtains all the time!

Hasan was nearly buried in their affectionate embraces. "Laud to the Lord who guides us into the path of deliverance and inclines fair damsels' hearts to us!" he exclaimed.

There were eager introductions now; but he could not remember all the elaborate names at once, and settled upon "Eldest," "Second," "Third," and so on down to the youngest, Rose, in his own mind.

Hasan was never alone after that, nor did he want to be. Even at night Rose would come and sit on his bed, the delightful younger sister, and tell him tales of old Serendip and of the marvelous kingdom in Sind, on the mainland. The others seemed to take turns with him during the day. At least, he found himself escorted by one or two, while the others busied themselves elsewhere, and never by the same girls on consecutive days. He kept his peace. He loved them all, and the constant variety and implied flattery were highly stimulating. Rose, of course, followed no rules; she had proprietary rights.

Eldest took him on a private hunt. She showed him the monstrous wild elephants browsing in the jungle, shy vegetarians despite their size, and great eagles soaring high above the hills. She trained him to the bow and spear and the short sword. When he shot an arrow into the flank of a happy earthgrubbing boar, far smaller than the powerful wild swine of the Bassorah swampland, and did not kill it with that shot or the next, he learned a lasting lesson. Suddenly the innocuous creature was a charging brute, and he had to finish it off desperately with his sword, overwhelmed by the vicious squeal and stink of it and its spouting blood upon his arms and chest. Now he knew that this was also the way of a man under attack, and was forever warned against the careless or inexpert application of weapons. As a True Believer, he could not even eat the flesh of the pig he had killed, since it was an unclean animal. He had won a pointless battle.

Second, a tall regal woman of classic beauty, showed him the palace. Room after room was filled with elegant furniture, rare colored glass, and panels of teak and ebony set with jewels of every type: sapphires and rubies plucked from nearby streams, and many less common stones. Pillared courtyards contained merry fountains and ornamental statuary, and pleasant fruit trees grew beyond sculptured arches. Careful geometric designs decorated every wall and hanging rug—reproduction of the human figure being forbidden—and even the common candlesticks were of ivory, and the lamps of ornate silver. Never had he seen such fabulous wealth, and his mind was overwhelmed with the vaults. Caliph Harun al-Rashid himself, the Commander of the Faithful and ruler of empire, could hardly display such opulence.

Third was a pleasant girl, plump of bosom and round of face, who took him to the gardens. All about the palace grounds were trees and shrubs of marvelous size and grace. Nutmeg, cinnamon, guava, fig and coconut-palm grew in the vast cultivations, and the strange jak tree with its heroic fifty-pound fruit hanging from the trunk, and its brother the breadfruit tree, in the guise of the champion of watermelon plants. She showed him the magnificent cultivated orchids on the walls, and in the pools the immense flat disks of lotus leaves, their pink and white floating flowers the harbingers of the narcotic lotus seed. And finally she showed him the small oranges of the most deadly strychnine plant, the same that Bahram had gathered for his nefarious purposes; her word of caution was unnecessary.

Fourth was robust, lithe and vigorous, and she led him a merry chase farther afield. She exposed him to the hills and dales beyond the palace, where solid carpets of exquisite nelu flowers stood knee-deep and concealed everything beneath. Ferns sprang up the size of small trees, and everywhere the crimson and gold flowers spread out their enchantments. And suddenly there was a sheer cliff, a smaller version of the rift at the Mountain of Clouds, where the monkeys gathered in the evening with incredible hullabaloo. On the way back they admired the large fan-palm, said to flower only once in fifty years, and whose leaf could be used as paper. Hasan asked her about the origin of the metal chains by which he had descended from the magician's trap; she knew of them, but not of their source. The chains had existed as long as anyone had knowledge of the mountain.

Fifth had a mouth like Solomon's ring and huge purple-painted eyes. She conveyed Hasan to an interior room that was dark even at noon, ignited naphtha torches set in the floor, and danced for him. As she moved her amber body under the almost transparent robe, the silken undulations accentuated her breathtaking breasts and liquidly supple hips. Muscles Hasan had hardly known existed flexed her abdomen, her buttocks, and he forgot the intricate art of the dance itself in his exceeding regret that he could never be her lover. Brotherhood itself was not the entire restraint, for adoptive siblings could marry; but she was one of seven. Love, in the physical sense, was a crime outside of marriage, and no man could take more than four wives, or marry two sisters. Concubines were limited only by his resources and ambition; but which of these princesses could he degrade to such status, and he a common merchant? But more: he would bring ruin upon them all if he were to violate the personal sanctity of these protected maidens, no matter how willing they might be. Sisters they were, irrevocably. But the dance awakened voluptuous longings, nevertheless. . . .

Sixth was the sister he had first met playing chess with Rose. She played the game with him also, but her moves and strategy were far more adept than his, and he was embarrassed to be so easily mastered by a woman. She took him to the library, where scroll after scroll was neatly rolled and filed. Here was documentation for the stories Rose liked to tell, and much more besides. But Sixth, unlike the others, expected him to contribute as well as receive: she made him dictate not only the details of his journey, but everything else he knew about geography and philosophy, while she gravely recorded the information.

She drew from the whole of his knowledge about the working of gold and other precious metals. Never had he felt so subtly inadequate, as his own voice exposed the pitiful paucity of his information. He had so much still to learn!

Rose was a constant joy. She it was who comforted him when he proved unequal to the task of bringing down game for their food supply, or selected inappropriate gems for some new palace decoration, or expressed his thought less than cogently for the library record. She answered his questions and listened raptly to his problems and cheered him with the honeydew of her lips, and he marveled that he could ever have existed without her passionate sisterhood.

"Why is your father determined never to allow you to marry?" he asked her. "I'm sure it wasn't just a matter of pride."

"Well, no," she admitted, not enthusiastic about this subject. "You see, Sind is far from Baghdad, and never was part of the Prophet's empire. My father was converted to the True Faith in his youth, when he traveled west, but his people haven't really changed. All of the neighboring Kings are Hindu. Daddy didn't want to embarrass those royal suitors by telling them that their religion wasn't good enough—"

"But why not? They should be ashamed to be infidels!"

"I *told* you. We're far from—"

"I see," Hasan said. "Now I understand. They're too far away to pilgrimage to the Holy City, and they probably expect you to adopt *their* cult. That would be intolerable."

"Would it?" she inquired in a rare pensive mood. "Is it really better to die a spinster than to accept another religion?"

"Of course. The curse of Allah would fall upon anyone who deserted Him."

"But what about the curse of Brahma?"

"I don't understand. What does Brahma matter?"

Sixth overheard the conversation and joined it. "I would marry an infidel," she said, "so long as he didn't interfere with my own belief."

Hasan was shocked. "An infidel!"

"In many ways the Hindus are just as devout as we are."

"How can you say such a thing!"

Rose got into the spirit of the argument. "Brother, would you refuse to marry a Hindu damsel if she wouldn't change her religion?"

"Certainly."

"Even if she were a princess, like us?"

"She couldn't be like you. An infidel!"

"And very beautiful?"

"No!"

"How about a Buddhist maiden?"

"No!"

"A Christian?" Rose teased.

Hasan choked. "A Christian! That's worst of all."

The two girls laughed. "Worse even than fire worship?"

Hasan suspected a trap, but they gave him no time to anticipate it. "Didn't you say you were going to marry Bahram's daughter?"

"Not after I found out about him," he replied uncomfortably. "Anyway, I don't think he has a daughter."

Sixth shook her head. "That man has been around. He may never have married, but he might have a daughter somewhere." This was the height of insult to the Persian.

"Well, I wouldn't marry her."

Rose studied him impishly. "She would be as fair as he is ugly, and a sorceress, of course. She could cast a spell over you and make your yard stand up, just like that." She made a magical gesture.

By this time the remaining sisters had appeared, and Hasan hastily changed the subject. "I thought you hated Bahram, after what he called you."

"What did he call us?" Eldest demanded.

"He made us all out to be ghouls and demons and devils!" Rose cried indignantly, remembering.

Eldest reddened. "We must surely slay him!"

"What connection did you have with him?" Hasan wanted to know. "He wouldn't tell me."

The princesses grinned. "He came here the first year we moved in," Eldest said. "He must have thought the palace was still deserted. He had this handsome young Moslem with him, as fair as the moon, all tied up. We freed the young man and drove off the magician, but next morning the lad was gone. Bahram must have tricked him into going on to the Mountain of Clouds. Foolish boy."

Hasan remembered the bones, but did not comment. He had been as easily deceived.

Hasan was sitting under the trees by the side of a fountain, idly looking down into the valley while Rose babbled merrily, when motion attracted his attention.

"Look—someone is coming."

"Get out of sight, brother!" Rose said. "It might be our father's party."

Hasan, in these months of relaxation, had almost forgotten the inherent liability of his position. He obeyed with alacrity, diving behind the fountain.

"No—those are camels," Rose announced, relieved.

Hasan stiffened. "Camels! That's Bahram the magician!" Suddenly the time he had spent in blissful company with the princesses was as nothing; the Persian was back, and revenge was a holy duty.

"I'll tell my sisters," Rose said, "and we'll arm ourselves and cut him down."

"No! I must do it myself!"

She looked at him with surprise, but did not argue.

That night they watched the magician's party camp somewhat beyond the palace. There were three camels—where did the replacement come from?—and a young man of surpassing favor. But Bahram cuffed and beat him, and the lad was in further difficulty because his hands were bound before him. He had to eat and drink by raising both hands together. His clothing, once elegant, had been soiled and torn from incessant use. Hasan saw himself, as he had been a year ago, in this handsome captive, and was hard put not to cry out in protest.

But Eldest was wiser than he. "Wait until he stops at

the Mountain of Clouds," she said. "Then we may come upon them while the magician is distracted, and he will not have time to harm the boy. If he saw us coming, he would surely use the Moslem as a hostage."

"All right. But I must be the one to kill him."

"Of course. Only have patience, brother, while we make arrangements."

"It is my right," he said uncertainly, put off by her ready agreement. "Allah has granted me revenge."

Eldest smiled with understanding, and Rose led him away.

Hasan spent a restless night, and even Rose could not pacify him. He remembered the first time Bahram had occasioned such turmoil, in Bassorah, with the dream of easy gold. Then came the first night as prisoner on board the ship, smarting from the cruel beating, bound for he knew not where and terrified for his life. Then that desolate night on the Mountain of Clouds, foully betrayed a second time by the magician and left to sojourn with the rotting bones of his predecessors.

And now the final night, precursor to revenge.

Next morning they brought out armor and fitted Hasan in a manner befitting King David. Under his tunic he wore a coat of mail, covering his body down to his waist and elbows. On his head rested an iron cap with bright feather headdress. He slung the jeweled scabbard of a sharp shortsword over his right shoulder. He rode upon an elephant.

It was noon before they were ready to ride. Sixth stayed reluctantly behind to watch the palace, and the rest rode with Hasan toward the Mountain of Clouds. They, too, were armed, and he could tell by the manner Eldest selected her arrows that she expected to use them. The princesses did not have quite the confidence in his prowess they professed.

Hasan was sick with impatience at the delays this preparation had caused—but he also could not conceal from himself the fact that he was still afraid of the magician. Thus he both chafed at and welcomed the passing hours that postponed personal decision, and fasted more because of an unsettled stomach than to obtain blessing from Allah.

As the elephant picked its way through the jungle with dextrous speed, reducing a day's journey to a matter of hours, Hasan had time to regret his insistence upon his sacred duty of revenge. True, this was in strict accord with the word of the Prophet, and he could hardly consider himself to be a man if he failed in this—but he was not a killer, however bold his fancy armor might make him appear. How could he take a human life?

Then he thought of Bahram's crimes against himself and countless other youths, and rage burned away the doubt. It was certainly no crime to slay such an idolator!

And yet again he wavered, wondering whether the Persian really did have a daughter who would thus be rendered an orphan. Was it fair to a beautiful damsel to—

Eldest watched him with compassionate but narrowed eyes, and fingered her stout bow. Hasan was ashamed, but could not say why.

They came upon Bahram's encampment in mid-afternoon. Two camels grazed at a distance; the third had already been slaughtered and gutted. A fire smoldered where the magician had baked his smelly cakes. The pretty youth was still bound, his frightened eyes peering over the gag as though it were a veil.

Bahram's high voice could be heard from a distance, cursing and threatening the captive. "Get in this hide, O cowardly cur of the gallows! Did I bring you all the way here to have you balk now? I will only release you when you agree to perform the simple task I ask; then you shall be free for the rest of your life. I guarantee this! By the Fire and the Light, I will beat you senseless and throw you in the carcass bound, if you will not do what I demand!"

The magician's back was to their party, and he was so transported by his simulated tantrum that he was not alert. Hasan forgot his fear, slid off the elephant, and ran up behind Bahram. "Hold your hand, O accursed!"

The Persian whirled around, amazed.

"O enemy of Allah and foe of the Moslems!" Hasan cried, almost slashing himself with the sword in his anxiety to draw it from its scabbard. "O dog! O traitor! O infidel of the flame. O you that walk a wicked path, worshiping the evil fire and light and swearing by the shade and the heat!"

Bahram's tone was abruptly mellow. "O my son, how did you escape? Who brought you to earth again?"

Hasan refused to be moved. "He delivered me who has now appointed me to take your life. I will torture you the way you tortured me, and all the other innocent youths. O miscreant! O atheist! You have fallen into your own trap, and your evil fire will never save you now!" He raised the sword, aware that he was talking too much instead of acting.

Bahram, surprisingly, did not draw back. He stepped forward. "By Allah, O my son, O Hasan—you are dearer to me than my own eyes. I called to you to come down off the mountain, and when you did not answer I thought you were dead. How glad I am that you are safe."

Hasan drew the sword back to strike. "Don't try to fool me with lies about your concern for my welfare. You broke the sacred bond of bread and salt!" But he was still postponing action. . . .

Bahram's eyes were wide and innocent. "O my son, how can you blame me for what you thought I did, when you yourself have done no less?"

Hasan's sword wavered. "What?"

"Look!" The magician whirled, removed his turban, drew out a package of powder and walked toward the fire.

"Stop him!" Rose cried. Hasan had forgotten the sisters standing not far behind him. "He intends sorcery!"

But still Hasan hesitated, and while he watched, Bahram threw the powder into the glowing embers.

The flame roared up. Smoke puffed out in a yellow mass, sweetly scented and forming a billowing ball. "Look, Hasan!" the magician cried, pointing.

A picture formed within the haze. Hasan recognized a

house—his own house in Bassorah, but with a difference. A tomb was set up in the middle of it, and before it crouched a woman, a hag so wasted away that her skin was a multitude of yellow wrinkles and her black shawl fit her shrunken body like a tent.

It was his mother.

The image vanished. "How can you talk of bread and salt when you dwell here in luxury, while your own dear mother mourns this very moment before your tomb?"

Hasan stood bemused. How indeed could he have been so callous toward the one who loved him most? He had never even thought of her these months.

The magician was before him, reaching out a skinny hand. "Now give me your weapon, son, and we shall—"

Hasan's defensive instinct took over. "No!" he cried, bringing the blade up in an attempt to ward the man off.

But Bahram was already leaping forward, the sympathetic mask discarded. The point of the rising sword pushed into his throat, and so desperate was his leap that the magician impaled himself upon it and severed the tendons of his own neck. Blood spurted over hand and blade.

"Magnificent, brother!" Eldest cried, hauling him out of the way as the corpse fell toward him. "Never have I seen a neater stroke! He didn't even have a chance to curse you before he died."

Hasan looked upon what he had wrought and felt the bile of his stomach distending his cheek. Eldest closed immediately and slapped him sharply across the mouth, concealing her action in a grandiose embrace. Hasan swallowed involuntarily. "You're a hero; act like one!" she barked into his ear.

Then they were all about him, congratulating him on his valor and prowess and marveling at his composure in the face of danger.

"O Hasan," Rose cried, "you have done a magnificent deed and avenged our honor and satisfied the thirst for vengeance that pleases the King of the Omnipotent!"

"I have?" But in the face of their unanimous acclaim

and evident disregard for the horror of the slaughter, Hasan could do no less than act the part. He strode over to the youth and untied him. "Everything here is yours," he said, while the young man gaped. "You may come with us or take the camels, whichever you wish."

Hasan opened the magician's pack, took out the kettledrum, and beat it with the strap. The two remaining camels came up immediately. "Do you know how to control these beasts?" he asked the youth. "Can you find your way back to the ship? You own it now, for the idolator's soul has returned to the fire. Pay off the crew and sell the merchandise you find aboard and you'll be a wealthy man."

The youth mounted a camel and left without a word. "I can't blame him for being afraid of us," Hasan remarked, watching him go. "After being tortured by the magician, and seeing the vision in the fire—"

"What vision, brother?" Rose inquired.

"Why, the house with my mother in mourning, and the tomb in the middle. Didn't you see it?"

Rose shook her head, looking at him with concern. "I saw nothing but a nasty cloud of smoke, all ugly and yellow. It's a good thing it didn't get in your eyes and blind you, so that Bahram could escape."

Hasan glanced at the others, the forgotten kettledrum dangling from his hand. None had seen the vision.

"Let's dump this corpse in the camel-carcass," he said. "This time the roc will have a meal, if it can chew it!"

Chapter 5. Bird Maiden

Hasan soon forgot the vision in the excitement of the palace celebration. After all, it had been a conjuration of an evil magician, a sight no one else had seen, and was probably only a false trick to stay his vengeance. But the ploy had failed. Now he felt like a man!

But a second trial of his strength was soon to follow. A cloud of dust rose from the plain beyond the palace.

"That's our father's host!" Rose said. "O Hasan, run to your room and conceal yourself—or if you prefer, go down into the gardens and hide among the trees and vines, for it is death if they find you here."

Hasan wasted no time. He went to his chamber and locked himself in.

He lurked behind the parapet adjoining his room and watched the cloud rise up until it darkened the welkin. Before long it opened, and beneath it was a conquering host like a surging sea, marching troops advancing on the palace.

For three days he suffered through the perpetual clamor of foreign troops being entertained, mad with jealousy because they ate at the banquet tables while he devoured scraps smuggled up by Rose; because their coarse voices laughed in the company of the seven princesses, while he had only stolen moments with one. It had seemed his own palace for so long that he suffered when reminded so blatantly that it was not; he didn't like being an imposter who had to hide lest his life be instantly forfeit. He who had killed the magician!

On the fourth morning Rose came to him with worse news. "We have to leave you, brother, for a while," she said.

"Leave! Why?"

"One of the kings is getting married, and we are expected to attend the festival. So daddy has summoned us home, so we can enjoy it all."

Hasan groaned. "How long will you be gone?"

"It may be two months."

"Two months!"

"But we'll be back just as soon as we can make it, Hasan. And you can stay right here in the palace, and no one will bother you, and everything will be all right. I'll give you all the keys."

"Keys!" he muttered, but there was nothing he could do.

She produced a massive chain of them. "But Hasan—"

"Yes?"

"You can go anywhere you want in the palace, except

one door. I beseech you, for myself and for my sisters—
your sisters—don't open that door. There is nothing there
you need, and I'm afraid there will be a great calamity
if—''

Hasan smiled. "Don't worry. I'll behave!"

She kissed him. "Keep your eyes cool, brother. Farewell."

She left, and within hours everyone was gone. Hasan
watched dolefully as the great party marched across the
plain, leaving nothing but drifting dust.

He was alone. Never in his life had he felt such continued isolation, as he tread the loud floors and gazed down
empty halls. He had not realized how terribly dependent he
had become upon the bright company of the seven cheerful
maidens, or how deeply he would feel their absence. Even
the living orchards were somber, and paradise without
companionship was torture.

He rode forth bravely by himself and slaughtered game
and prepared the meat and ate it, alone. He visited each of
the princesses' apartments in turn, fancying he could somehow commune with the owners; but their rich trappings
and feminine adornments only served to remind him that
the girls who used these things were gone.

He tried to divert himself by exploring the less familiar
chambers of the palace, for there were many reaches and
hallways he had never penetrated. He found behind one
door an open court with a garden like that of the angels;
the trees were of freshest green with shining yellow fruits,
and pretty little birds were singing pleasantly. He walked
among them and smelled the delicate breath of flowers,
and almost believed he could hear the praises of Allah in
the avian melodies.

He opened another door and faced what resembled a
spacious plain set with tall date palms and watered by a
running stream whose banks were rich with flowery shrub-
bery. It reminded him of his home city, Bassorah, the city
of dates, but did not ease his isolation.

In other rooms were bulky colored marble artifacts and
decorations of precious stones and sandalwood and other

wonders beyond remembering. But physical wealth alone
could never take the place of human fellowship. How he
longed for his sisters' return!

Only one thing took his attention from his loneliness:
the thought of the forbidden door. If there were wonders
such as he had seen in the open portions of the palace,
what might not lie behind that secret portal?

"My sister would not have asked me to stay away
unless there were some tremendous secret!" he told himself. "But what could she have to hide from *me*?"

He remembered her dire warning against this door, and
resolved to restrain his curiosity and inquire when the
princesses returned. But then it occurred to him that they,
having concealed it from him this long, might refuse to en-
lighten him later. If he really wanted to know the secret,
he had no choice but to discover it now, while there was
no one to stop him.

"By Allah!" he said, then paused because he knew he
was taking the name in vain. One should not invoke Allah
to witness an improper deed. "I will open that door and
learn what it conceals, though death is there!"

He took the key and unlocked the forbidden door. He
stepped back. Suppose there were some ravenous beast
inside, waiting with bared fangs? He should have come
armed!

He locked it again, unopened, and went to don mail and
sword. He returned, turned the key again, pushed the door
open with his foot while raising his sword defensively, and
stood ready for the rush of whatever might come.

In that, at least, he was disappointed. No creature
emerged, no sound, and the gloom of the room was abso-
lutely still. Why hadn't he thought to bring a lamp or torch?

He ran to fetch one, cursing himself for his stupidity.
He lit a torch and came back—to discover he'd forgotten
to close the door! The thing might have escaped!

Cautiously he poked his head in, ready to leap back
instantly. There was nothing, as the light flickered to the
farthest corners. The chamber was empty.

He shut the door, locked it, and tried to reason out the meaning of this mystery. Why had Rose made such an issue over *an empty room?* Had this been set up as a joke, and were the sisters laughing even now to imagine his confusion? Rose was certainly capable of such a thing— but somehow he could not believe that she would have tricked him this way when she was not on hand to watch the result. She liked to appreciate her little jests personally. No—she had been serious, and must have had a better reason to put him to this torture of uncertainty.

Or had the room been occupied? He had left it open; if a demon lurked within, it would hardly have sat idle when escape was offered. Did it creep stealthily along the passageways at this moment, waiting for him to pass? Was it cunning, knowing that he must sleep sometime? Was this the disaster Rose had feared, already loosed upon the palace?

Hasan looked nervously behind him. Was that a noise? Had he seen something, something that vanished just before he turned?

Already he heartily regretted disobeying his sister's instruction. But if he was to live, he had to undo the damage he had done. First he had to learn what kind of thing it was, so he could devise some means to kill it. Assuming it was a *live* creature.

Perhaps it had left a footprint.

He unlocked the door a third time, lifted his sword, and looked in with frightened boldness. Once again the torch brightened the corners. This time he saw that thick dust lay everywhere. There were no footprints. It was obvious that no one had occupied this room or even visited it for many months.

Either there had been no inhabitant, or—

A fragment came back to him suddenly. He had mentioned a remarkable bird, thinking of the roc, and they had reacted strangely. It had not been the roc that worried them. Had it been a bird in this chamber . . . or some other flying thing?

Yet a bird would have had to perch sometime, and it would leave droppings. . . .

He moved into the room, glancing apprehensively into the upper corners. There were no ledges or perches. Featureless walls met a featureless ceiling. His own tracks in the deep dust were the only sign of molestation.

His tracks! They would betray him! He would have to sweep out the entire chamber to erase them, and hope that no one would check until as even a layer had formed again. Meanwhile, he should search every foot of the room for whatever clues there might be. He had only guessed it might be an animal; probably it was something else entirely. Some magic object, perhaps. Some dangerous magic relic.

He glanced into an alcove. "Idiot!" he cursed himself. He had missed the obvious again. There was a stair ascending from the alcove, winding up in a vaulted spiral into the dark. The secret was not in the room itself; it lay above!

He was fully committed now. He dared not stop until he knew the exact nature of the danger that confronted him. He mounted the stair, the torch flickering with the shivering of his hand. His fear increased as the space constricted and the minutes passed without any break in the still tension. What if a sinuous dragon lay above, waiting to roast him in a downward spiraling column of fire? He could never retreat in time.

The stair coiled around like the stomach of a python. He could not see the base below or the termination above. Where was it leading?

Light! After two complete loops, the end was coming in sight. He climbed into an open dome that overlooked the roof of the palace.

He hardly dared feel disappointment. He still had no idea why he had been warned away from this. He looked about.

The roof was a terrace, and as he gazed upon it he was amazed to see the entire palace grounds laid out before him. To one side the wall dropped off to expose the rising towers and minarets, and the open pits of the courtyards with the cultivated trees spreading their gentle foliage up. To the other side—

A new world greeted him. The main roof of the palace was a garden more magnificent than any he had seen below, set with trees and flowers and softly flowing streamlets and even a shining lake, the wavelets shimmering across its surface in the breeze. Beside the lake was a pavilion constructed of alternate courses of bricks; two of gold to each one of silver, studded with jaycinth and emerald. Four alabaster columns rose to support the ruby dome, and within it a mosaic marble platform extended into an interior pool, a soft veil of green silk above the crystal waters.

"This must be the thing my sisters forbade me!" Hasan said, marveling at the beauty of the scene. But still he wondered why they should not have wished to share the ultimate glory of the palace with him. Surely the sight of such beauty would not in itself bring destruction?

He approached the pavilion and discovered that it was even richer than he had supposed. The center, around the sparkling pool, was a sitting room whose benches were thrones of polished stone latticed with red gold and inlaid with enormous pearls and symmetrically disposed gems. Above the pool was a trellis set with jewels the size of pigeons' eggs and on it was a climbing vine bearing grapes like rubies. Brilliant birds fluttered upon it, of a type Hasan had never seen on Earth, and their warbling seemed to celebrate the glories of Allah with throats of miraculous sweetness.

"What king could own a place like this?" Hasan exclaimed. "Or is this Many-Columned Iram, the property of no mortal man?" And he sat down within the pavilion and glanced around him in continued amazement, hardly aware of the passage of time during his contemplation. Had he once dreamed of mundane gold?

He was roused from his reverie by motion in the distant

sky. Quickly he rose and ran to the stair . . . in case. But it was only a flight of birds approaching from the heart of the desert plain, and he could tell by the steadiness of their passage that they intended to roost on the palace roof and refresh themselves there. They were beautiful creatures with spreading white wings, and he did not wish to frighten them away. He ducked down and hid inside the little dome sheltering the stair, concealing himself as well as he could while keeping an eye on the formation.

They came, beating the foliage with the wind from their spectacular wings. These were enormous birds. They were smaller than the rocs, but larger than the eagles or buzzards. They lighted on a mighty tree by the water, then dropped to the ground and paraded toward the pavilion.

There were ten of them, and their leader was a hen of remarkable beauty, sleek and haughty and a veritable queen among birds, strutting and pecking at the lesser ones who did service to her. Hasan was not surprised to see that birds had their royal personages, just as men did; this was the natural state of the kingdoms of Allah.

They filed into the pavilion and perched upon the great stone couches there. Hasan craned to see what went on inside, but the pillars interfered with his view at crucial moments. They were doing something, stretching out their wings and twisting their torsos with the most unbirdlike gyrations and clawing at their downy breasts. Had they come here to slay themselves with exercise?

Lo! The shapes of the birds collapsed, and suddenly Hasan pawed at his own eyes to relieve them of an impossible vision. For there were no longer birds in the pavilion, but people! How had this happened?

Too stunned to move, Hasan watched as the ten daughters of Adam stood up, maidens whose beauty shamed the brilliance of the full moon. They wore the filmiest of gowns; but in moments they drew off even these and threw them aside and plunged naked into the pool.

Hasan stared as they bathed, and not merely from surprise. These were high-bosomed virgins as lovely as any he had seen. The vigor with which they washed and sported, shrieking and splashing each other, only served to enhance their youthful pulchritude. Most striking of all was the princess—for such she had to be—who sashed and dunked the others, but upon whom nobody laid hands in turn.

As he watched, he remembered with a hot rush what had been missing from his happy life with the seven sisters. They were his sisters, which was the trouble. There was that a man could not do with his sister. They *were* beautiful—but there were beauties a man could not view in his sister. He loved them all—but there was love that could not be shared among sisters.

Hasan stood behind a post, gazing upon the maidens while they thought themselves unobserved. The sight of their dancing breasts and wetly quivering thighs excited his mind to lecherous promptings. His loin grew hot. He sighed to be among them in that pool, touching what he could only glimpse at the moment and caressing what he could only dream about. He felt a flame that could not be quenched and a desire whose signs might not be hidden.

The chief damsel tired of the sport. Bidding her companions to remain, she stepped out of the pavilion and stood, unknowingly, directly before Hasan's blind. She stretched her sleek limbs and combed out her long hair, dazzling him with the splendor of her person.

Her body was exquisite in the afternoon sunlight, gleaming with dripping water and seeming to shine with its own sublimity. The luster of her face outshone the resplendent moon; her damp hair curled around a bosom whose outlines were no less than the masterwork of Allah. Her neck was a bar of silver smoother than that of a gazelle; her teeth gleamed, perfect hailstones in the sun. Her belly was softly rounded and delightfully dimpled. Her buttocks projected generously, resilient as cushions filled with ostrich-down, and strove against each other when she walked, shaping and reshaping the darker shadows of their separa-

tion. Her thighs were heavy and firm, expanding columns
embracing that same shadow.

She sat upon the low wall of the pavilion and lifted her
lithe legs so that she could brush the sand from dainty feet,
and there was revealed to Hasan, as from behind a cloud,
what lay between her thighs.

It was midafternoon when Hasan was startled from his
trance by the clear voice of the royal maiden. She spoke in
a lovely language he could not comprehend, but his imagination filled in the words. They were obvious in the
context: "O daughters of kings, the hour is late and our
home is far away. Come—we must depart."

The girls arose and went to the benches in the pavilion.
They were dressed now, but they took up the feathered
suits and behold: they were birds again! They filed out,
spread their wings, and ascended into the sky.

Hasan stood bemused, unable to credit his senses. Had
the damsels really transformed themselves to birds before
his eyes, or had he suffered another delusion like the one
Bahram had shown him in the fire? Could he really have
looked upon the naked glories of an incredible woman, even
to that which no unmarried man was privileged to see?

Only when the last speck vanished beyond the clouds
did he think to ask himself the basic question: could he
really have fallen most passionately in love with an alien
princess who could transform herself into a bird?

Hasan hardly remembered dragging himself down the
stair and back to his own chamber. He lay without appetite
or thirst, drowned in a solitude suddenly magnified ten-
fold. For it was true: he was smitten by the beauty of the
bird maiden, and he was unable to rest in her absence. All
night he tossed about, finding no comfort, and he wept and
moaned with frustration until morning.

When the sun rose he rushed out of his room, entered
the forbidden chamber with no thought of danger, and
mounted the spiral stair to the roof. All day he waited,
growing faint from the heat of the terrace and from lack of

nourishment, but the bird-maidens never came. When his hope at last expired, he fell to the ground in a fainting fit. There was no one to comfort him.

The cool of the evening roused him. He crawled down the steps on hands and feet and dragged himself back to his room. There he passed out again, and lay on the floor all night, dreaming of beauty and sorcery.

On the following day he made his way to the terrace once more, but the pavilion was deserted. His love was gone. After that he stopped looking. His life became a delirium of melancholy, lamentation and unrequited love.

For the first time, he was sorry he had not died on the Mountain of Clouds. He had approached the forbidden door with a raised sword to guard his body—but it was his heart he should have protected.

When the seven sisters returned from their visit to their homeland, Hasan roused himself and hid, ashamed to show himself to them and wishing only to die. For they had warned him, and he had stubbornly violated their trust, and now he had to bear the penalty of his deceit. He no longer deserved their company.

Rose didn't wait to doff her traveling-gear, but dashed immediately to Hasan's room. She found it sadly disarranged, and her brother nowhere in sight. She searched everywhere in growing anxiety—and finally found him slumped in a closet, thin and feeble. His body was so shrunken and his bones so wasted by starvation and fatigue that she hardly recognized him.

"O Hasan!" she cried. "What has happened?" But his sunken eyes only flickered in the pale face. He did not answer.

She gripped his emaciated shoulders and dragged him bodily to the bed. "O my brother—I would give my life to save yours! Tell me what illness has befallen you."

Hasan felt her sympathetic embrace and wept. What could he say to his well-meaning sister? His mouth opened.

When parted from the thing he loves
A man has naught but woe to bear.

"But Hasan—"

Inside is sickness, outside doves;
His first mere fancy; last, despair:

"What are you saying, Hasan? I don't understand!"

Her confusion was natural; he himself did not comprehend what was happening. Still he found himself unable to state his case.

Rose fluttered her hands, thoroughly shaken. "You're dying, O beloved. How have you fallen into this terrible plight? We told you we would come back—"

The birds took flight and went away
And gave me Love's death blow.

"The birds took—"

I'll keep my secret while I may—
Ah, but Love's needs must show!

Rose stared at him, appalled. "Hasan—you opened the door!"

It was out. Now would come the punishment he deserved, the censure he had brought on himself.

Rose cradled his head against her bosom, crying wihout shame. "O Hasan, Hasan—we meant to spare you this. I should have thrown away that key!"

But in a short time her natural exuberance reasserted itself. "By Allah, O my brother, I will not abandon you now, though my life be forfeit! Tell me everything, and I swear by the bond that binds us together I will help you somehow."

Now everything that was within him poured out, and he told her of the terrible passion he had conceived for the beauteous bird-maiden, and how he had been able neither to eat nor to sleep since seeing her. "My heart is gone," he finished. "She has flown with it, and I have no wish to live any more."

Rose wept for his misery, not condemning him at all, then brightened again. "O my brother, be of good cheer and keep your eyes cool and clear. You'll see her again, and if it is the will of Allah Almighty you might even win her. I'll help—"

"But what can you do? She's gone."

"I don't know, Hasan; but whatever it is, I'll do it. Now you've got to eat something. Promise me you'll eat if I sneak some fruit to you. I can't get anything else while my father's troops are downstairs."

Hasan promised, encouraged by her certainty, and shortly she was back with an armful of breadfruit and coconut. "But remember, Hasan—don't breathe a word of this to my sisters. I'm afraid of what they might do if they found out. If they ask you about the door, you must tell them you never went near it."

"But how shall I explain my illness?"

"I'll think of something. My sisters won't see you until the escort departs. You must stay here and try to get well. We can't do *anything* if you don't get strong again, Hasan."

It was the turning point. Hasan was weak and uncomfortable, but he did begin to eat. When the King's troops left, the other sisters came to see him as a group.

"You have not been exercising, brother," Eldest said, and Fourth nodded agreement. The others looked concerned, for this careful understatement could hardly justify his obvious emaciation.

"I *told* you, sisters," Rose said. "Our severance from our dear brother left him desolate, for the days we have been absent were longer than a thousand years to him, a stranger in the palace and solitary, with none to keep him company or cheer his lonely heart. He is just a youth, and maybe he remembered his poor mother, who is very old and ugly, and thought of how she weeps for him all day and all night, mourning his absence. We used to bring him solace with our society and keep his mind off such things. But when we deserted him—''

''We understand, sister,'' Eldest interrupted gently.

They gathered around him, comforting him and offering dainty tidbits for him to eat. They bemoaned his yellow color and shrunken flesh and promised never to desert him again. They told him of the wonders and rarities they had seen on their journey and of the splendor of the wedding in Sind. And if they had reservations about Rose's story, they did not say so in words.

A month passed, but though Hasan's health improved, his melancholy hardly abated. When he closed his eyes he saw the face of the bird-maiden, her mouth as magical as Solomon's seal and her hair blacker than the night of estrangement after his own love-despair. Her brow was as bright as the crescent moon on the eve of a feast after long fasting, and her eyes were those of an innocent gazelle. Her nose was straight as a cane, her cheeks like a bright anemone, lips like coral and teeth like strung pearls. She was perfection.

> Her lips are sweet as honey, in their virginity;
> Keener than a scimitar, the glance she cast at me!

His body had recovered, yes, but his spirit remained waxen. All of his longing and the extemporary couplets spawned by it could not make real the intangible vision. The bird-maiden had cast no glance at him, and had no inkling of his existence. If she had seen him, she would have flown that much sooner.

At the end of that month, Eldest organized a hunting and birding party of several days' duration. Rose declined to accompany them. ''By Allah, O my sisters, I cannot join you while my brother is in such plight, too ill to take proper care of himself. I must stay and comfort him until he is well again.''

Eldest replied with a half-smile. "Allah will reward you for your efforts on behalf of our brother."

The six princesses rode forth without delay, carrying with them supplies for well over a fortnight. "Perhaps he will be better when we return," Eldest said wisely as they parted. Rose missed the significance.

Rose watched them until they were well out of sight and the noise of their animals faded. Then she went eagerly to Hasan. "Come, brother," she said. "Show me the place where you saw the maidens."

Hasan, too, had observed the departure of the hunting party. "Yes, sister," he agreed. He jumped to his feet and promptly collapsed. His enthusiasm was greater than his strength, despite the improvement of his color.

Rose put her arms around him where he sprawled, letting his head rest between her breasts while she hauled him upright. An observer might have suspected that she took more time than was necessary. "Just hold on to me, Hasan. I'll get you there somehow."

He found that he could walk well enough, with her support, and his strength gained steadily, now that they were taking positive action. They stumbled through the forbidden room—his old footprints still plainly visible, for he had forgotten to dust—and up the spiral stair to the terrace. "That's it," he said, pointing to the splendid pavilion.

"Now show me just where they came from, and where they went, and describe everything you saw them do."

Hasan obliged, sparing no detail. He paid particular attention to the chief bird-maiden and the marvels made manifest by her nudity.

Rose paled, obviously upset. "O my sister," Hasan inquired, "what is the matter? Why are you so wan and troubled?"

"I am *not* jealous," she snapped. "Let's get out of here."

Hasan had to make his own way down the steps. Rose led the way briskly to the library. "I didn't have a chance to look while my sisters were here," she explained, "but there must be some information on this. All I know is that those bird-maidens come every month or so to spend a day sporting in the pool, and we leave them strictly alone because there is powerful magic about them. We knew you'd get into trouble if you saw them: That's why we tried to keep you away. Something awful would happen if they caught a man spying on them."

"I must have her," Hasan said.

Rose paced around the library. "We have books on everything. If only I knew where to look."

"What's that scroll on the table?"

She picked it up. "This must be something my sister forgot to put away." She glanced at the title. "Hasan! This is it!"

"Glory be to Allah, the Omnipotent!" It did not occur to either of them to question this coincidence.

"Listen to this, brother," she said, excited, and began to read. "She who visiteth the pavilion on the roof of the palace with her handmaidens and damsels of the courts is the daughter of the sovereign of the jinn, the most puissant of their kings, who hath dominion over men and jinn and wizards and chiefs and tribes and cities and islands without number. He hath immense wealth in store and kings are his viceroys and vassels and none may avail against him for the multitude of his troops and the extent of his empire and the muchness of his moneys. He hath assigned his daughters a tract of country a whole year's journey in length, a region gird about with great rivers and oceans, and thereto none may attain, nor man nor jinni, without his cognizance. He hath an army of women, smiters with swords and lungers with lances, five and twenty thousand in number, each of whom, whenas she mounteth steed and donneth battle-gear, eveneth a thousand knights of the bravest."

"I knew she was a princess." Hasan said.

"Moreover he hath seven daughters, who in valor and prowess excel the amazons, and he hath made the eldest

Queen over the country aforesaid. She is the wisest of her sisters and in valor and horsemanship and craft and skill and magic excels all the folk of her dominions. There is none more beautiful than she, and. . . ."

Hasan nodded agreement as Rose plowed through the description with something less than perfect grace. "She is my love," he said.

"But Hasan—it is death to desire her. Her father would send his jinn to smash this palace and everyone in it, if you even admitted to looking at her. She *can't* be as desirable as all that."

"I'll die if I don't possess her."

Rose glanced further along in the text. "Hasan . . ." she said quietly. "She is not of the True Faith."

"My soul is hers," he said simply.

Chapter 6. Marriage

"Now this is my plan," Rose explained a few days later. "According to what I have learned, your bird-maiden will be here again before my sisters return from the hunt. You can never catch her as long as she has the plumed skin, the cloak of feathers, because that is the handiwork of the jinn. But we can overcome that if you follow my instructions exactly."

"Yes, O my sister!" Hasan said. His responses were considerably faster now, and he felt stronger.

"You must take your place at dawn and stay well hidden until they come. Don't let them see you, or we will all lose our lives. We're lucky you didn't bring calamity upon us all the last time. Stay close to the pavilion, though. When they take off their feather-suits, make sure you know which one belongs to the damsel you love. Then steal it and hide it, without being caught yourself. She can't return to her country without her suit; when you master it, you master her."

"But suppose they *do* see me?"

"They'll kill you. Then they'll fly home and tell the King, and he'll destroy us all, and our father's kingdom too."

"Why wouldn't she take one of the other suits?"

Rose squinted thoughtfully. "I don't think the magic works for anyone else. I mean, it has to be tuned to the individual . . . I don't know what I mean. We'll just have to try it and see. If I'm right, her companions will take off without her. Only then can you safely approach. By that time she'll know that it isn't just an accident. Don't let her beguile you with sorrowful words, either. She'll say 'O thou who hast robbed me of my raiment, restore it to me, for I am at thy hands and at thy mercy!' If you relent—"

"She speaks a different language," Hasan pointed out.

"I know. With ostrich-down hind-parts . . . Anyway, if you relent and give back her suit, she'll arm herself with its magic and kill you and bring the vengeance of her sire upon us. Better not let her know you have the suit at all; hide it and keep it, and she will be your prisoner. Then carry her down to your chamber, and she will be yours."

Hasan was pleased with her advice. His sorrow left him and he felt up to the most difficult task. He kissed her, ate a hearty supper, and slept well that night.

He woke before dawn, took food and drink, said his prayers, and went to the terrace. He decided immediately against trying to hide inside the pavilion itself; they might approach it from any direction and sniff him out before the transformation. He could not trust the tree nearest it, either, because they landed there. He finally stayed right where he had the first time: under the shelter at the top of the stairs.

Nothing happened. At dusk Rose brought him meat and drink and a change of clothes, and he slept right there on the terrace. It was the same the following day, and the next, but he did not give up hope. On the contrary, his vigil seemed to improve his outlook, and he felt better than he had in a month. He rejoiced when he saw the new moon come, for he remembered that this had been the time of the month when he had spied the maidens before.

And the birds came! Once more they arrowed across the plain from the distant ocean, circled the palace, perceived nobody, and alighted in turn and trooped into the pavilion. Hasan hoped the calamitous beating of his own heart would not betray him.

Again they doffed their suits and stood revealed as beautiful girls. The loveliest of all was the princess. Hasan never took his eyes off her until she set aside the feather-suit; then he fixed the place in his mind with exceeding care. If he made a mistake, he would get the wrong girl . . . and the princess, warned by the episode, might never return.

He waited, tense with excitement, as one by one they entered the pool. The last to go was his love. For agonized moments he was afraid she wouldn't swim at all, this time. She finally joined the others.

Hasan clenched his teeth to prevent their chatter in the violence of his emotion, and crawled toward the pavilion. He was in plain sight, now; if one of them happened to look this way, he was done for. But they shrieked and splashed each other merrily, oblivious to everything outside the pool.

Their noise even covered the involuntary sounds he made crawling through pebbles and brush. Allah was with him—so far.

He reached the wall of the pavilion and hunched beside it, invisible for the moment unless one of them chose to come and look over the edge. But the hardest part of his task was just ahead.

He crawled cautiously to the place where the surrounding wall dropped down to form the entrance. He would have to go inside, for the suit he was after was beyond his reach from the outside. Why hadn't he thought to attach a hook to a line, and fish for it!

He paused. Would it be better to retreat, and wait for the following month with better preparations? He could lose everything by his precipitous urgency. Then he heard the glad laughter of the princess, and his heart was charged with renewed determination. He had to have her now!

This was the key move. He could not tell whether they

were looking his way except by poking out his head. Once
he did that, the spear was cast. Either they spied him or
they did not; it was the chance he had to take.

He moved, and saw the pool, scarcely twenty feet away.
One girl was facing him! He froze, panic-stricken, as she
squinted her eyes, brought her hand up. He heard her say
something in that strange language. Then another girl came
to her and peered into her face.

Relief! She had a speck in her eye. He crawled quickly
into the pavilion and hid himself behind the nearest bench.
Success was so close, now; he had only to circle a quarter
of the way around the pool and grab the feather-suit from
behind this protection. If only they stayed in the pool!

The happy squeals continued. The backs of the benches
farthest from the entrance were hollow. It seemed that the
builder had economized on the expensive stone and brick.
Hasan approached the suit, reached up . . .

There was a sudden lull.

"What's the matter, Mistress?"

The language was foreign, but that was what the tone
said. Had he been spotted?

The noise and laughter resumed in a burst. He had
worried for nothing; apparently it had been some momentary girlish game, damming up the twitter only to release it
all at once. He had to remember that: the words he thought
he heard were homunculi, and could not be trusted.

He reached up again, found the suit, took hold of its soft
material, and yanked.

It came down with a thud, the feathers rattling against
the stone. This time the abrupt silence was no mistake.
They had heard!

How could he have been so stupid! He should have
brought the cloak down gently, a contour at a time, so that
no noise could result. Now—

There was a burst of chatter. Hasan lay where he was,
translating the sounds with a certainty that went beyond
language. "What was that noise?" "Someone is here!"
"Kill him!" Should he jump up and run for it now?

No—they could easily catch him, and that would be the end. Even if he made the stairs, and slammed the door and escaped today, all would be undone when they reported to their King. Not only his own life. The lives of all his sisters, and their father too.

What could he do? Their steps were already sounding on the pavement circling the pool. He was trapped.

He could play dead! Perhaps, that way, they would at least spare the palace, thinking that a stranger had died on the roof without the knowledge of the sisters. Of course, they would quickly detect the warmth of his body . . . but he was still a little sallow from his illness, and if he pretended unconsciousness, this would be all the more evidence that no one had cared for him. He hoped.

He straightened, lying prone on the tile—and rediscovered the space under the bench. He rolled into the cavity without thinking.

The bricks were solid on the side facing the pool, meeting the polished stone without a chink. Appearance was everything, fortunately. He was invisible again. He might yet escape, if they didn't search too carefully.

If there weren't any snakes or spiders or leeches lurking in this dust. . .

There was the slap of wet feet against dry brick, and another exclamation. "Princess—your suit is gone!" What else could they be saying?

A soprano hubbub immediately over his head. Bare toes, dainty and beautifully manicured, coming to rest inches from his face. In spite of his predicament, Hasan thrilled to the satin smoothness of that foot, the slender perfection of the ankle. This was the foot of the princess, tantalizingly close. He was strongly tempted to slide forward and kiss it, and to Tophet with the consequence!

His nose itched. The smell of the feathers was—

He bit his tongue. The pain seemed to stave off the oncoming sneeze, for the time being.

"My cloak—it fell off the bench!" What a delightful

voice belonged to that foot! Such a voice, incomprehensible or not, was well fit to die for.

Tapered fingers descended, grasping the cloak. Hasan's breath stopped in his throat as he thought of the nakedness of that hand and that foot and the body connecting them. What might he glimpse if he poked his head out and looked up now? Was death too great a price to pay?

Melodious laughter. "That was all—your suit fell down!" "We were worried over nothing!" The foot withdrew, flicking a last droplet of water onto Hasan's nose, and the crisis—and opportunity—was over. They were returning to the pool.

But he still didn't have the suit. And now, he could not be sure which one was hers.

Hasan sent off a fervent prayer to Allah, reached up once more, casting about blindly upon the bench—and touched the feather-suit. She had not moved it.

He brought it down—carefully—and maneuvered his body to head in the direction of the exit. This was not easy to do without sitting up, and the magic robe encumbered him. It was light—as light as a feather—but bulky, and although he knew it was his enemy he could not bring himself to damage any part of it. This was an article of *her* clothing, that had once clung to her marvelous . . . but nothing she had touched deserved destruction at his hands.

The return-plunge through the entrance, the anxious hesitation outside the wall—these were things he must have done, but he was never able to remember them. The worst was over. They had not discovered him, and he had the suit. If they continued bathing just a little longer. . . .

They did, and Hasan made it safely to the shelter of the stairs. It was merely a matter of time, now, before he achieved his desire.

But the suit! What was he to do with it? If he kept it here the damsels would see it, and all his exploits would be rendered meaningless. If he took it into the palace, the princess might escape during his absence.

Escape? They could do nothing in his absence that they

couldn't do as readily in his presence. He must secure the
feather-suit first; then he could do what he liked.

He descended the steps and carried the cloak to his
chamber. He emptied the clothing from his largest chest,
laid the beautiful feather-dress in the bottom, piled other
things on top of it, and closed the lid and locked it.

The girls on the terrace had not missed him. He stood
concealed by the stairs and waited for the inevitable.

This time the princess—actually, he supposed she was
the Queen, but she seemed so young—took a walk in her
delectable green dress, arranging her hair with strokes
from a jeweled comb. Hasan had never imagined anything
so lovely. Looking upon her noble serenity, he was sorry
that it was to be so short-lived. Not for anything would he
hurt this elegant creature . . . but he had to capture her and
tame her before he could worship her.

Midafternoon, and the group prepared to fly. Now at
last the shrieks began in earnest. Hasan stayed hidden,
watching as the princess beat her breast and tore her
elegant raiment; but her magic plumage was gone, and she
was helpless. Her handmaidens wept and searched every
cranny of the pavilion and the water and shore and vegetation around it—but as the shadows lengthened, they donned
their own suits and departed.

Hasan felt a fierce sympathy for the princess, for this
scene brought poignant memories of his own hour of
dismay, years ago. He had been a young heir in Bassorah,
and friends had congregated daily at his house to share the
feasts. Then, when his carelessly-spent wealth ran out,
they had deserted him—as these maidens were deserting
their mistress in her hour of need. Had they stood by her,
he would have been able to do nothing. They could have
ransacked the palace and recovered the feather-suit. But not
one of them cared to risk her life by staying the night.

Dusk, and the princess was alone. She sat naked on the
wall of the pavilion, silent in her despair. Briefly she
raised her head and spoke desolately to the one she must
have known was listening, and once more Hasan seemed

to understand. "O who has taken my dress and stripped me cruelly, I beseech you to restore it to me and cover my shame, for the night is upon me and I am alone." Then she wept.

What empathy he had with her! He could not treat her thus. He would fetch back the—

She heard his motion and spread her arms as if to fly, helplessly. The time had come.

Hasan stepped out from his hiding-place and stood before the damsel. "Do not be afraid of me," he said soothingly. "Daughter of majesty, I love you."

She had been beautiful in serenity and lovely in sorrow; now she was tantalizing in fright. She leapt up and ran around the pavilion, her long tresses sailing out behind. Hasan was afraid that in her desperation she might forget again that she could not fly and fling herself off the palace roof. He had to catch her immediately.

He chased her. She screamed and tried to hide behind a tree; his action was compounding her terror. How had he gotten into this? Wouldn't it have been better to let her fly in beauty, than to kill her through terror? He could still return to his chamber, bring out the suit—

She plunged headlong for the edge. He leaped, reached out his hand, and caught her rich black hair. She was snared. He brought her, birdlike, to him, and circled her slim waist with his arm so that she could not escape.

She fluttered and fought, her ruby mouth open in a soundless scream, breasts heaving in pathetic but alluring panic. But the loss of her feather-suit had robbed her of vitality. Her struggles diminished and ceased.

Never had Hasan felt so much like an unclean swine.

Captive, she walked passively beside him as he brought her to the stair. She was beautiful even in pathos. He hooked his hand again in her hair and kept his eyes away from her body as she preceded him down into the palace. He was ashamed, now, to look at her.

Hasan guided her to his chamber, set her on his bed, and threw a striped silken cloak over her. He left her there,

weeping and biting her hands in grief. He locked the door
and rushed to find Rose for further advice.

Rose met him in the hall. She was carrying his nightly
meal, not realizing that this had been the day. "I've got
her!" he shouted. "Now what do I do?"

Rose accepted the news with limited enthusiasm. "I was
afraid it would work," she said. "Well, I'd better go talk
with her. *You're* not good for much, right now."

She set course for Hasan's room, still bearing the tray.
"What about my—" he began, hungry now.

"Go find your own," she told him sharply. "*She* has to
eat too, you know." He retreated to a garden and plucked
some fruit, feeling ashamed.

Time passed. Night came upon the palace, and still
Rose did not emerge from his chamber. Dim light shone
under the door, which was locked against him. He had a
key, of course, but took the hint. He put his ear to the door
and listened.

Rose was talking. ". . . so he took the feather-suit and
burned it, and waited until you were alone so that he could
bring you in. He did not mean to harm you, or even to
frighten you; he did all this only because he was mad with
love for you. You know how these Arabs are. Otherwise
he would not have pined away without eating or sleeping,
all for your sake, and almost died before we found him."

A muffled weeping was the only reply.

"Now I know you can't understand my words any more
than I can understand yours, except that we both are
women," Rose continued steadily. She employed the tone
she would have used to soothe a wild bird. "When my
sisters return, we'll see about teaching you our language. It
is only the will of Allah that we are able to talk with
Hasan, you know, for most of the people we know in Sind
speak the dialects of the continent. But that's another
story, and you don't want to hear about language and geography right now, do you. I'm going to leave you here for
the night, and you'll see that no one is going to hurt you.
And if you can understand anything at all that I'm saying,

think about this: woman was not made except to be loved by man. Hasan isn't bright, but he is handsome and he loves you and he will make you a perfect husband. He is naive but very nice, and that is exactly the way a man should be. If you respond to him and treat him decently, he will be your slave for life—and that is more important than all your father's palaces and troops and magic. I would gladly change places with you, but Allah did not grant this thing to me. You are the one he loves, and the sooner you come to terms with this the happier you'll be. You think you're the captive, but the truth is that *he* is the captive. Have pity on him and give him the chance he deserves. You could have been served with more bitter fruit."

Hasan tip-toed away.

The bird-maiden was subdued in the morning, and appeared to be resigned to her fate. Rose brought her food and talked to her and dressed her in a clean robe, and moved her into a chamber of her own so that Hasan could recover his room. This relieved his alarm lest the captive discover the feather-suit, so near at hand all night. He stayed well clear of the proceedings, dismayed that his sister should have to promote his suit, but certain that he would botch things horribly by himself.

Two days later Rose summoned him. "She's doing better now," she said, but something in her attitude renewed Hasan's feeling of guilt. "I think she knows more of our language than she pretends. It's time for you to talk to her."

"Right now?" Hasan asked, immediately bashful.

"You have to meet her *sometime*, Hasan." Rose took him firmly by the arm and trotted him to his room. "First I'll have to make you presentable, though. No woman would find you attractive if she saw you the way you usually hang around the palace." She covered the catch in her voice by bustling through the collection of robes they had provided him. "Put this on. And comb your hair. And clean off those sandals—here. I'll find you better ones. Go take a bath.''

Hasan was changed and groomed willy-nilly. "Men have no taste in clothing," Rose complained. "They'd never get married at all if it weren't for women." She led him to the bird-maiden's chamber. "Now speak softly to her, Hasan—remember, she has to be tamed. And take her a present—here, I'll get you something suitable."

"Maybe I'd better wait until tomorrow—"

He found himself before the forbidden door of the captive's chamber, an attractive bouquet in his hand and utter confusion in his mind. "I can't," he whispered, shaking.

Rose paid no attention. She opened the door, pushed him inside, and slammed it behind him.

The princess reclined on a divan, so astonishingly lovely he could hardly look at her directly. She wore a light veil which only increased her allurement, and a dress of scarlet satin that set off her coal-black hair in a manner that took Hasan's breath away. Most notable was the robe she graced; it was thrown loosely over her other garments and was decorated in red gold with figures of wild beasts, and birds whose eyes and beaks were gems and whose claws were red rubies and green beryl. Her neck was embraced by a chain of great round jewels, and even her slippers sparkled richly.

Hasan stumbled across the room and held out his bouquet. She ignored it. He was left awkwardly supporting the flowers in sweaty, trembling hands. "Princess," he began, but could think of nothing more to say.

Dark lashes flickered contemptuously. How could he ever have aspired to such a woman! She was the daughter of a mighty king, while he was nothing but a merchant's son. He could not even speak in her presence without choking over his stupid tongue. He was not worthy to kiss her feet.

Kiss her feet. The vision of her bare ankle beside the pavilion bench came back to him. He had almost been ready to sacrifice his life for the privilege of a single gesture, then. Could he do less now?

Hasan dropped to his knees, put a quaking hand to her outstretched slipper, and took it off. He set the flowers aside and gently massaged the sole of her foot. Arabian women, he knew, were quickly mellowed by such treatment. He kissed it, and suddenly the words were undammed.

"O princess of the fairest, life of the lovely sprites and delight of all who behold you, be easy in your heart, for I come to you only in order to be your bondsman till the Day of Doom. I might have captured one of your handmaidens, but not one of them compared to yourself in beauty and grace, and indeed there is not in all the world a fairer maiden than you.

"O my lady! I have no desire except to take you as my wife, after the law of Allah and the practice of His Apostle, and to journey with you to my own country. And I will buy you handmaidens and chattels, and my mother, who is the best of women, will do you service. There is no finer land than mine; everything there is better than elsewhere, and its folk are pleasant and bright. Only consent to come with me and let me worship in the light of your smile, and—"

She had not spoken a syllable or moved a toe, but he had to break off at the sound of knocking from below. Someone was at the front gate! The sisters had returned!

He was tongue-tied again. Quickly he replaced the slipper, as though tidying furniture, and stood up. He left the flowers on the floor.

"I must go," he said, backing away. "But I love you."

She made no sign.

Downstairs he found the six sisters in their hunting clothing, soiled and tired and laden with game. "Welcome!" he cried.

"You look much better, brother," Eldest said, eyeing his elaborate outfit. He had forgotten to change! "We'll join you shortly." And the six retired to their rooms to clean up and don more feminine apparel.

Hasan looked at their collection of game. They had taken gazelles and wild dogs and leopards and even a small bear. It had been a good hunt.

In due course the sisters emerged from their chambers, refreshed and delicately robed. Hasan went up to each in turn, kissing her and expressing great affection. "Why so friendly, so suddenly?" Fifth inquired, flattered. "Did you have a fight with Rose?" Second asked. "I'm glad to see you so much improved, Hasan," Sixth said. "I wonder whether we came back too soon," Eldest said, "or too late."

Hasan was abruptly overwhelmed by his own deception, seemingly so transparent. Why had he wooed a foreign damsel, when these were his true friends, his dear sisters? The hot tears came to his eyes. He was unworthy of them.

They quickly noted his distress, and turned inquiring glances to Rose, who had just appeared. But Rose remained aloof, letting Hasan solve his problem himself.

"We thought you were over this sadness, brother," Third remarked. "Do you miss your mother and your native land? We would not hold you here against your will. We love your company, but rather than see you weep, we will equip you and send you home again."

Hasan looked about, startled. "By Allah, sisters, I could not leave you!"

"Which of us has vexed you, then?" Second asked, softening. "Why are you so troubled, when we thought you were doing so well?"

Hasan stood silent, unable to come up with any reply. How could he tell them the truth? They might be furious, and cast him out and kill the princess. . . .

He noticed that Eldest and Sixth stood a little apart, no longer participating in the questioning. They suspected!

Rose finally filled the silence. "Maybe our brother caught a bird from the air, and wants you to help him tame her," she said maliciously. "A very pretty bird."

"Is that right, Hasan?" Fifth asked him. "Show her to us! We'll be glad to help. Tell us everything. How did you snare her? What does she look like?"

Hasan cast about in total confusion. How could he avoid telling them? Yet he was unable to begin. Why was Rose baiting him now, when she had done so much to help?

He went to her and got down on his knees and kissed the hem of her skirt. "I am ashamed," he said. "Please help me."

Now the tears came to Rose's eyes. "No Hasan—I am the one who is ashamed. Get up; I'll tell them." She led him to a couch and put her arm around his shoulders.

"O my sisters, when we went away to visit our father and left alone this unhappy one, the palace was too quiet for him and he fell to exploring all the rooms and courts of the palace for some diversion. He opened the door to the staircase leading to the roof—"

"Didn't you tell him not to—" Fifth broke in, alarmed.

"Perhaps I forgot, sister. He sat upon the roof, hoping to see the first sign of our return, and also to make sure no enemy came upon the palace unawares. Suddenly he saw ten birds approaching, and they lighted on the brink of the basin which is in the pavilion. He watched these birds, for they were marvelously strange, and saw among them one goodlier than the rest, who pecked the others, but against whom none of them dared to put out a claw. Presently they set their nails to their neck-collars and rent their feather-suits and became damsels like full moons. They fell to playing in the water, and the one who was the chief-damsel was fairest in favor of them all, and our brother was distracted by her charms and his heart was afire with love for her. Then they donned their feather-suits and flew away home, and he fell sick with longing and repented that he had not somehow captured her. He abode on the palace-roof abstaining from meat and drink and sleep for a whole month when behold! the birds appeared again. So he stole the chief damsel's feather-suit and burned it and when the others flew away he seized her and carried her into the palace."

"You mean she's here?"

"Locked in a special chamber," Rose replied.

"What does she look like?"

"She is fairer than the moon on the fullest night and her face shines brighter than the sun. The dew of her lips is

sweeter than honey and her shape is more slender and
supple than tall cane. Her eyes are black as the night and
her brow white as a flower. Her bosom—'' here Rose took
a breath as though to suppress a tinge of envy. ''Her
bosom is as bright as a jewel, and her breasts are two
pomegranates and her cheeks apples. Her waist has beautiful dimples and her navel is as smooth as carved ivory and
her legs are alabaster columns. Surely she is goodly of
shape and sweet of smile, and ravishes all hearts with her
splendid symmetry.''

''In other words,'' Eldest said dryly, ''a pretty girl.
Hasan, you'd better show her to us.''

Where was the shock, the outrage? They hardly seemed
surprised. Dumbly he led the way to the princess's chamber and ushered them in. The bird-maiden seemed not to
have moved a muscle since Hasan had left her in the
morning, but the flowers had been removed.

They stood in a semicircle studying her, while Hasan
fidgeted. What would their judgment be?

Eldest turned to him and clamped her hand upon his
shoulder. ''Brother—you have excellent taste in women.''
She smiled.

The trial was over almost before it had begun. It was all
right! They had accepted the bird-maiden.

''Well, let's not dawdle.'' Eldest was gruff. ''What's
happened has happened, and obviously Hasan will have to
marry her. Sister, you know something of her language,
don't you?''

Sixth, the librarian and scholar, nodded. Hasan had a
retroactive suspicion about the book left so conveniently
on the table, and indeed, about the entire series of events
following the sisters' return from their visit home. How
much had they known?

Sixth spoke unintelligibly. The bird-maiden's head lifted.
She looked sharply at Hasan, first with royal indignation
and then, slowly, with heavy-lidded appraisal. He wondered just what Sixth was saying to her. Finally the prin-

cess inclined her head, and Eldest stepped to her side.
What was going on?

Sixth beckoned to him. "Brother, go to the storeroom
and fetch a good handful of gold. Hurry."

"But—"

She shoved him out the door and closed it behind him.
This was the second time this had happened today, and he
still wasn't quite certain what it signified. He heard animated conversation behind him as he went for the money.

When he returned, his sisters were seated in a circle on
the floor, and Rose was quietly crying.

"Put the money on the table, Hasan," Sixth directed,
and he did so. It came to him like a dawning sun: this was
the betrothal! The bird-maiden had agreed to marry him!

"Sit down," Eldest said, indicating a space immediately before her. He crossed his legs and sat. She raised
her right hand and clasped his, pressing her upraised thumb
against his.

Sixth came over and dropped a handkerchief over the
joined hands. "Glory be to Allah, the Compassionate, the
Merciful, and blessed be His Prophet, in whose name we
perform this ceremony," she intoned solemnly.

"I hereby betroth to thee," Eldest said, tightening her
grip on his hand, "the damsel for whom I act as deputy,
Sana of the Isles of Wak, for the dowry duly presented."
Sixth translated for the watching bird-maiden, who nodded.

It was Hasan's turn. "I accept from thee her betrothal to
myself," he said, hardly believing it.

They recited the opening chapter of the Koran, and it
was done. "Come—we feast!" Eldest said, and guided
Hasan down to the banquet-hall where everything was
miraculously spread out.

Hasan was able to remember almost nothing of the
celebration that followed, except that it lasted all afternoon
and well into the night and matched the splendor of any
royal wedding. Sweet sherbets were served instead of the
forbidden alcoholic beverages of corrupt courts, yet somehow his head spun more dizzily with every glass he downed.

That evening he entered the nuptial apartment, and she was there, standing in her bridal gown, waiting. He removed her veil, the veil that would never conceal her face from him again, and once more was dazzled by her beauty.

She lifted off her silken dress and showed him her breasts, delights fit for caliphs, half-hidden by the flowing hair of her head. She dropped her petticoat trousers and revealed to him her remaining delights, this time intentionally.

Hasan became a man of action. He rose and threw her on the bed and rent the veil and opened the gate and broke the seal and pierced her every secret; nor was it misery that kept him sleepless throughout that marvelous night!

Perhaps it was well that he did not remember that his sisters were standing outside the chamber door, thankful for the sounds of his good fortune and remarking upon them . . . but nostalgic for the similar joys forbidden to each of them.

Hasan stayed at the palace with his bride for forty days, and his affection for her and delight in her love increased. He did not question the sudden ease with which she had yielded herself to him, nor worry unduly that the joys so readily gained might as readily be lost again.

Bit by bit he learned her language, and she learned his, and his satisfaction mounted as he came to comprehend her mind as well as her body. She was clever but docile; her learning had versed her in many things, but once she had given herself to him, these things were his.

The seven sisters eagerly assisted the couple, making every day a holiday and every meal a feast. They congratulated him upon his marriage, and Sana the bird-maiden upon hers. Even Rose became reconciled, discovering that the sharing of affection did not after all diminish it, and she remained as close to Hasan as she had ever been.

It was the happiest period Hasan had ever known. Sana, too, seemed content; she never spoke of her lost feather-suit or of the mighty kingdom left forever behind. She had known from the start that the handmaidens who had de-

serted her at the pavilion would never dare return home; all
of them would have been executed for their betrayal.

Perhaps it was Sana's royal training that gave her the
courage and spirit to accept her situation. Certainly she
never hinted otherwise.

Chapter 7. Mischief

At the end of that forty days Hasan had a dream. He
saw his mother mourning for him. Her bones were wasted
and her complexion had turned to yellow parchment. She
was near to death from sorrow, while Hasan was in
excellent health. She saw him, and cried: "O my son, O
Hasan, how is it that you live such a life of ease and
luxury, but forget your old mother? Look at my plight
since you were taken from me! My tongue will never cease
repeating your name until I perish, and I have made a
tomb in my house, so that I cannot forget you. O my son,
if only I could have you with me again!"

Hasan's joy deserted him. He woke with tears in his
eyes and sorrow in his heart for the great wrong he had
done his mother by neglecting her. More than once he had
been reminded, but each time he had selfishly put the
matter from his mind. What if she died before he saw her
again? This time he would have to act: he would have to
make it right.

But how could he leave his beloved sisters, who had
done everything for him and even obtained for him his
lovely bride? He tossed on the bed, and could not return to
sleep though the dawn was long in coming.

In the morning Rose came in with a smile on her face.
"Get up, Hasan," she said. "Man's work may last all
night, but not all day as well. Give your poor wife a rest."

When Hasan did not reply, she turned to Sana. "What's the
matter with him? Didn't you treat him properly last night?"

Sana shook her head in bewilderment. "He scream in

dark," she said, still slow to pronounce the unfamilar
words. "Roll over, not say word, not sleep."

"Didn't you ask him?"

"Not talk to me. Sad, silent."

Rose plumped down on the bed beside Hasan. "Come,
brother, tell sister. What ails you?"

Hasan groaned, but roused himself and told her his nightmare. Rose listened, understood, and ran from the room.

Soon all seven sisters appeared. Their countenance was
grave. Eldest took the initiative: "Brother, we shall not hinder
you from visiting your mother. Do as you will, in Allah's
name, and we will help you by whatever means we may."

"We've had you for over a year," Rose added, muffled. "It couldn't last forever."

"Go with our blessing," Sixth said. Her voice also had
a catch. "But you must promise to visit us, if only once a
year."

"I promise!" Hasan exclaimed, suddenly relieved. "To
hear is to obey. Thank you, thank you, O my sisters!"

They made immediate preparations for the trip. The
sisters gathered an immense store of wealth to give the
traveling couple; entire chests of gold and silver and precious jewels, wardrobes of costly garments for Hasan and
queenly raiment for Sana, and other gifts defying description. There were more than fifty caskets in all, not one of
them light, and he despaired of transporting them the great
distance to his home in Bassorah.

"Have you forgotten the magician's drum, brother?"
Rose inquired sadly. "I'll show you how to use it."

Hasan *had* forgotten the drum. "But how can three
camels carry all this?"

"You don't know much about magic, do you?" she said
with a spark of her old enthusiasm. "Beat the drum."

Hasan obeyed, sitting beyond the gate and pounding it
rhythmically with the strap in the way he had so often
observed Bahram doing it. The sound of it bothered him,
for it brought recollections of an experience that had not
been happy. Before long the three dromedaries approached.

Three? Twice he had seen one killed. . . .

"Don't stop, Hasan—that's only the beginning."

Mystified, he continued, although the animals were standing right in front of him. Then he understood.

More beasts were coming, and not only camels. There were oxen and mules and horses and elephants—creatures from every part of the world, summoned unerringly by the drum. The plain was covered with their tracks, and an army of them milled about him.

They selected the finest animals and formed them into a caravan, loading each with the proper burden of gear. It took several days to complete the arrangements.

The seven sisters accompanied Hasan and his bride for the first three days, according to the dictates of royal etiquette, during which time they accomplished a journey north that matched the one he and the magician had made in a fortnight. The animals were magically swift, when prodded. Apparently Bahram himself hadn't known very much about magic. . . .

They approached the section where the sea barred the way. Far across the restless waters Hasan could see the mountains of the land beyond. "Here we must leave you," Eldest said, "for we dare not go beyond the limits our father has imposed upon us. But stay firm on the backs of your mounts, and they will carry you safely across."

Now was the hour of parting, and it was unbearably difficult. Each sister kissed Hasan affectionately while Sana looked on with an indifferent expression and each bade him fond farewell. Rose was the last; but though she approached bravely with her little chin uplifted, her composure broke when she touched him. She flung her arms around his neck and wept as though her soul would fly.

Hasan held her, deeply touched; but the animals were impatient and he had to loosen her embrace. She slumped against him, her head lolling. She was unconscious.

Eldest came to pick her up, but Rose recovered at once from her faint and stood by herself. "O my brother," she said with pathetic calm, "if anything happens to you beat the drum and choose the swiftest camel and come to see us as fast as you can.''

''I will, my sister.''

''And remember you promised to visit us every six months.''

''Whenever I can, my sister.'' Now was not the time to quibble over the agreed period.

''And never forget that we love you and——''

Eldest led her away, still talking. Hasan covered up his own tears by shouting at the caravan of animals. They plunged into the ocean and drove for the opposite shore.

He looked back once, and saw the seven watching forlornly, Rose with her hair tumbled over her face in grief. Eldest waved—or perhaps she was gesturing him on—and that was all. He turned his face resolutely forward and did not glance back again.

It was a long and adventurous journey over plain and desert and mountain and valley, through burning sun and torrential rain, past elegant cities and deserted wilderness; but the blessing of Allah was upon them and after months of travel they reached Bassorah without calamity.

Hasan brought his caravan to the door of his house and dismounted. The domicile seemed oddly small, after his absence, though he knew that he was the one who had changed. As he put his hand to the door he paused. He heard weeping, as though someone within were fainting from sorrow and on fire with grief. For a moment he thought of Rose, inconsolable in her lovely palace, day and night; but of course she was not here.

He entered—and found his mother wailing before his tomb, exactly as the magician had showed him in the vision. She was emaciated beyond description, and he was amazed that she was still alive.

''Mother,'' he said, inadequately.

She looked up at him with staring eyes. ''Hasan,'' she said, and fell to the floor in a faint.

He rushed to her and lifted her dry husk of a body and carried her to the divan, where he bathed her hands with water. As quickly as she had passed out, she recovered, and embraced him and kissed him. "Where have you been these two years, my son, and how did you escape the terrible Persian?"

"I slew him," Hasan said, his chest inflating slightly. "And now I have come home with riches not even the Caliph can match, and the most beautiful bride in the world!"

She was shocked. "Hasan! You married without consulting your mother!"

Hasan smiled to see her revert so rapidly to normal. "It happened suddenly, Mother, or I never would have neglected you. May I bring her in?"

"You brought that hussy *here*?" she screeched with a fine store of indignation. She jumped up as alertly as her state permitted and bustled about the house, attempting to abolish in a minute the disorder of two years.

Hasan went outside, unloaded the camels and other animals of his caravan, and dismissed them. He took Sana by the hand and led her into the house, heavily veiled.

"A wife!" the old woman was muttering. "I will not share the roof with—" Then she saw that it was too late. She collapsed on the divan, wringing her hands.

Hasan reached up to remove Sana's veil, since she was inside now, but his mother objected strenuously. "No!" she exclaimed, turning her back. "I will not look at her."

Hasan smiled and set his wife on the opposite divan. "Let me tell you of my adventures, Mother; then perhaps your heart will soften, for I know you are generous and forgiving." And while his mother sat with face averted, he recounted the whole of his adventures since his involuntary departure from Bassorah: the ocean voyage, the flight in the camel-skin, the betrayal by Bahram, the delight of the seven sisters, the revenge against the magician, his capture of the bird-maiden and the dream which brought him home to Bassorah again.

His mother relented enough to rise and examine the baggage, and when she saw the immense wealth and knew that they would never be poor again, her disposition improved somewhat. At last she condescended to look upon the King's daughter, Hasan's wife, grumbling all the while.

Hasan removed the veil and let Sana's beauty shine forth. The old woman halted her monolog abruptly, stunned. She stared for several minutes.

At length she recovered and put out her hand. "My son has mistreated you terribly," she said. "Imagine forcing a lovely child like you to ride a camel across the ends of the earth! Come, my daughter—I'll take care of you."

Next morning Hasan's mother took Sana shopping and bought her the finest furniture in the city, together with elaborate new clothing and utensils of solid silver and gold. No praise was too extravagant for the adorable bride, and no reprimand too sharp for the callous son.

Hasan bore up under the abuse with suitable dignity, hardly concealing his secret pleasure. He would not have had it otherwise.

But he was not allowed to relax. "O my son," his mother said, "we cannot tarry in this town with all this wealth, for we are poor folk. Already I have heard the neighbors whispering of alchemy. They will make trouble for us, be certain of that."

Hasan was appropriately contrite. This problem had already occurred to him—but his mother would never have budged if he had suggested that they move to escape the fury and avarice of jealous city-folk. "What can we do, Mother?"

"We must depart for Baghdad, where everyone is wealthy and we may dwell in the Caliph's sanctuary. Then you shall sit in a shop and buy and sell in the sight of Allah—to Him all might and majesty!—and no one will suspect the source of your fortune."

"Excellent advice, Mother! I shall do exactly as your wisdom prescribes." Hasan had not dealt with a magician, seven royal sisters, and a captive wife without learning something of diplomacy.

He swung into action. He sold the house, summoned the

dromedaries, and loaded them with all their goods and gear. Then he took his mother and wife down to the great docks, where the two mighty rivers joined, and hired a craft to carry all their possessions.

The sail up the Tigris took ten days. The land on either side was flat and featureless, palm trees projecting on the horizon. Huge rafts of cut reeds drifted slowly downstream, twice the length of their ship but bearing only two or three men apiece. Camels traveled the banks of the river wherever the ground was solid enough to sustain them.

The marshes dwindled imperceptibly, and the irrigation ditches became sloppy and finally nonexistent. Toward the end of the trip the signs of civilization reappeared, and they came in sight of Baghdad, the fabulous Round City, with its elegant towers and minarets and spires showing above the mighty wall. This was the richest capital in the world. Only the chief city of Byzantium, in the land of the Christian infidels, was said to rival it in splendor. Hasan discounted such claims; every True Believer had to be wary of the lies of Greeks and Christians.

Along the river were many miles of wharves, and hundreds of vessels were docked there: merchant ships, pleasure craft, ships of war and even exotic colored boats from the lands beyond Hind. Local rafts of inflated sheepskin drifted down from Mosul, and on toward Bassorah.

Hasan, who had been here in his youth, described to Sana the manner in which the city was constructed, with triple brick walls rising almost a hundred feet above the plain and surrounded by the deepest moat. Four ponderous gates opened on highways that spoked the length and breadth of the empire. In the center of the city was the green dome of the Caliph's palace, the tallest structure in the city.

Sana said nothing, but Hasan fancied he saw a glint of respect in her expression. At any rate, she was looking intently at the palace.

They docked, and instantly had to fend off the throng of petty merchants, beggars, retainers, jugglers, fortune-tellers,

money-changers and thieves—though the last term could
be applied comprehensively. Horses stamped nervously in
the street, camels cried, and famished dogs prowled everywhere, looking for tidbits.

Hasan wasted no time in hiring a storehouse. He transported his goods there and left them under guard, then
found lodging for his wife and mother in the khan—a
place where shelter was available, but no food or service.
Both women objected stenuously, but he turned a deaf ear.
Next morning he changed his clothes and went into the
city to inquire for a reputable broker.

Judicious disposition of coin soon brought him the man
he wanted. "O my master, what is it that you lack?" the
broker asked.

"I want a house—the most handsome and spacious one
you have available for immediate occupancy."

The man appraised him unobtrusively, noting the quality
and fit of his dress and the impartial certainty of his
manner. Then he showed the way to a high-class merchant's
domicile. Hasan took one tour through its halls and frowned.
"If this is your best, I am dealing with the wrong broker."

Without a word the man brought him to the mansion of
a former wazir, the ranking minister to the Caliph preced-
ing Harun al-Rashid. It was fashioned of quality brick and
rare stone, with handsome pillars beside the massive front
entrance, and pointed arches showing the way to a fine
central court with palms and flowers and a clear flowing
fountain. It hardly rivaled the palace of the seven princesses, but Hasan was satisfied that it was the best he
could expect in Baghdad. He purchased it immediately for
a hundred thousand golden dinars.

He proceeded next to the storehouse and had his goods
moved into the residence while he went to the market and
bought carpets and household vessels and a complete staff
of servant-girls and eunuchs, and one little Negro boy for
the house. Then he brought Sana and his mother and let
them exclaim as they might.

They were settled in Baghdad.

*   *   *

Three years passed in peace and happiness. Sana bore Hasan two graceful sons, one of whom he named Nasir and the other Mansur, and he could not have asked for a more sanguine existence. The old lady was as delighted with her grandchildren as with her daughter-in-law, and ran the household with taste and dispatch.

One day Hasan brought himself up short and realized that he was bored. He possessed everything he had dreamed of as an immature youth—but he missed the adventure he once had known. He had sadly neglected his dear sisters, the princesses of Serendip, and had broken his promise to visit them regularly.

The memory brought irresistible nostalgia. He had to visit his dear sisters without delay! Obsessed with longing, he went to the market and bought trinkets and costly material and delicious confections and all things calculated to delight girls who could not go shopping for themselves.

"What are you up to, Hasan," his mother wanted to know. "We don't need those things."

"I propose to visit my sisters, who showed me every sort of kindness and gave me all the wealth we presently enjoy. I owe them far more than this."

His mother looked uneasy, but could not deny his logic. "O my son, go if you must, but do not stay away from Baghdad too long."

Hasan was relieved that she offered no more protest than this. "Where's Sana?"

"I left her sleeping on a couch. I'll fetch her for you."

"No," Hasan said quickly. "There is something I must tell you about her privately." She leaned close, eager to receive the confidence. "You know, O my mother, that my wife is the daughter of a King who rules over the jinn, and who has more troops and treasure than any monarch we know of except the Caliph himself. She is the dearest of her father's children. She is high-spirited, and I'm afraid of what she might do if she went out into the city alone, for she was not born to the True Faith and only

wears the veil because I command it. Yet I love her with all
my heart, and I would quickly die if anything happened to
her. I'm afraid for her safety even when the wind blows.''

''I understand, my son.''.

''But more than this, I must tell you a secret I have
revealed to no one. When I captured her I threw her
feather-suit into the bottom of a trunk and told her I had
burned it, so that she could never escape. I don't think she
would have married me, if she had known that her feather
cloak still existed. I didn't burn it; it was too beautiful, and
it would have been like burning part of her—a thing I
could never do. I buried that chest in a storage closet in the
back of the house. Watch over it, in case she should
happen upon it. If she recovered that feather-suit she might
fly away and take her children with her, and we would
never see them again. Make sure you never say a word
about this to her.''

''Allah forbid that I do such a thing!''

Neither of them saw Sana retreat from the curtained
doorway, or heard her quiet return to her couch. When
Hasan came to bid her farewell, he mistook her subdued
smile for a pleasant dream.

There was no premonition in his mind of the disaster he
had wrought by his carelessness. He went outside the city
a reasonable distance, beat the magic kettledrum, loaded
the dromedaries, mounted, and rode for Serendip at a great
rate, never pausing longer than he had to.

The princesses were overjoyed to see him. Rose threw
her arms about him once more and wept, this time for
happiness, then proceeded to berate him soundly for neglecting them so long. They set up a mighty feast, and
everything was as it had been before, with hunting and
sporting and kissing and merrymaking and endless delight
from one day to the next.

Three months went by, and Hasan could no longer
extend his visit. He missed his wife and two sons, one two
years old and the other one year. He took his leave of each
of the sisters, as he had before, and Rose wept and fainted

from the agony of separation as she had before, and it was all highly satisfactory. They gave him five more camel-loads of gold and five more of silver and one of food for the trip and let him go, making him promise not to forget them so long next time. It was a promise he would keep.

Saddened but eager, he impelled his mount toward Baghdad. In due course he arrived, entered his house, and called for his family.

No one answered him. Alarmed, he searched from room to room, finding them all deserted. Finally he came upon his mother in the courtyard, kneeling before three graves and crying bitterly. Her body was worn and her bones were wasted; she was so miserable that she fainted when she saw him.

Hasan knew disaster was upon him. Mechanically he unloaded the camels and dismissed them, trying to calm his emotion. He went to the storage-closet and found the door open, the chest broken, and the feather-dress missing, and understood that his wife and children were gone. He tore his clothes and buffeted his face and threw himself to the floor like a madman; his head struck a tile and he knew no more.

When he woke his mother was tending him. Rage overcame him; he bounded to his feet, lifted the giant scimitar he still wore from his journey, and advanced upon her. "Tell me the truth!" he roared. "What happened? How did my wife get hold of the feather-dress? Confess at once, or I'll strike off your head and then kill myself."

She recoiled in terror, knowing him mad enough to do what he threatened. "O my son, do not do such a horrible deed! Put away your sword and sit down, and I will tell you everything that passed while you were gone."

Hasan was suddenly shamed by his violence, knowing that his mother would never have betrayed him. He sheathed the blade and sat down beside her, listening to the story she told.

*   *   *

Sana stayed quietly with Hasan's mother for two days after he left for Serendip, tending her sons and saying nothing. On the third day her manner changed.

"Glory be to God!" she exclaimed, and the expression of her mouth had little element of worship. "Have I lived with this man for three years and never had a bath?"

"O my daughter—I cannot take you to the Hammam, the public bath, for Hasan made me promise not to take you out in the city or expose you to any danger. But I will gladly draw water and heat it for you and wash your head in the bath we have here in the house."

Sana's eyes flared. If Hasan's mother had ever doubted the girl was of royal blood, she would have been instantly convinced by the queenly wrath that now appeared. "If you had spoken this way to one of the slavegirls, she would have pleaded ill-treatment before the magistrate and demanded to be sold on the open market!"

"But your husband said—"

"Men are foolishly jealous, especially husbands. You have to allow for their ignorance, because they are afraid that any woman who leaves the house will get into trouble. But women are not all alike and you, as a woman, know it. If a woman has a mind for trouble, no man has the power to keep her from her desire. She will do what she wants, and nothing restrains her except her reason and her religion." Then Sana wept and bemoaned her isolation and cursed her fate, until Hasan's mother was sorry for her and became convinced that there was nothing for it but to let her have her way.

She committed the affair to Allah and made ready perfumes, clean linen, and everything else they would need for the bath. Then she took Sana and her two little boys to the Hammam, since it was ladies' day there.

The Hammam comprised several apartments with mosaic pavements of black and white marble and fine red tile. The inner apartments were covered by domes, with small round windows to let in the light.

They entered the disrobing room and stripped off their

clothes. No one looked at the lank old limbs of Hasan's mother, but all the women were amazed at Sana's beauty, and they gathered around and exclaimed in delight.

They left the little boys playing on the cushions of the benches and went on into the main baths. The chief room was an extensive oblong, with a central pool-area the shape of a cross. In its center was a robust fountain of hot water rising steamily from a marble base.

The heat was oppressive at first, but their bodies soon adapted to the pervasive atmosphere, and the hot vapor was very pleasant. Attendants massaged the women and brought them sweets to eat. Sana looked about with interest at the taps and boilers in the corners, while a maid carefully plaited her unbound hair,

Other women admired Sana's symmetry and grace. "Surely there is none like her in all the city!" they whispered. "And she has two children, too!" The women of Baghdad seldom retained their sprightly figures after child-bearing: to be a mother was generally to be soon ugly.

Word of her loveliness spread beyond the Hammam, and before long more women were coming in to see for themselves. The bath became so crowded they could hardly get around.

"We'd better go," Hasan's mother whispered anxiously. "We're creating an unwholesome distraction."

Sana pretended not to hear her.

A slave-girl approached and studied Sana with particular attention. "Glory be to Allah for the fair forms He creates!" she said. Sana smiled complacently and ignored her.

At length they left the bath and returned to the outer chamber to dress. When the women saw the fine apparel Sana donned they were amazed all over again, for she became even more beautiful. The slave-girl followed.

Sana gathered in her sons and accompanied the old woman back to their house, much pleased with herself. But the slave-girl continued to follow them until she saw where they lived.

Then that slave-girl, who belonged to the palace of the
Caliph (explained Hasan's mother angrily) returned to her
mistress, the Lady Zubaydah, and kissed the ground between her hands. "O Tohfah," said the mistress, "why
did you tarry so long in the Hammam?"

"O my lady, I have seen a marvel! Never have I
witnessed anything like it before, and so I had to learn
more about it because I knew you would be interested."

Zubaydah was the chief wife of Caliph Harun al-Rashid,
and his cousin. This double relationship to him gave her
enormous power. She was famed for her beauty, munifi-
cence, and cleverness. She wore the costliest fabrics in the
empire and refused to eat from any platter which was not
gold or at least fine silver. She was devious: only last year
she had presented the Caliph a gift of ten exceedingly fair
and pliant slave maidens, in order to distract him from a
rival favorite in the court, and it was said that several of
these were already anticipating royal offspring.

Everything that happened in Baghdad was Zubaydah's
concern, particularly the influx of attractive women. Splendid palaces had been built in her name, and she was
constantly heaped with honor—but she did not rely on
beauty alone to maintain her favor with Harun and her
power over him.

"And just what did you see, Tohfah?" Zubaydah asked
her slave, interested.

"O my lady, I saw a damsel in the bath who had with
her two little boys like moons, yet never eyes beheld the
like of this woman! She is without peer in all the realm.
By Allah, O my lady, if the Commander of the Faithful
were to learn of her, he would surely slay her husband and
take her for his own, for her like is not to be found among
women!"

"Indeed?" Zubaydah's eyes narrowed. "What else did
you learn?"

"I inquired who was her husband, and they told me he
was called Hasan of Bassorah, a man of much wealth. I
followed her and discovered that she lives in the house of

the wazir that retired some years ago, the house that has a gate opening on the city and another on the river. Indeed, I fear lest the Prince of True Believers hear of her and break the law and slay her husband and make a liaison of love with her!''

"You are repeating yourself," Zubaydah snapped, hardly pleased. "Now let me understand you clearly: you say this damsel is so beautiful that one look at her would capture the Caliph himself?"

"Yes, O my lady."

"Then I shall have to take a look at her, and if she is not as you describe, I'll have my eunuch strike off your head."

The girl gazed at her appalled.

"O strumpet!" Zubaydah said. "There are three hundred and three-score slave-girls in the Caliph's harem, one for every day of the year, each a jewel unpriced and a filly unridden save by the Caliph—but not one of them would distract his attention from me for a moment, did I choose to claim his interest. Now you tell me this merchant I never heard of has a wife, not even a virgin, that—''

The girl groveled. "O my mistress, she is lovelier than any of them, than any woman in the world!"

"Than *any* woman?" Zubaydah repeated ominously. "Woe to you if that isn't true. You have just staked your life upon it, girl. Now get out of here and fetch Masrur."

The slave scrambled away, terrified.

Masrur was the Caliph's eunuch, the most important and trusted slave in the dominion. He performed the most personal tasks for Harun, and was especially favored for executions.

Masrur kissed the ground before her. Zubaydah, despite her pretensions, was well aware that this was purely a matter of courtesy. The eunuch owed allegiance to no one but the Caliph—and if the Caliph were to order him to behead the leading lady of the realm, the slave would surely do it.

"Go to the old wazir's house, the one with the two

gates, and bring me the damsel who resides there, as well as her two children and the old woman who lives with her. Waste no time.''

"I hear and obey, my lady." Masrur didn't mind running errands for pretty women, when he wasn't otherwise occupied. Eunuchs were not sexless, and were capable of a good deal more than the ignorant supposed.

Masrur proceeded to Hasan's house and knocked on the door. "Who's there?" the old woman demanded before opening.

"Masrur, sword-bearer to the Commander of the Faithful.''

At these words she was afraid to deny him admittance, and opened the door. He saluted her with a handsome salaam. "The Lady Zubaydah, daughter of Ja'afar bin Mansur and queen-spouse of the Caliph Harun al-Rashid, the fifth of the sons of Al-Abbas, paternal uncle of the Prophet—whom Allah bless and keep!—summons you to her presence, you and your son's wife and her children; for word has reached her of the damsel's beauty.''

Hasan's mother was alarmed. "O my lord Masrur, we are foreign to this city, and the girl's husband, my son, is abroad and far from home, and he has strictly charged me not to let her go out during his absence or let anyone see her." She took a breath. "I'm afraid if anything happened to her he would kill himself. I beseech you, O Masrur, do not ask us to do what we are forbidden.''

"O my lady, if I knew there were anything to be afraid of, I would never make this demand. But the Lady Zubaydah only wants to see the damsel, to assure herself that she is as lovely as is claimed; after that you will be free to return. So do not protest and do not worry; I will bring you back safely myself.''

"You are taking the lamb to the crocodile, who only wants to look at her!" the old woman muttered, but saw that she could not disobey this order. She resigned herself and hoped for some intervention from Allah while she made Sana ready.

They followed Masrur to the palace of the caliphate, where they were duly escorted into the presence of Zubaydah.

The Caliph's wife sat on a couch of ebony inlaid with gold and silver. To her right and left hung multiple necklaces of jewels, turning in the breeze from fans her slaves beat, and shining brilliantly. Ornate tapestries covered the walls, set with gems, and her own robe was so copiously worked with precious stones that it was impossible to single any one of them out.

Hasan's mother was highly impressed, but Sana acted as though such trappings were commonplace.

"Will you remove your veil, so that I may look upon your face?" Zubaydah requested politely enough. "There are no men here."

Sana removed her veil and allowed the queen to look upon her features. Immediately the ladies of the court gave a great sigh, put to shame by the light of her countenance, which was brighter than the moon and fairer than a day in spring. Zubaydah and all her company stared at Sana without uttering a word.

Finally the queen arose and brought Sana to her couch, embracing her and seating the visitor beside herself. She called for a rich robe and took down the most splendid necklace for her guest. If there was malice in her mind, no trace of it showed in her attitude. "O liege lady of fair ones, you astound me and amaze my eyes. Surely Allah created you to give his followers a foretaste of paradise! Do you have any special skills?"

"O my lady, I have a dress of feathers of unearthly handiwork. If I could place it before you, you would see something marvelous indeed, and all who witnessed it would talk of its wonder until the day they died."

"By all means. Where is this dress of yours?"

"My husband's mother has it. Ask her for it."

Zubaydah summoned the old woman, who had overheard only a trace of this conversation. "O my lady the pilgrimess," she said, using the honorable address for aged females. "O my mother, go and fetch us the feather-dress, that we may appreciate the marvel she promises."

Hasan's mother saw that all was lost, but she did her best. "O my Lady, this foolish damsel is mistaken. Who ever heard of a dress made of feathers? Only birds possess such things!"

"She has it," Sana insisted. "She keeps it in a chest buried in a storage closet, in the back of the house."

Zubaydah took from her neck a chain of jewels worth the treasure of an empire. "I conjure you, O my mother, accept this necklace and bring the dress to us. Afterwards you may take back the dress but keep the necklace."

"I never saw such a dress! I don't know what she's talking about!"

Zubaydah's patience, never extensive, puffed away. "Masrur!" she called, and the giant eunuch strode into the hall. "Take this hag's keys and go back to the house. Inside you'll find a storage closet, near the back. Open it and see if there is a chest therein. Take it out and break it open and bring me what you find within it."

Masrur took the keys and departed. Despairingly, the old woman followed, weeping and moaning with regret that she had ever listened to Sana. The crafty maiden's clamor for a bath had been nothing more than a trick leading to this! She watched the slave locate the feather-suit and wrap it carefully in a napkin and carry it to Zubaydah, who took it out and turned it over in her hands. She marveled at the beauty of its structure and the cleverness of its workmanship.

Zubaydah passed it to Sana. "Is this the garment of which you spoke?"

"Yes, O my lady!" She took it at once, joyfully. She examined it in detail and rejoiced to find that it was exactly as it had been before, whole and without a feather missing.

Sana wrapped herself in the suit and lo! she became a spectacular bird. "Glory be to Allah, to whom belong all might and all majesty!" Zubaydah exclaimed, and all present were wonderstruck.

Sana walked up and down the hall with a graceful and swaying gait looking so much like a bird that no one who had not seen the transformation would have recognized her as human. She danced and sported and spread her fair white wings so that every feather stood out, making patterns like enormous fans.

"What do you think of that, my ladies?" she inquired, and her bill moved in the talking and her voice was the chirp of a bird.

"We have never witnessed such a thing!" they replied.

"What I am about to do is better yet!" And now she spread her wings and flapped them strongly and rose from the floor, flying toward the queen in a great swoop, while everyone stared in disbelief.

"And even more," she chortled grandly. She stood up, opened her suit so that she became half-woman again, and picked up her two sons. Nasir and Mansur clung to her, and she folded them to her bosom and closed the suit over them. She spread her wings and flew up into the high dome of the palace, where she perched on the sill of an open vent.

"What a rare exhibition!" Zubaydah said. "Come down now and return to your lovely human shape and we shall celebrate this incredible occasion."

"Far be it from me to return!" Sana cried, her voice now a cackle. "I will not give up my freedom so easily, now that I have recovered it. I'm going home!"

"O my daughter!" Hasan's mother cried. "How can you desert Hasan, who loves you with all his heart and who will die wretchedly if he loses you?"

Sana paused. "O mother of my husband," she chirped, "indeed it irks me to part from you, for your heart is good; but your son surprised me in my innocence and captured me by force, and there was nothing I could do but yield myself to him after he had seen my shame and deprived me of my freedom. Moreover he is not my husband, for I am not a Moslem, nor do my people recognize your marriage-customs. But if your son grows lonely and desires to see me again, let him come to me in the Isles of Wak!''

With that she took flight and disappeared from their view, while the old woman wept and beat her face and swooned away from misery.

Zubaydah caught her up and led her to the couch. ''O my lady,'' the old woman cried, ''what have you done!''

''O my lady the pilgrimess, I did not dream this would happen,'' Zubaydah replied. Somehow she didn't sound as miserable as she might. Certainly *she* had no problem remaining. The Caliph would never see the bird-maiden now. ''If you had told me everything and warned me of her powers, I would never have given her the feather-dress. I did not know she was of the flying jinn. But what good are words? I intended no evil; please forgive me for the injury I have done you.''

There was nothing the old woman could do except to answer shortly ''I forgive you!'' and go home.

And at home she fasted in sorrow and spent her days in misery, pining for her lost daughter-in-law and grandchil-dren. She cursed the queen and cursed herself more, afraid of what would happen when Hasan returned. She dug three graves in the courtyard to represent the lost members of the household and spent her days and nights in a mournful watch, unable to assuage her grief.

Chapter 8. Quest

''O my brother,'' Rose exclaimed with mixed emotions. ''What is the matter, that you should come again so soon after we saw you last? It has hardly been two months.''

Hasan had certainly ridden hard. ''I've lost my wife,'' he said, then clung to her for support.

Rose screamed, and the other princesses gathered around, not knowing how to comfort him. The thing had happened while he was visiting with them, and they felt in part responsible for his misfortune.

"By Allah!" Rose swore bitterly. "How many times I meant to make you burn that feather-suit. Some evil spirit made me forget. Don't you have any idea at all where she went?"

"All she said was 'Let him come to me in the Isles of Wak.' "

Eldest brightened. "Wak? That's her home."

Sixth, the librarian, was not enthusiastic. "That doesn't help us, sister. She may be there, but no one else can follow her."

"But I must!" Hasan protested. "I cannot live without my wife and sons! Is there no one who can help me?"

The sisters exchanged bleak glances. Suddenly Rose jumped up. "What about Uncle Ab? He knows everything!"

Eldest nodded thoughtfully. "He could tell us whether it is possible, at least."

"What are you talking about?" Hasan asked.

Rose threw her arms around him. "He's our father's brother, Abd al-Kaddus. He wasn't given a kingdom, so he practices magic. He's not a Moslem, so it's all right. He's the dearest old gentleman!"

Hasan was impressed. "Where can I find him?"

"You don't have to find him. He'll come here."

"But if your family finds out that I'm here—"

Rose laughed. "Not Uncle Ab. He wouldn't turn us in. He knows all about your stay with us."

"Your father's brother?" Hasan was incredulous.

"He and Daddy don't ride the same elephant. He always did say we should all get married to Hindu princes and raise big big families." She paused reflectively. "I wish—"

"Rose!"

"Well, anyway, he'll help us if anyone can. We'll summon him right away."

"Right away tomorrow," Eldest said firmly. "Our brother must have some rest."

Hasan's misery abated, now that hope existed, and he joined them in a sumptuous meal. It was several tomorrows before they made the necessary preparations, and in that time he recovered much of his health and strength.

They gathered in a court and built a small fire. When it was blazing merrily, Eldest produced a delicately carved wooden box and took a small pouch from it. From this she shook a minute amount of pungent powder into her palm. "O Abd al-Kaddus, come to us!" she intoned, and cast her powder into the flame.

A perfumed cloud of smoke drifted up reminding Hasan uncomfortably of Bahram's evil magic. "Are you sure you can trust him?" he asked.

"You'll find out," Rose said, and guided him outside.

Across the plain came a cloud of dust very like the miniature smoke-ball they had just quitted. An elephant emerged from it with a white-bearded gentleman perched in a howdah on its back. The man waved and made signals with his hands, and the elephant trumpeted. The sisters waved back; but apparently fearing that they hadn't seen him, the man kicked out his feet and signaled with them too.

Presently he drew up and dismounted. Eldest ran over and threw her arms about him in a feminine display Hasan had never seen her exhibit before. "Welcome, Uncle Ab!"

The man embraced her with affection and patted her behind. "You're getting to be a big girl," he said. "Time you got married."

"Uncle, you *know* our father—"

"Hm, yes—but he *is* a fishbrain. Why do you listen to him? My daughters never listen to *me*."

"Uncle—you don't *have* any daughters!"

Ab considered. "Must do something about that, one of these decades." He saluted the remaining sisters in turn, making remarks which brought dainty blushes to their cheeks. At last he came to Hasan.

"My, you're an ugly one," he remarked.

"Uncle—that's Hasan," Rose protested.

Ab looked again. "I did think there was one too many," he admitted. "But then, why should I notice anyone who doubts me?"

"O Shaykh Abd—" Hasan began, using the polite title.

"Don't 'Shaykh' *me*, junior. I distinctly heard you remark, just after my niece summoned me—"

It was Hasan's turn to blush. "I told you," was Rose's smug reminder.

"There I was, sitting at ease with my dear wife, your aunt, when I smelled the perfume and knew my nieces needed me. And what do I hear but this—"

"He's sorry, Uncle," Eldest said.

Ab smiled at her, mollified. She was obviously his favorite. "Well, if you say so, my dear. Why did you call me?"

"O Uncle, we longed to see you, since you haven't visited us for over a year."

"Hm. Well, I was busy, but I was going to visit you tomorrow."

"And now our brother Hasan has a terrible problem, and only you can help him." And they told their uncle everything that had happened.

"Wak, eh?" he muttered. He shook his head and bit his finger thoughtfully. Then he squatted and began to make marks in the earth with his finger-tips.

"If you could just tell me how far away it is—" Hasan began.

"How far?" Ab shook his head again. "Not far, lad, as the roc flies."

"But the roc can cover a year's journey in a single day," Rose said.

"Nineteen hours," Ab corrected her absently. "Anyway, someone's been scaring those poor birds by jumping out of camels, or something. Must put a stop to that. Bad for their morale." He lapsed into silence, looked right and left, and shook his head a third time.

"Please give us some answer," Eldest urged him. "Our brother is sorely afflicted, and we hardly know how to console him."

Ab looked at her. "If I were you—"

"Uncle!"

Ab sighed. "O my daughters, you have no way to

console him, then, for he cannot gain access to the Isles of Wak.''

''But Shaykh—''

''Between this place and those isles lie seven mighty mountains and seven tremendous gorges and seven turbulent oceans. A mortal man could not make his way there though he had the flying jinn with him and the wandering stars. Far better you consider your spouse and sons to be dead, and turn back to your home and stop tormenting your spirit. I give you good council, if you will only accept it.''

Hasan cried out and fell to the ground, and the princesses wept for his sorrow. Rose tore her clothes and buffeted her face and fainted from the stress of her emotion, landing neatly beside Hasan.

''Oh, be quiet!'' Ab said, disturbed by the spectacle.

''Will you help us?'' Rose inquired from the ground, momentarily recovered.

''I don't have any more sense than your father!'' Ab growled.

''Oh, thank you, Uncle!'' the sisters cried together, embracing him *en masse*.

''Clear out. Stand on your own fourteen feet!'' he grunted. ''Take heart, lad, and you will win your foolish wish in spite of these creatures, if it be the will of Allah.''

''But you don't worship Allah, Uncle.''

''Still a perfectly good name to swear by. Rise, O my son, collect your courage, and follow me.''

''O Hasan, you're leaving us again!'' Rose cried.

Ab cut her off. ''Desist, girl. We'll never get moving if you start all that again.''

''At least stay the night,'' Eldest pleaded. ''We'll have music and a feast.''

Ab paused. ''Never could stand your music.''

''Daddy wouldn't approve, anyway,'' Rose said.

''I don't give a fig in the fire what that coconut-head approves! Where's my room?''

Next morning, or perhaps the one following that, Hasan

mounted the elephant behind the venerable gentleman and waved good-bye to his sisters once again. Partings seemed to come more frequently now, but each one wrenched his heart all over.

The elephant ambled along for three days, during which time Abd al-Kaddus did his best to dissuade Hasan from his venture. Hasan suspected that the trip would have been much shorter, otherwise, since the man had already demonstrated his ability to travel almost instantaneously. "Know, O my foolish son, that the Isles of Wak are seven in number, inhabited by a mighty host, all virgin girls. The inner islands are peopled by demons and marids and warlocks and various tribesmen of the jinn, and whoever enters that land never returns—at least, none have done so yet. So return to your people with the blessing of Yahweh, and—"

"Yahweh?"

"Zorothustra, then. Forget this damsel you're smitten with, for she's no damsel at all but the daughter of the King of all the Isles, and you can never aspire to her. Listen to me, my son, and perhaps Brahma will replace her with a better wife."

"O my lord," Hasan said. "They could cut me in pieces and my love would only redouble. There is no help for it; I must enter the Isles of Wak and come to the sight of my wife and children. I'll return with them or never at all!"

"My boy, think of your poor weary mother and your seven fine sisters. Don't make them spend their lives in torment because of your idiocy."

"I'll die anyway, if I don't recover Sana."

Ab shook his head, resigned, and the elephant journeyed on.

At length they came to a vast blue mountain whose stones were azure. A massive iron door was set in its base with curious inscriptions upon it.

Hasan studied the mysterious writing. "That's the language of Confucius," Ab said. "I stole that door from—"

"You stole it from a god?" Hasan was dismayed, forgetting that there were no gods but Allah.

"Confucius isn't a god. Whatever gave you that idea? Anyway, I never knew the gentleman personally." He raised his fist and rapped the metal.

A monstrous black slave opened the door from inside, as fierce and hairless as an ifrit. He carried a sword in his right hand and a steel shield on his left arm. "Master!" he cried, kneeling to kiss the Shaykh's hand.

Ab led Hasan inside, and the slave drew the door shut behind them. They were in a huge and spacious cavern, lighted in some enchanted fashion, through which ran a towering corridor. They traveled along this for several thousand paces, until it abutted upon a large open space. Then Ab angled off toward an elbow of the mountain and stopped before two huge doors cast of solid brass.

The old man went up to the left door and set his shoulders. "Wait here," he said ominously, "and I'll be back presently. On no account are you to follow me inside."

Hasan agreed, uncertain what was about to happen, and sat down against the wall between the doors. Ab opened the portal a crack, slid within, and drew it firmly closed. There was silence.

Hasan sat for a full hour, fidgeting. He admired the enormous dripping vaults of the cave. Ponderous swords of stone hung from the ceiling, many times the size of a man and pointed at the tip, so that he was afraid to pass underneath. Rows of colored rock rose from the floor: dragon's teeth, perhaps. Was the dragon near? He did not feel easy, here.

A crash, a snort, and the door burst open. Hasan bounded to his feet, reaching for his dagger—but it was only Abd al-Kaddus, leading a spirited black stallion. It was a beautiful horse, with sleek flanks and a short nose, bridled and saddled with velvet trappings. Its prancing hoofs scarcely seemed to touch the ground, and Hasan could tell that this was the swiftest of animals.

"Mount!", Ab panted. "This beast is uncontrollable without a rider." Hasan mounted, and felt the eager surge of the stallion beneath him. What a horse this was!

"Keep tight rein on him, or I won't answer for your safety," Ab warned him. He opened the second door.

Beyond it was an endless desert, burning and barren. Hasan guided the horse outside and held it steady.

Ab handed him a long roll. "O my son, take this scroll and go where this steed will carry you. When he stops at the door to a cavern like this, dismount and throw the reins over the saddle-bow and let him go. He will enter the cavern, but you must stay outside. Stay there five days, and don't go away. On the sixth day a black shaykh clad all in sable, with a long white beard flowing down to his navel, will come out. As soon as you see him, kiss his hands and seize his shirt and lay it on your head and weep before him, until he takes pity on you and asks you what you want. Then give him this scroll. He will take it without speaking and return to his cavern. Wait outside another five days. If the shaykh comes out the sixth day himself, all is well; but if one of his pages emerges, depart in all haste, for he comes to kill you. Then may the mercy of Buddha be upon you, for he who takes such chances risks death; on the other hand, he who won't gamble can't win. Do you understand?"

"Yes, Uncle," Hasan said more bravely than he felt.

"Now you don't have to risk your life this way, you know. If you'd rather return to your friends, the elephant is still here. You can ride back——"

"I must go on."

"That's what I thought. You're lovemad. Well, in this letter I have presented a strict account of your case to Abu al-Ruwaysh, son of Bilkis, daughter of Mu'in, for he is my mentor and my teacher, and all men and all jinn humble themselves before him and stand in awe of him. And now go with the blessing of—who is it?"

"Allah—I think."

"With the blessing of Allah!" Ab slapped the flank of

the horse and it galloped away with a surge that rendered any formal leavetaking impossible.

Hasan was on his way.

He rode. The stallion raced all day across the desert, never changing direction or easing his pace. Hasan looked about him at first, wondering whether he was still on Serendip; but as the hours passed he grew weary, and his thighs chafed with the steady movement.

Night came, but still the steed pounded on, flinging back occasional spume from its flaring nostrils.

Hasan nodded sleepily. When was this ride going to end? Did the horse never tire? He looked down—and knew he was dreaming, for the flashing hoofs appeared to be galloping over deep water. Water!

The long night passed; the sun came up on his right. Hasan's legs were throbbing with fatigue, and he was desperate for a call of nature. The horse was running through strange country, up a long coastline with the ocean to the east.

Mountains rose to the west, and the land was a wild deep jungle. But evidently the mountains in sight were not his destination.

Hasan sat up straight and hauled on the reins. The stallion bucked and skittered, unwilling to be restrained, but it slowed and finally came to a halt in a deep forest.

He was about to dismount, but remembered Ab's remark that the beast was uncontrollable without a rider. Yet he had to get off for a few minutes, at least. Why hadn't Ab told him the trip was going to be so long?

He searched through the saddlebags. In one was a folded tunic. He drew it out, but was surprised to discover that it was not after all an article of clothing, though of rich design. It was an oddly shaped sack.

A sack—or a hood? Suddenly he remembered the way Eldest controlled her falcons. Would it work on a horse?

He leaned forward and dropped the hood over the stallion's head. There was no complaint. This had to be it!

He dismounted, keeping his hand on the bridle, but the horse did not move. He retreated among the trees and did his business; then he located a small stream and performed the morning ablutions. His legs were stiff and very sore, but at least the most pressing discomfort had been eased.

He was hungry! He had not realized this until drinking from the cool stream. He'd better find something to eat. There was no way to tell how long this journey would be.

He walked around the horse and delved into the opposite saddlebag. There were packages of something. He withdrew one, opened it, and looked at the brown lump inside. Bread? It didn't smell like it. He took an experimental bite.

The stuff was dense and chewy, but not unpleasant to the taste. How could he be certain it was edible?

Hasan took out another package, unwrapped it, and poked it under the covered nose of the horse. The animal sniffed, then took a gigantic bite that just missed his fingers. This might be horse feed, but at least it should be safe. He attacked his own chunk in earnest.

Strength flowed into his arms and legs. He felt full of fire. He could run for miles without tiring. He neighed.

It was horse feed all right. Hasan checked his appetite as he led the stallion to water. Best not to eat too much of the stuff.

He rode. Days shot by under the flashing hoofs, and scenic lakes and valleys and mountains passed in review. The ocean to his right disappeared, but the sun showed his route to continue north. Occasionally the horse skirted native villages, the dark-skinned tribesmen staring curiously. Could any of this country be Sind?

The land opened out into a mighty plain with rich black soil. They crossed a river as large as the Tigris. Now Hasan became assured that the steed was magic, for it ran on the surface of the water as though it were sand.

On what Hasan estimated was the tenth day a vast mountain range arose ahead, walling the world from east to west. The peaks were towering and white at the tops;

Hasan was sure that nowhere else on earth did their like exist.

The stallion neighed exuberantly as it approached the forbidding range and there were answering neighs. Horses flocked to it, mares as numerous as drops of rain on the monsoon wind. They thronged so tightly that their backs made a restless sea; they pressed against the flanks of his steed. What did this mean? Abd al-Kaddus had not advised him of this situation, either.

It occurred to him that there were many things in life that friends could not or did not predict.

There was nothing he could do except maintain his seat and fare forward, hoping for the best. And so at last he came to the mountain cavern accompanied by thousands of mares.

The stallion drew up at the entrance and Hasan dismounted. He threw the rein over the saddle and let the animal go, half expecting it to frolic among its companions. That feed was potent stuff. But it trotted up to the door, opened it with a blow of its front hoof, and disappeared inside.

Hasan waited, but the door did not open again. Once more he grew hungry and thirsty—but Ab had told him not to leave this spot. He dared not disobey the instructions. Magic was involved, and his perils were great enough already. But he would starve before his vigil was up, since it was scheduled for five full days, with five more to follow that. It was cold; what would the nights be like?

He thought of Sana and his children, and recovered strength. He would survive somehow. Allah would provide a way. There were horses, waiting at the door for their stallion to return. He could kill one and live off its flesh. He could squeeze juice from the fruits of the bushes. He would survive.

But no such drastic measures were necessary. Several of these mares had foals. He caught and milked them, careful not to take from the same one twice in succession, so that there would be milk for the foal as well. At night he bound one and curled up beside her, using the heat from her body to drive away the cold that would otherwise have destroyed him.

This was not his idea of luxury, but he was man enough now to sacrifice convenience for the sake of his objectives. The thought of his family bore him up. Unless he prevailed, his children would grow up fatherless and his old mother would die alone and unmourned. There was grief enough without failure on his part.

The prescribed time passed. The door opened. A man came out, his robe as black as his face. Hasan recognized him as the Shaykh Abu al-Ruwaysh, and threw himself at the man's feet.

"What do you want, O my son?"

Wordlessly Hasan handed up the scroll. The Shaykh accepted it and re-entered the cavern, making no reply.

Five more days passed. Hasan's nervousness increased as he thought about his situation. If the shaykh did not come out the second time, his quest was a failure. He would have either to escape or kill the page, then make his way home, never to see his lovely wife again. It was too horrible to contemplate.

On the sixth day the door opened and a white figure emerged. The page! Hasan staggered back, stricken, but reached for his sword.

The figure made no hostile sign, and Hasan relaxed. It was the shaykh after all—this time in a white robe. His petition had been accepted!

The old man took him by the hand and brought him into the cavern. This was even more extensive than the other. Sputtering torches lit the cold passages, and twists and turns were so numerous that he soon lost track of direction. It seemed hours before they stopped at an arched doorway with a panel of a steel for a door. The shaykh opened this and led the way into a vestibule vaulted with onyx, arabesqued with gold and blessedly warm.

They passed through this and came to a wide hall, paved and walled with marble. In its midst was a flower-garden

containing a variety of trees and flowers and fruits, with
birds warbling on the boughs and singing sweetly. There
were four daisies facing inward, and in each a jetting
fountain at whose corners stood golden statues of lions
spouting water from their mouths into the basin.

On each dais stood a chair, and in each chair sat an
elderly sage with a library of books before him and golden
censers containing fire and perfumes. Students gathered
around each elder, reading the books to him.

When Hasan and Abu al-Ruwaysh entered, the sages
stood up and did the shaykh honor. The shaykh gestured
them to dismiss their scholars, and they obeyed promptly.
The four then seated themselves before him and inquired
about Hasan.

The shaykh turned to him. "Tell this company your
tale—everything that has happened to you from the beginning of your adventure until the end." Hasan obliged,
relating the manner in which Bahram the Persian magician
had appeared and tricked him with promises and dazzled
him with gold and kidnapped him into a mighty adventure.

"You are one of the lads that man sent up to the
Mountain of Clouds in camel-hides?" they asked, amazed.

"I am."

They turned to the shaykh. "Never have we heard of
someone surviving that ordeal. How did he get down?"

"Tell them, Hasan."

So Hasan continued his story, leading up to his marriage
with the princess of Wak and her subsequent escape.

"Verily," the sages exclaimed, "this youth is to be
both admired and pitied. Surely, O elder of elders, you
will help him to recover his wife and children."

The old man pulled sadly at his beard. "This is a grave
and perilous matter. This youth is determined to throw
away his life. The Isles of Wak are very hard to reach, and
no one can go there without risking his life. The empire of
Wak is very powerful. Moreover, I have sworn an oath not
to tread the soil of that land or transgress against its people

in any way. How then shall I help this man to come at the favorite daughter of their King?

"O shaykh of shaykhs, this man is consumed with desire for his family, and he has already risked his life to come to you from our brother-in-scholarship, Abd al-Kaddus, who has importuned your help. He has endured the trial of ten days without the gate, which few men survive. How can you deny his plea?"

Hasan went to the old man and threw himself down before him. "I beg of you—reunite me with my wife and children, though it cost me my life and my soul!"

"It is liable to, Hasan—that is why I hesitate."

But the four elders continued to plead for Hasan, and finally the shaykh relented. "This willful youth little comprehends what he's getting into," he murmured, "but we'll help him to whatever extent we can."

Hasan and the elders rejoiced. Abu al-Ruwaysh took up his pen and a sheet of fine paper and wrote a letter, which he rolled up and sealed and gave to Hasan. Then he produced a pouch of perfumed leather which contained incense and firesticks and similar magic. "Take strict care of this pouch. If you get into trouble, burn a little of the incense and speak my name, and I will come to you and help." He spoke to one of the elders. "Fetch me a flying ifrit."

"One of the jinn?" the sage asked, startled. "As you wish."

Hasan marveled. Could these sages actually summon a jinni?

The elder left, to return shortly with a horrendous ifrit in tow. Hasan had never seen such a creature before. It resembled a huge, grotesque man, with a muscular body, two descending tusks, and mighty wings. Yet, stripped of these special features, it would not have been unhandsome. Certainly it was more closely related to man than to the animals, and perhaps its sympathies would normally also lie with man. Of course it had no soul, but—

"What is your name?" the shaykh asked the ifrit.

"Dahnash bin Faktash," the creature boomed.

"Come over here."

The ifrit approached, and the shaykh put his mouth up to its ear and said something. "I accept, O elder of elders!" Dahnash said.

The shaykh spoke to Hasan. "Arise, O my son, and mount the shoulders of this ifrit, Dahnash the Flyer. But be careful: when he ascends into the heavens and you hear the angels glorifying God with their hymns, don't you try to imitate them, or you will both perish."

"I won't say a word," Hasan said. "No, never."

"O Hasan, after faring with you all today, Dahnash will set you down at peep of dawn tomorrow in a land cleanly white, as though it were made of camphor. That is as far as he can go; you will have to walk the rest of the way. After ten days you'll come to a city. Enter the gate and ask for the King. When you come into his presence salute him and kiss his hands; then present to him this scroll and pay careful attention to his advice. Farewell!"

"Farewell," the four elders echoed. Hasan was getting accustomed to the abrupt manner of acquaintance and leave-taking in these enchanted realms, and accepted his dismissal gracefully.

"Hearing and obeying," he said, and climbed onto the ifrit's broad shoulders, trying not to bang his wings.

"Take care of him, Dahnash the Firedrake!" the shaykh called, and the powerful wings spread and raised a confusion of dust.

"I'll take care of him!" the ifrit muttered as the world tilted dizzily. Hasan didn't like the sound of this; but by the time he got his bearings they were above the mountain, rising into a calm morning sky.

Hasan was perched on the ifrit's shoulders, seated between the wings with his feet dangling on either side of the thick neck. This had seemed secure enough when the ifrit stood upright in the cavern; but high in the air and horizontal it became the most precarious lodging. He glanced down, saw the mountain features passing far below, and

instinctively drew back—almost losing his balance in the
other direction. He was not on the Mountain of Clouds; he
could not retreat from the dangerous drop-off so easily,
this time!

"Sit still, mortal—want to throw us into a tailspin?" the
ifrit demanded.

Hasan sat very still. He kept his eyes fixed to the sky
above, trying to imagine that he was riding a camel on the
ground. This helped. Why should he believe that he had
not only seen a demon of the air, but now rode the back of
one? Nonsense—but don't look down.

The experience of air travel was not unpleasant. The
atmosphere was cool—chill, in fact—but the wind whis-
tling around his ears was invigorating. How unfortunate
that man would never be able to fly without the aid of the
birds or jinn! He watched a cottonpuff cloud come down—
they were still climbing!—and was irrationally seized with
the desire to tread the spongy surface. He had always
wondered what plants might grow on the sunlit tops of
these floating islands. What a delightful castle might be
built on such a paradise, subject to no monarch and forever
free of bad weather!

"Dahnash," he said.

"Yes, mortal?"

"Can we park on that little cloud ahead for a moment?"

The ifrit's body shuddered. Hasan was alarmed. Had
something happened? Then he realized that the creature was
shaking with laughter. "Park on a cloud!" Dahnash exclaimed. "Ho ho!"

Hasan was nettled. "The shaykh didn't forbid it, did
he?"

"Watch, mortal."

The ifrit came up level with the cloud and accelerated
toward it. Hasan had to cling frantically as the wind tore at
his body.

The cloud loomed larger. Far from being a tiny puff, it
was an immense boulder of material, white at the top and
with a flat gray bottom.

"Dahnash! You're going to collide!"

"Back-seat driver. Ho ho!" the ifrit laughed, and swooped ahead faster. The outlines of the cloud grew hazy, as though it were surrounded by an atmosphere of its own.

Hasan stared, terrified. Had the demon betrayed him? Did it plan to kill him by dashing him against the cloud? Why had the shaykh trusted him to its care?

They were in the foglike outer fringes. The cloud was so close he couldn't make out the solid outlines at all. Everything was grayness and fleeting mists.

Then the sun reappeared. Dahnash had dodged it after all! He had only skirted the edge.

"You see, mortal?"

"You certainly frightened me," Hasan admitted, deciding honest flattery was the safest policy. "But I still don't understand why you think it's so funny to land on a cloud. Does something dangerous live upon it?"

Dahnash craned his head around to look at Hasan. "You serious? That was the cloud, mortal."

"But all we touched was a little mist."

"Now don't take offense, mortal—but you are ignorant as hell. That's all a cloud *is*. Mist."

"I can never believe that!"

"Brother!" the ifrit sighed. "Some company *you* are going to be." He sighed again. "And they say men are going to take over the world!"

Hasan was embarrassed and angry. "If you're so smart, why do you have to obey the shaykh? He's a man."

"Mortal, there are men and there are men. The shaykh is the greatest of mortals, while I am the least of immortals. There is a certain minimal overlap. Anyway, he offered a pretty good deal."

"Well, why do they say one man is worth a thousand jinn? If you're so powerful—"

"*Who* says that?"

"*Men* say it. Everyone knows—"

"*Men* say it," the ifrit mimicked. "What preposterous audacity! What phenomenal delusions of grandeur! Did you ever hear an *ifrit* say it? Did you ever hear Allah say it? Can you document such a statement?''

''Well, we have souls don't we? You don't.''

''Mortal—we *are* souls!''

Hasan was disgruntled. ''What did the shaykh offer you for this job?'' he asked, trying to modify the subject.

''Ah, that.'' Dahnash was silent for a moment, and Hasan thought he wasn't going to answer. ''He promised to put in a good word for me with the council of marids. I'm eligible for promotion, and—''

''Marids?'' Hasan was concerned. ''You mean those big black funnels that tear ships apart?''

''Funnels? Mortal, when a marid tears loose he doesn't bother with trifles. He sweeps across the ocean with the power of a thousand thunderstorms, blacks out the sky, sinks every ship on the sea and destroys entire cities with the force of his breath.''

''His breath! You mean he *blows* down houses and . . . Allah strike you down for such a story!''

''You'd be in pretty poor circumstances right now if Allah *did*,'' Dahnash observed dryly, glancing down. Hasan involuntarily followed his gaze, and felt immediately sick. They were very high. Suddenly he didn't feel like arguing any more.

''I suppose I don't know much about the jinn,'' he said.

''Never fear, mortal—you have inquired at the proper stall.'' Dahnash took a deep breath and launched into an extemporaneous lecture. ''Know, O child of Adam, that Allah in his wisdom—yes, I am a True Believer—and omnipotence created three species of intelligent beings to dwell upon the earth. From the light He made the Angels, who are sanctified from carnal desire and the disturbance of anger. They don't know what they're missing, if you ask me. They disobey not His will; their food is the celebration of His glory, their drink the proclamation of His holiness, their conversation the commemoration of His name, and their pleasure His worship.

''From the Fire he made the Genii, ranked in five

orders: the lowest are the Jann, who have little power; next are the Jinn (though this term is over-used generically); then the Devils; then Ifrits; and finally the most powerful of all, the Marids. Each of these groups maintains its representatives on land, in the sea and in the air. I am a flying ifrit—and it is from *my* group the whirling funnels come. We are second only to the marids.''

''But you have nearly human shape,'' Hasan said, fascinated.

''Do you want me to change?'' Dahnash demanded, and Hasan hastily demurred. ''We can assume any shape we wish, except that the larger it is, the more diffuse it becomes. I could become the size of an ant—but I would be an exceedingly heavy ant, and have strength to crush stone in my pincers. I could become a hundred feet tall— but I would have no more substance than the cloud we flew through. That's why our form changes so much. The size determines it. A man-shaped, hundred-foot ifrit would be blown all out of shape by the wind, unless he really *was* that big in solid state.''

''You mean you couldn't destroy a ship, in your funnel-cloud form?''

''O mortal, I could destroy a ship—but it would be a lot more difficult than it looked from the outside. If it were easy, I assure you that there would be very few vessels left on the ocean! An ifrit in that shape is invisible. What he has to do is exert himself to start the air moving and circling about. Once he gets it going, he can increase the velocity bit by bit and make the whole affair larger, until water or sand is sucked up and mortals can look upon him. If he moves over a ship *then*, he can do much damage while he has his inertia going for him.''

''His what?''

''You wouldn't understand. Just think of it as one of the magical attributes. Inertia. Anyway, it does take pretty careful preparation to accomplish something spectacular, like the destruction of a ship, and I want you to appreciate that.''

"O Dahnash, I do!" Hasan said, and did.

"The water ifrits have some success with great circles of liquid that suck down everything on the surface of the sea. Same principle. And you should see the spectaculars put on by some of the earth-ifrits! I don't know how they do it, but they come up with cones of fire, red-hot rock, and sometimes they shake the ground so hard the houses of mortals fall down. What sport! I tell you, not in thousands of years will your kind avail against such things!"

Hasan was silent, impressed in spite of his conviction that the ifrit exaggerated considerably. So much of what he had been told about the magical realms was exaggerated. He had heard no angels singing, for example.

Time passed. The ifrit landed once, upon request, to allow Hasan a rest-stop and some food, then resumed the long flight. The day darkened, and still the flight continued. Hasan clung as well as he could and hoped sleep would not tumble him off.

"Where are the angels?" he inquired, hoping the conversation would keep him alert.

"Mortal, it isn't safe to fly that high. I'd be incinerated and dashed to the ground long before I reached heaven."

"I thought you were immortal."

"I am—but that doesn't mean I can break the rules. Haven't you seen the shooting light of chastened ifrits being abolished from heaven? Just a flash in the night, and they're gone. They live—but not as flying ifrit any more, you can be sure. The smart ones stay well within the three-mile limit."

Hasan *had* seen the occasional streaks among the stars on cloudless nights. It was amazing the way everything fell into place, once he understood the causes.

"You said there were *three* intelligent species on earth," he said, remembering another little mystery. "You've told me about the angels and the jinn—"

Dahnash laughed and laughed. "Ho mortal—if you don't know, I am not the one to tell you!"

Hasan was not so easily put off. "Can the third species fly?"

"No, mortal."

"Can it perform feats of magic?"

"Very little—and most of those are illusion."

"Are there many around?"

"Very many."

"What *can* this species do?"

"It can reproduce, mortal—that's why there are so many. Ho ho!"

Hasan was frustrated by the ifrit's too-obvious satisfaction. "It doesn't sound like anything worthwhile to me," he said.

"My opinion exactly, mortal!" Dahnash laughed. And laughed.

Chapter 9. Shawahi

In the morning the ifrit landed in the middle of a white desert. He set Hasan down, still chuckling, and departed. For a moment Hasan thought he saw a funnel rising in the air, but it was gone immediately with a faint "Ho ho!"

He was on his own again.

He hiked, foraging what he could from the land and bearing directly toward the rising sun. The hills were gentle and rolling, and as he marched the land became flat, and was cultivated extensively with rice. Some of the dwindling hills were terraced with more rice growing on the additional levels.

At length he arrived at the city. It was a handsome one, whose architecture differed from everything he had encountered before and whose people were yellowed-skinned. They spoke a language totally different from his, as he discovered when challenged at the gate.

For a time he was afraid they would slay him or imprison him as a stranger, and felt nervously for the pouch with the fire and incense to summon the shaykh. But surely the man had known about such difficulties, and would not have sent Hasan hither unless he also knew they would be resolved. What was obvious to a magician was seldom obvious to Hasan. But determination and on-the-spot ingenuity had prevailed so far.

This time he did not overcome the problem. The people of the city did. They brought a translator.

"What is your business here?" the yellow man inquired, once he settled upon Hasan's dialect.

"I must see the King. I have a message from the Shaykh Abu al-Ruwaysh."

The man nodded. He recognized the name. After due formalities Hasan was ushered into the presence of King Hassun, Lord of the Land of Camphor. At least, that was the way Hasan understood the title. It appeared to suffer somewhat in translation.

"So you come from the mighty sage of the mountain, the Father of Feathers," the King said. Again Hasan wondered how much distortion was engendered by the indirect mode of communication. "A wise man. He sent a letter?"

Hasan gave him the scroll.

The King read it with interest, shaking his head. It was in the King's language; Hasan had peeked, and seen the peculiar paint-brush symbols resembling those on Uncle Ab's stolen door.

The King looked up. "Take this youth to the lodge of hospitality," he said.

For three days Hasan resided in the guest-house, royally treated and fed delightfully exotic meals. He told his entire story to the King, who was suitably amazed to converse thus with a citizen of a country so far removed from civilization.

On the fourth day they discussed Hasan's mission. "O traveler," said the King, "you come to me seeking to enter the Isles of Wak, as the shaykh of shaykhs advises me. I would send you there today—but on the way are many perils and many terrors, and I am afraid you go only to your death."

"O King—I must go, for my wife and sons are there."

"So I understand. We certainly comprehend the ties of the family. Have patience; I shall help you in whatever humble way I can. I have devised a plan that at least gives you an even chance, and that is the best I can do, even for the sake of the venerable Abu al-Ruwaysh, whom I would dislike to disappoint."

"Thank you, thank you, O auspicious King!"

"I am not certain I am doing you any favor," the King said sadly. "But since you insist upon this adventure I will put you on a ship going in the direction of the Isles. I would take you to Wak myself—but although I have a mighty host of fighting-men, I can not hope to prevail against the forces of Wak. You will have to enter surreptitiously."

"Only tell me what to do," Hasan said, undismayed.

"I will place you on board with a note in my own hand designating you as a clansman of mine, so that no one will interfere with you. But my protection ends the moment you leave the ship, for it sails beyond my domain, and my name cannot help you at Wak. Now as soon as the captain bids you to land, go ashore, for this will be your closest approach to the Isles. You will see a multitude of wooden settles on the beach. Choose one, crouch under it, and do not stir a muscle. When dark night sets in you will see an army of women appear and flock about the goods, for this is the way we trade with that empire. One of them will sit upon the settle you have chosen. Then you must put forth your hand to her and implore her protection. And know, O traveler, that if she accords you her protection, you stand an excellent chance of continuing your quest; but if she refuses, you are a dead man. You are risking your life, and will probably lose it, and I can do no more for you—but Allah (here the translator considerately supplied Hasan's word for God) has smiled on you so far, or you never would have achieved this much. Perhaps he will smile again."

"O mighty and puissant King, when are the ships coming here?"

"It will be a month, and it will take time for them to

complete their business here; but you are welcome to stay with me that time.''

Hasan thanked him and spent a pleasant month in the Land of Camphor, learning something of its language and custom.

He also strained to remember the speech of Wak that he had learned from Sana, and improved upon his knowledge of it by studying with a linguist who spoke it. His experience with the King had impressed upon him the need to know other tongues than his own.

The ships arrived, among them one huge vessel with four masts, enormous square sails reinforced by horizontal rods of bamboo spaced every two feet, and sixty tiny cabins, each sufficient living-quarter for a single merchant. The sides of the boat were brightly painted, and the whole affair was spectacular and quite entertaining to the stranger. Hasan was unable to count the number of people upon it; there were hundreds.

The days of unloading and reloading were interminable, for these traders did not rush things, and put protocol before convenience. Hasan stamped fretfully around the docks, unable either to wait or to hurry up the process. At last the King sent for him, gave him attractive gifts, and equipped him with the things he needed.

Next the King summoned the captain of the largest ship. ''Take this youth with you in your ship, but do not let any man know he is there or what his purpose is. Put him ashore where you trade with the amazons of Wak, and leave him there.''

''Leave him there! Is your headsman ill, that you must resort to this manner of execution?''

''This is no convict, Captain, but an honored guest, who desires to travel to Wak.''

The captain looked at Hasan and blew out his moustache. ''To hear is to obey,'' he said doubtfully.

''And Hasan,'' said the King. ''Don't tell anyone aboard anything about yourself, in case someone sees you. If news of your mission preceded you to Wak—''

Hasan agreed wholeheartedly. He made his farewell to the King, who wished him the best and committed him to

the care of the captain. The captain put him in a chest,
loaded it into a dinghy, and hauled it aboard the ship while
the crewmen were busy preparing for the voyage. No one
doubted this was special merchandise.

Hasan had the run of the cabin. It hardly seemed larger
than a casket. He peeped out to watch the shoreline pass,
and was reminded of the time so long ago when he had
been a captive on his way to Serendip. Phenomenal adventure had waited for him there. Would it be the same this
time—or worse?

The days went by; Hasan lost count at ten. At length the
fleet of ships hove to in a natural harbor with a long white
beach lined with a number of ornate benches, or wooden
couches, all unoccupied. The crewmen conveyed the trading goods ashore and picked up, in return, certain other
goods waiting on the beach, while the captain ferried
Hasan quietly ashore. The men returned to the ships; the
vessels set sail, and Hasan was left once more to his own
devices.

Hasan walked along the beach from chair to chair,
noting the workmanship and splendor of each. He would
have to hide under one of these—and upon his choice
depended his life, not to mention the success of his mission. There were hundreds of them; how could he locate
the proper one? *Was* there a proper one?

Some settles were larger and finer than others. He had
to assume that this was an accurate indication of importance. The commanding general should have the most
elaborate one of all. Should he select an insignificant chair
on the theory that its owner might be young and sympathetic? Or a fancy one, knowing that its occupant would
have more power?

A young woman might agree to help him more readily,
but probably wouldn't have the authority to do much. The
moment her superiors found out, he would be lost. And,
possibly, she would be jealous once she learned his mission. A veteran would be much harder to move, on the

other hand. She would be capable of killing him outright. The leaders of armies were callous creatures.

Dusk was falling. He had to make his decision soon, before the women came, or he would be lost before he started. Already he heard a distant clamor. They were here!

He ran pell-mell for the mightiest chair, a veritable throne, and thrust himself under it.

The noise increased. Hasan peeked out from his hiding place and saw a multitude of warriors approaching, wearing strangely-wrapped garments and unusual helmets and swords. This was the fabulous army of women he had been told about!

They spied the merchandise on the beach and gathered about it with delighted exclamations. Warrior-women were still women, Hasan reflected; the strangeness was only in his own view.

After a while their lights ceased to move and bob, and the women came to their chairs to rest. One seated herself upon the settle under which he crouched, and he knew his moment had come. He offered a silent prayer to Allah and grasped the hem of her garment.

"What is this?" the woman exclaimed in the Wak language, and he was thankful for his recent practice in it.

He crawled out and threw himself to the ground before her. "O Amazon!" he cried. "Your protection! Your goodwill!"

"Who are you? Stand up and let me look at you."

Her voice was sharp with command, though he could not see her face. This was a leader, without a doubt.

Hasan stood up. "O my mistress! I throw myself under your protection."

She peered at him in the light of her torch. "Why— you're a man. Don't you know we kill any man who sets foot in our camp?"

"Have pity on one who is parted from his people and his wife and his children! I have traveled across the world to rejoin them, risking my life and my soul for their sake. I beg for your help—otherwise all is lost."

The merchant-warriors in the neighboring chairs turned to see him standing there. "Get out of sight before they learn you are a man," she whispered harshly. "They'll kill you if they find out. Hide where you were."

Hasan immediately crawled under the settle again. "Mind—" the woman said, to the air but loudly enough for him to hear, "I have not decided what to do with you yet. I want to hear your story first. Stay there until morning; after that I'll transport you to my tent."

"O my mistress! Thank you, thank you!"

"Don't get effusive. I may have to kill you anyway."

She stood up and went down the beach, as did the other women. They lighted new torches—flambeaux of wax mixed with aloes-wood and perfume and crude ambergris— and passed the night in celebration, while Hasan watched and slept fitfully and wondered what was to come.

At dawn his benefactress returned with an armful of clothing. "Put this on," she said. "Hurry."

Hasan stood up and donned a light jacket of mail, a helmet, a clasped girdle and footwear that was obviously intended for no man. The armor was certainly shaped to other specifications than his, and quite uncomfortable. He slung the sword over his shoulder so that it hung under his armpit, and took the spear in his hand.

"Cover your face," she directed. "Your shape is bad enough—but no amazon wears a beard on her chin."

Hasan had seen that the amazons also did not wear veils, but he was hardly in a position to argue the matter.

"Now follow me," she said. "Don't say a word—your barbarous accent would destroy you."

It was not light yet. Hasan both blessed the murk for the concealment it offered and cursed it for making it so difficult to distinguish his benefactress amidst the troops. He didn't even know her name, and hadn't seen enough of her face to make it recognizable.

The armed women crowded around him as they followed a narrow road from the beach; severe campaigners alternating with lovely young first-termers. They chatted and joked with considerable crudity, and bumped into each other and himself, causing him much apprehension. Even if he had not been fearful of discovery, he would not have enjoyed the company of such masculinely attired women. The mail suits suppressed their charms considerably, both physical and intellectual.

They approached the amazon camp. Military tents were pitched amid the trees, each carefully pegged and ditched to keep out insects and water. The women dispersed, each to her own tent. Hasan looked around—and could not find his patron!

The aisle between the tents was almost deserted now. He wandered along, uncertain what to do. He couldn't just stand outside—the sentries would notice. But how could he risk entering the wrong tent?

He offered up another silent prayer and headed for the largest tent. This was his only chance. He entered.

The woman inside had thrown down her arms and was lifting off her mail. She paused as she saw Hasan, and he paused too, ready to bolt.

"Come in before someone sees you, young man," she snapped. It was the right tent!

She finished drawing off her armor, and Hasan did likewise, glad to get out of the pinchy and bulgy costume. They faced each other in the light of the interior lamp.

Hasan had not known what to expect in his companion, but he was nevertheless disappointed. She was a grizzled old woman with straggly hair, wrinkled eyes, bald eyebrows; gap-toothed, big-nosed and hoary-headed. Her face was a pockmarked calamity, but her body rivaled it for ugliness, with limbs like dry sticks and breasts like empty pouches.

They conversed. She was commander-in-chief of the amazon army with a name and title he found difficult to pronounce or comprehend. He settled upon an adaptation he could remember: Shawahi the fascinator, Mother of Calamities. "The calamities are visited upon the foe, despite appearances," she reassured him. "Now tell me who

you are and how you came to this country, for I can
plainly see you are a stranger.''

Hasan summarized his story for her. He had told it to so
many people in the course of this journey that it was
beginning to sound uninteresting. He refrained from add-
ing embellishments, however; he wasn't trying to impress
this woman, but to obtain her protection and help.

''A princess of Wak?'' she repeated, and sniffed. ''Every peasant girl is a princess when she meets a handsome
stranger. I daresay we can run her down without involving
the court.''

It had not occurred to Hasan that Sana might be less
than she had claimed—but of course she *hadn't* claimed to
be a princess. Rose had read it in a book, and he had never
questioned it. Sana had come accompanied by servants,
and was so obviously highborn that—

It didn't matter. He had married her for her beauty, not
her royalty. ''Whatever she is,'' he said, ''I beg of
you—help me find her. Otherwise I shall surely die.''

''Don't worry, lad,'' the crone said. ''I like you, and I
have decided to help you to achieve your desire. You are
fortunate you encountered me, because no one else would
have helped you.'' And she questioned him closely on the
details of his story.

Hasan answered with complete openness, but remained
nervous. At last she was satisfied. ''I will show you how I
will help you, O my son,'' she said. Hasan's distress
abated; by addressing him as ''son'' she had indicated that
her own interest in him was compassionate rather than
romantic. This was a necessary reassurance, for he had
heard tales. . . .

Shawahi clapped her hands. Young attendants appeared
at the front of the tent. ''Summon the captains of the army
to my presence,'' she said.

The captains came and stood before her. ''Go out and
proclaim to all the troops that they shall assemble tomorrow at daybreak. Let no one stay behind, for she who tarries
shall be slain.''

"We hear and obey," they replied.

All day Shawahi gave directions and organized the army for travel. The goods were packed and loaded on beasts of burden, and food for the journey was hunted, prepared and stored. Hasan ascertained this by the sounds about him, since he never left the tent.

At dusk Shawahi rejoined him. "I am not a practicing Buddhist," she said, "for the religion of peace is difficult for warriors and the royal-born. Yet I would solve your problem without violence if I could. It would not be easy for you to recover a girl from Wak itself."

Hasan had many questions, for he knew nothing of this religion to which she didn't belong, yet disliked thinking of her as an infidel. He wondered what her plan was. But he held back his queries and accepted the mat she laid out for him in the corner of the tent. She had agreed to help; that was enough, for now.

At dawn the troops assembled. Shawahi made Hasan dress in an all-enveloping shawl, with a kerchief over his face so that nothing showed but his eyes. "Now I want you to stand beside me and tell me if you recognize your wife among my girls, for it is possible that she is among them," she said.

"But how shall I know her, in armor?"

The old woman smiled. "Perhaps they will remove some of it," she said. "Come."

Hasan followed her to the beach, where she sat upon her settle and bade him stand beside it. The captains shouted orders and the troops moved, unit by unit, past them and down toward the water. There each woman removed her armor and the rest of her apparel and went into the water to bathe. Naked, buxom girls paraded before him in all their natural charm.

Hasan concealed his astonishment, knowing that the amazons never would have exposed themselves in his presence had they suspected his identity. They washed their fair skins and frolicked in the water, no longer the tough warriors he had seen before. It was amazing how much of a woman's pretensions vanished with her clothing! These damsels were beautiful; clean of limb and firm of breast, with long dark hair streaming down their backs.

Hasan studied them closely, trying to recognize the face and feature of his beloved . . . but the sight of their nudity and the soft and rounded decorations between their prancing thighs gave him a tremendous erection.

Shawahi chuckled. She was watching him, not her amazons. "They have attractive . . . faces, don't they, Hasan?"

"They—yes," he agreed, embarrassed. "But I don't see my wife among them."

Shawahi signaled, and the first company emerged from the water and marched, naked, directly in front of the settle, on their way back to their armor and camp. Hasan found it painful to stand still—but none of these was Sana.

All morning the amazons bathed and marched past him; but though each company seemed more remarkable than the last, and his gaze lingered increasingly on the flexing buttocks retreating toward the tents, his disappointment grew as he despaired of finding his wife among them.

At last the officers bathed. Most of these were less attractive than the lower-ranking girls, but there was one among them who stood out like the moon among stars. She had many waiting-women, and entered the water in the company of slavegirls of surpassing beauty. She fell to splashing and ducking them, while they did not dare return the gesture, and Hasan felt hot tears of remembrance come to his eyes as he remembered his first vision of the bird-maiden and her sport in the pool.

"This girl is very like my wife," he murmured, admiring her high bosom and broad thighs as she came from the water to don precious ornaments and clothing threaded with gold.

"Ah—have you recognized her, then?" Shawahi inquired.

"No, O my lady—this is not my wife, nor have I ever seen this damsel before. For a moment her grace and symmetry suggested the appearance of my wife, but not one of these girls is her like.''

The old woman frowned. ''Describe her to me, then. I know every girl in the Isles of Wak, for all are required to serve under me before taking husbands. Perhaps I will know her from your description.''

''My wife has the fairest face and form of grace,'' he said, plunging into the task with enthusiasm. ''Her cheeks are smooth and her breasts are high; her calves and thighs are plump to the sight and her teeth snowy white, her speech a delight; her gifts are moral and her lips red coral—''

''Are you quoting something?''

Hasan flushed. ''We of Arabia get poetic when emotion overcomes us,'' he admitted. ''When I bring to mind the imagery of my love—anyway, on her right cheek is a mole, and there is a sign on her waist under her navel. Her waist is so small her hips seem to be a heavy weight. Her face is brighter than the moon and the touch of her lips is a draught from the fountains of paradise.''

Shawahi's eyes narrowed speculatively. ''Now give me a detailed account,'' she said.

Hasan obliged, while the damsel before the water dressed in leisurely fashion. When he finished, the old woman bowed her head.

''I would have been happier without this knowledge,'' she said. ''I recognize this woman by her description.''

''O Pilgrimess! You know her!''

''I know her—but this is no cause to rejoice. Of all the women it might have been, this is the worst. For you have described the eldest daughter of the Supreme King of Wak.''

''Yes—I told you she was a princess!''

''If I had believed you, I would never have agreed to help,'' the old woman said bitterly. ''I allowed for youthful exaggeration. That was a mistake.'' She faced Hasan, her knowledgeable eyes boring into his. ''Now listen, young man. If you're asleep, wake up. If this woman is indeed your wife, it is impossible for you ever to obtain her. If you came to her somehow, you still could not possess her, because the distance between your station and hers is the distance between earth and heaven. If you even attempt to win her, your life and the lives of all who help you will be forfeit."

Hasan was plunged into despair. "O my lady—how shall I turn my back now, after coming this far? I never thought you would forsake me like this!"

"O my son—believe me, if you persist in this quest you can only sacrifice your life. Go home; you are too handsome to die like this! You have seen all the girls of my army naked. Tell me which of them pleases you, and I will give her to you in lieu of your wife, and you can return to your country in safety and comfort. That damsel lingering on the beach—surely she is to your liking? She is of royal blood herself, and—"

But Hasan hung his head and would not be consoled. "I cannot live with any but my beloved," he said. "And my sons."

Shawahi sighed. "I don't know what I'm going to do. If I take you before the Queen you say is yours, I will lose my own life as well, because she will blame me for admitting you to her lands, and her wrath is terrible. I will give you a fortune in treasure and fair women, if you will only reconsider."

"I don't want anything but my wife and children," Hasan said.

Shawahi saw that it was no use. "This is death for both of us," she said, "but I will take you to the Queen."

Hasan started to thank her, but thought the better of it. She did not want thanks; she was only honoring the letter of her promise to assist him.

"This, then, is the journey lying before us," she told him. "From here to the chief city of Wak is a distance by foot of seven months. We fare first to the Land of the Ferals, where tigers and bears and crocodiles and all manner of fearsome creatures prowl. Then we travel on to the

Land of the Birds, where the noise of their wings and screeching scarcely allows anyone to talk or sleep. After that we come to a third country, the Land of the Jinn, where our ears are deafened by their cries and our eyes blinded by the sparks and fire of their mouths. At last we approach the main section of Wak, the largest island, and cross a mighty river and pass an enormous mountain, Mount Wak, where a tree grows which bears fruits like the heads of the sons of Adam. When the sun rises on them the heads cry out 'Wak! Wak!' and at sundown they cry out again. And yet these things are nothing compared to the power and wrath of the Queen when she finds out—'' she broke off, shuddering.

The empire of Wak extended far beyond the seven principle islands. Hasan had been landed at its farthest extremity, just south of the Khmer empire that lay between them and the Land of Camphor. Their route would skirt the Khmer demesnes and circle a great sea bordering the long northern peninsula that reached down toward Wak itself.

They marched. The soil underfoot abruptly changed to deep, bright red, as though a dragon had been slain and bled of its vengeful life directly into the earth. They kept mainly to the shore, following the white sandy beaches whenever possible.

Giant mangrove trees thrived here. At flood tide only the trunks and crowns showed in the water, but during the ebb the bizarre prop-root structures were exposed, three to five feet long and converging upward toward the stem. Individual sections stuck out of the mud, going nowhere.

The serpentine coastline wound in and out, fringed with forested islands and mangrove swamps. Hasan hardly knew which direction he was going, because their route seemed to bear in all directions. He knew he could never have negotiated this country by himself.

The land near the shore was fairly level, but he could see tall mountains rising inland. Rivers came from them to the sea, edged thickly by bamboo forests and more sparsely

by coconut palms, papayas and banana plants. Elsewhere
the trees were bare; carpets of brown leaves many inches
deep covered the forest floor.

"Why are all the trees dying?" Hasan wanted to know.

Shawahi laughed and explained that it was the dry season, when the parched forests lost their foliage. "Things
will change when the monsoon comes," she said. "And
we'd better be across the plain before it does."

"But the rains bring no harm."

"Stranger, trust me to know my business. After the
rains come the floods. All the plain is covered with dirty
water, a sea of it, with nothing but sugar-palms rising out
of it to show where the land was. You can't even tell
where the salt ocean begins. The native houses are built on
stilts to keep them dry—but we are on foot. It would not
be very comfortable traveling."

Hasan shut up, chastened. Still, he maintained a certain
skepticism, until such time as he saw such a wonder for
himself. He had seen floods in Bassorah, but nothing on
this order.

They entered the Land of Ferals. Hasan was disappointed; its appearance was much the same as what he had
already seen. But of course he should have expected the
animals to be in scant supply during the dry season, and
should be thankful for it.

Yet why did reality always turn out to be so much less
than anticipation?

He kept his eyes open and did see animals—elephants,
bears, boars, monkeys and a solitary tiger. Deer bounded
away on sight, and a jackal skulked after the party, scav-
enging for their remains. There were crocodiles and turtles
in the rivers, and at night the sharp-pointed porcupines
roved among the trees. Rats were common, and their
prettier cousins, the squirrels. Several times he saw lithe
black panthers, and of course there were many snakes of
all sizes.

He suspected that the Land of Ferals would be much
more dangerous for an individual traveler. As it was, in

the midst of an armed party of many hundreds, the trip was dull.

They crossed the plains. The outlines of the mountains faded far to the north and the land became level and monotonous. Drowsing buffaloes stood near the water, the helpful weaver-birds picking parasites out of their fur. There were villages here: the clusters of houses were indeed on stilts, and the little island-like collections of dwellings were surrounded by bunches of thorny bamboo and palms.

Shawahi took the party through one village, stopping for supplies, and Hasan got a closer look at the natives and their way of life. The huts were fashioned of bamboo and grass, with peaked roofs of matted hay, and stood three or four feet above the ground. The men wore the phanung: a long wide cloth wrapped around the body from waist to knees, with the two ends passed between the legs and tucked into the waist in back to form serviceable panta-loons. The women wore tunic-like dresses, colorful tur-bans and silver rings around their necks. Little boats were in the water, with domes over their decks like barrels laid sidewise.

The market-place both fascinated and repelled Hasan. There was none of the vociferous bargaining he was accus-tomed to. The shopper either paid the price or he didn't; the shopkeeper didn't seem to care. How could anyone do business that way? Later he was to realize that much of what he took to be indifference was in reality the extreme politeness of the people here, and come to appreciate this quality very much; but this first experience left him cold.

The floors were covered with fresh fruit and vegetables. There had to be some cultivation in spite of the dry season, Hasan thought. Did they irrigate? Bright green cone-shaped lotus-pods stood in piled pyramids. Flattened dried frogs were pressed together in bunches. Turtle eggs and edible lizards were displayed, together with pugnacious live crabs and even live octopuses squatting in bowls of water.

Some food was already prepared: octopus entrails and

tentacles served as a side dish to steaming boiled rice. Hasan looked at the obvious suction pads and moved on, unhungry.

Some of the young village girls wore fancy belts under their blouses. "The quality of the belt shows her value on the marriage market," Shawahi explained. "Good system," Hasan agreed.

That night Shawahi treated him to a special delicacy of the region: a royal fruit called the durian. It was green and thorned on the outside, almost the size of a man's head. She cut it open to expose the creamy meat inside and an odor of garlic, rotten cheese and camel-urine wafted up. She handed a thick slice to him. "Eat your fill, Hasan—you will seldom get to feast on a delight like this!" she said mischievously, while Hasan gagged on the stench and eyed the brain-like convolutions of the surface.

Shawahi ate with gusto. "You'll find it melts in your mouth," she said, cutting a second slice from the large center fruit stone. "Isn't this an unforgettable experience?"

Hasan agreed wanly.

Egrets rose lazily as the army marched from the village, and hawks circled high overhead. There were cities along their route, but Shawahi intended to avoid these. Next was the Land of Birds.

Hasan wondered whether his mouth would feel clean by the time they reached it.

Chapter 10. Queen

He was thoroughly weary of the plain by the time they reached the forested mountains. Though the sun beat down mercilessly, there were signs of change. The monsoon season was approaching.

The transition was abrupt. Suddenly they were in the thickest and rankest rainforest Hasan had ever seen. Here grew the gigantic yang trees: the enormous trunks branchless for well over a hundred feet, topped by broad crowns of small leathery leaves. Bamboos were the size of trees,

seventy-five feet tall with culms a foot in diameter. A
handsome tree with long, narrow silver-green leaves bore
greenish-yellow flowers on stems sprouting directly from
the trunk. The undersides of the leaves were reddish.
Hasan studied it and was reminded of Serendip; then it
occurred to him that this could be the tree that bore the
durian fruit, and he lost interest.

The party plodded single file through the jungle along
narrow trails shut in by walls of green. Herbs and shrubs
rose up to great heights, and sizable tree-trunks stood close
together. Elephants made these trails, Shawahi explained;
they were indefatigable path-makers, contouring them around
peaks and along valleys.

"A rhinoceros will try to burrow under tangled vegetation," she said, "rather than walk over it. But the elephant
is at home in the forest. It can go anywhere a man can go, and
we are not too proud to use the good trails it leaves for us."

Hasan looked at the deep growth of climbing and twisting plants surrounding many of the trunks and festooning
the spaces between them, and was glad she felt that way.

Broken tree-trunks lay on the ground, and some dead
trees were so entangled they could not fall. They leaned,
defunct and rotting, upon other trees. Luxuriant moss covered these, and from this moss sprang beautifully colored
orchids. Cup-shaped palms grew where they could, and so
did the tree-ferns. The upper foliage of the forest was so
dense that it was impossible to see the sky from the
ground. Only occasionally did the canopy part to admit the
blinding sunshine, which reflected from the shiny surfaces
of the lower leaves. The forest air was humid and musty—a
hothouse of solid greens.

This was the Land of Birds. Near the water were small
white egrets, storks and ibises. Hasan stood at the edge of
a brook, where the sunlight fell from the side and made
every leaf turn toward it, and watched a red-headed crane
take off from behind a tree-trunk bridge. The bird was
almost as tall as he was, standing, with uniform gray plumage and a bright wine-red head.

The birds of the forest were much prettier than those of

the plain and swamp. There were brilliant kingfishers, flocks of noisy green parakeets, and jungle hens with rusty red feathers and a metallic sheen in the tail. There were pheasants, crows, falcons and buzzards; peacocks perched over the streams, and the pied hornbill was frighteningly large in flight. Hasan's favorite was what he learned was the long-tailed broadbill: it had a green back, yellow throat, blue tail, and a black cap with a bush of blue and yellow feathers. Shawahi also pointed out the small swifts, from whose nests soup was made.

But birds were hardly the only creatures here. The jungle resounded with the calls of unseen animals and the chatter of families of gibbons. The shrill mass-chirping of the cicadas began at dawn and filled the air until the hottest part of the day. Then it stopped—no one begrudged the insects a rest—and began again in the afternoon until it reached a deafening crescendo at dusk. Even at night it did not stop; the noise abated only gradually as the hours of darkness passed.

The mountainsides were steep, and high up Hasan encountered nests of sticks half the height of a man. No, not for birds—these were built by wild pigs to protect their burrows from predators. Flying lizards moved between the trees, and bats appeared in every size. "Wait until you see the flying centipedes of Wak," Shawahi said.

Hasan had thought he had seen the most spectacular refuge of wild-life and wilderness in Serendip. Now he realized that there was a great deal yet to appreciate.

The monsoon came as they crossed the valley between the long mountain ranges, to the western side of the peninsula. The rains beat down with devastating force, drenching everything with elemental savagery. This was one of the wettest spots in the world, Shawahi said, and Hasan believed it.

They moved on south, day by day. Brilliant flowers were everywhere. Plants climbed trees, reached up through the crowns and out into the sun. Some plants even lived in the high foliage entirely, with their roots dangling in the air below. Butterflies fluttered about, and even fish climbed trees.

Land appeared across the ocean to the south. This was the major island of Wak itself—the land where Hasan was to meet his fate.

They crossed in long double-hulled boats, the amazons taking paddles and rowing vigorously in their enthusiasm to be home. All day they rowed, and did not touch land again until night; Hasan was glad there was no storm that day, for the ocean seemed exceedingly wide and deep for such tiny craft.

They landed; but the journey was hardly over yet. They had yet to traverse the Land of the Jinn.

Great mountains lay to the south and west. The countryside did not seem to change, except for one notable feature: the top of the largest mountain they passed was white. Hasan remembered this effect from the mountain of the black Shaykh.

"What's the matter with that peak?" he demanded, gesturing.

Shawahi smiled. "That is snow."

Hasan fidgeted in the heat, looking for the joke. "But snow is cold."

She nodded agreeably.

Hasan gave up. Evidently he was missing something again.

They marched inland now, through thick forest. Animals and birds of every description were present, and Hasan gaped at bamboo stalks over two feet thick, and fly-covered flowers the same size. The soil was uncommonly rich and black, but still—!

At night he woke with a shock: the ground was shaking! "What's happening?" he shouted.

"Go back to sleep, lad," Shawahi mumbled. "I told you this was the land of the Jinn."

The jinn! So it was true. The flying ifrit Dahnash had said that the demons of the earth could shake the ground. . . .

"Do they really make cones of fire?"

"Of course," the old woman said. "Go to sleep."

"How can I sleep when the jinn are walking?"

Shawahi sat up. "Listen, Hasan—all that a man needs for happiness is a horse, a knife, a wife and a singing bird. That's a proverb of ours. Worry about your wife. That's all you're missing. You don't need to concern yourself about the doings of the fire-spirits. You'll see enough of that tomorrow. Now sleep."

Somehow he wasn't reassured.

In the morning they marched uphill. The jungle opened out and they stood before a ragged mountain of ominous appearance. "That's your cone," Shawahi said. "One of the largest in Wak. See—there's a little fire now."

Hasan looked anxiously. The top of the mountain leveled off, and above it was a cloud of smoke. As he watched, an expanding ball of blackness puffed up from the mountain itself.

"That's really a ball of steam and ashes," the old woman said. "Just a little innocent practice. Sometimes Magma is angry; then the fire shoots out and the ashes fall everywhere, and the terrible burning rock flows down the side. When that happens, you must get as far away as you can." She smiled reminiscently. "But it doesn't happen often."

"Magma? Who is—?"

"Magma is the marid of the mountain. You haven't seen power until you've seen a marid in action. But don't be alarmed—our temple to Buddha is nearby, and while the holy men hardly serve the marid, there seems to be a pacifying influence."

"What kind of temple does—Buddha—have?" Hasan was still curious about this strange religion that never faced Mekkeh.

"You'll see it when we pass beyond the mountain. There are holy relics and the sacred ashes of our dead. You can hear the bells for many miles, and it is a sanctuary for all who are in need."

"But why so far from your cities? You said we still have to travel many—"

"Buddha loved the forest. A tree may be as holy as a temple. Isn't that true in your land?"

Hasan shook his head, amazed. "And Buddha permits a marid to menace the temple?"

"Buddha is tolerant," she said simply. "Even the jinn have the right to seek destiny in their own fashion."

He found it hard to comprehend such an attitude. But in a land where mountains bore snow in the heat or belched fire from their summits, strange beliefs had to be expected. Or were the jinn so powerful in their own land that even a god—an *infidel* god, he corrected himself mentally—had to defer to them?

Whatever the situation, he had a nasty premonition that the fire-demons, large and small, would not stay pacified until his quest was over.

Yet the old woman hardly seemed to be concerned about such things. Instead she worried about the reaction of the Queen. If the Queen of Wak were really Sana, his wife, why should there be such concern? He knew Sana did not have the heart for vengeful measures. She had seldom been able even to reprimand a household slave. Whatever her reputation might be here, he was confident that once he found her and talked with her, she would agree to come back to Baghdad with him.

Shawahi had said that the woman he described as his wife was the Queen—but somehow the personalities were entirely different. How could this terrible Queen be his wife—and if she were not, where *was* his wife? Surely there could not be two on earth like her.

As Hasan's journey neared its conclusion, his apprehension and concern increased. Something was wrong.

The house was large and strange to Hasan, though he had learned to take strangeness as a matter of course. Its timbers were of dark hardwood, much of it carved and painted in intriguing artistry, and suspended mats of bam-

boo formed certain walls and the peaked ceiling. From the
outside he could see that the structure was square at the
base and topped by a fantastic sway-backed thatch that
curved up into a decorated pinnacle at either end. The roof
reminded him of the saddle of a giant—but he would not
have cared to be the giant who bestrode so knifelike a
support.

"O my mother!" Hasan exclaimed as Shawahi entered.
"What did she say?"

She eased herself into a seated posture, looking old. "O
wretched man, would I had never seen your face."

Hasan stood back despondently. "The Queen is not my
wife?"

"Hasan, I would do a ritual dance for joy that would
rattle my brittle bones apart if I were only certain that she
was not."

"Then she *is* my beloved!"

Shawahi fixed him with a dour stare. "O ill-fated one,
be silent and hear my story."

Perplexed, Hasan sat down and listened.

Shawahi left her house (she narrated) in the morning
with bitter foreboding. She had brought the foolish youth,
Hasan, into the city disguised as a handmaiden—indeed
the fairness of his complexion assisted the subterfuge—and
hidden him in a room apart, lest any should come to know
of him and inform the Queen and bring the stroke of the
sword upon them both, and she hoped he appreciated this
properly. She had served him herself while striving to
instill in him the fear of the awful majesty of the Supreme
King, the father of this woman he claimed as his wife, but
he had wept before her most piteously and said, "O my
lady, I choose death for myself and loathe this worldly
life, if I unite not with my wife and children: I have set my
existence on this venture and will either attain my aim or
die."

What could a tired old woman do in the face of an
attitude like that? A lover never harkened to the speech of
one who was fancy-free. If he was determined to throw his

life away, she would simply have to cast about for some way to make it less suicidal. Thus she repaired to the Queen with her mind tumbling with abasements and petitions, hoping that the royal heart might in some way be softened.

The Queen was the eldest daughter of the Supreme King, who had put her in charge of the state while he visited with his six remaining daughters, all virgin maidens. The Queen had absolute power here in her city; but Shawahi had a claim upon her favor because she had reared all the King's daughters and trained them in weaponry and tactics until they were the finest of amazon warriors. Now she needed all the good-will there might be in store, for the Queen was not going to be pleased with what the old woman had to relate.

Shawahi was admitted readily to the presence and fell down and kissed the floor before the Queen.

"Come, beldame, rise and sit beside me," the Queen said, embracing her formally. "I haven't seen you in a year. Did you have success in your trading expedition?"

"O my lady, it was a blessed journey, and I have brought you a gift which I will present to you very soon. But O my daughter, Queen of the age and the time—"

"Speak, woman."

"I have a favor to ask. But it is a delicate matter, and I pray it will not upset you. I hesitate to bring it up—"

"Come, mother—tell me, and I will accomplish it for you. My troops, my kingdom and myself are at your disposition."

But the old woman trembled and quivered like a dry reed in the wind of the monsoon. "O protect me from the wrath of the Queen," she murmured fearfully to herself. Then, to the Queen: "O my lady, a man hid himself under my settle in the North District and begged my protection. He said he was searching for his wife and children, and would die if he found them not. Never have I seen a braver or more handsome man. I tried to discourage him, but—"

"And so you brought him here . . ." the Queen said

softly. "Concealing him carefully from your troops while you kept him in your tent."

"O my lady!"

The Queen contemplated her thoughtfully. "And the favor you crave of me is this: that I now permit this mannequin of yours to achieve his desire."

Shawahi maintained the silence of terror. She knew too well the mannerisms of the Queen.

The storm broke. "O ill-omened beldame! Have you come to such a state of lewdness that you now must sneak strange males to the sacred isles of Wak and flaunt them before your Queen? Have you no fear of the mischief I should wreak upon your head for such treachery? By the head of my father the King, but for your service in my youth, I would immediately put both you and this man to the foulest of deaths, and set your corpses beside the gates of the city so that travelers might take dire warning by your fate. O accursed! None dares do the like of this outrageous deed!"

A glimmer of hope lit the old woman's face. The Queen had not stated that she *would* execute them, only that she might. "O mistress of the ages! Surely it behooves your power and generosity to grant this suffering traveler some token. At least give him audience before sending him on his way. He hails from Baghdad, throne city of the Caliph Harun al-Rashid."

"Baghdad? I know of no such city." But Shawahi knew by the subtle nuances of her manner that the Queen did recognize the name.

"O my Queen! It is a rich and powerful empire with armies like the sands of the sea, and Hasan is a prince of—"

"A prince? Then why did he have to beg your aid?"

"A prince of merchants, O my lady." Shawahi was no longer certain how much the Queen knew. Could she actually be Hasan's wife? At any rate, it obviously wasn't safe to try to pass him off as royal born, however helpful that might have been. "All he desires in the world is the recovery of his wife and two sons. A small thing to grant, to one of your—"

"I will be the judge of what is small." But she was interested now. "He has two sons, but sent his wife to Wak? What kind of man is this?"

"He did not send her. She escaped without his notice and flew with her children to Wak, leaving word for him to follow if he desired. And now he is here, having braved the most—"

The Queen cut her off with a gesture. "I don't have time to see him. But his case is curious, and I will grant him what he says he wants. Summon all the women of the city and parade them before him tomorrow; if he knows his wife among them, I will deliver her to him and send him home with honor."

"But my lady—"

"And if he knows her not in the morning, I will crucify him over your door that very afternoon. Such is my decision."

"And this is the calamity you have brought upon yourself!" Shawahi said to Hasan in conclusion. "Now that the Queen knows of your presence here, there is no escape. Tomorrow you must view the assembled women of the city."

"But that's no calamity. The Queen is helping me."

Shawahi sighed, as she did so often when reasoning with him. "O for the innocence of youth! She has sentenced you to death, Hasan."

"But I can recognize my wife in a moment."

She closed her eyes as though in meditation. "You will view all the women of the city, no more. This city. Do you know how many cities there are in the empire of Wak?"

"Why, I thought—"

"But let's say she is in this one city, of all the hundreds in Wak. What makes you think you'll see her?"

"But you said all the women would be—"

"All but one, Hasan."

He gazed at her, confused. "One?"

"The Queen herself."

"Well yes, you did say my wife was very like the Queen, but—"

"Can there be two like her in all the world?"

"No! No one could match my wife!"

Shawahi spread her hands. "So it is death."

"I don't understand."

She opened her eyes and stared at him somberly. "The woman you describe as your wife must either be the Queen or one very like her. Believe me, there is none like her in the city. So if she is not your wife, you will not find what you seek among the women of the city tomorrow."

"Well, I suppose not. But—"

"Could the Queen be your wife and not know it?"

"Of course not!"

"Then, if she knows she is the one you seek, why should she set up this parade of damsels? Why condemn you to death for failure—*knowing you must fail?*"

Hasan was shocked. "My beloved would never do that!"

Shawahi looked upon him with the compassion of the very old for the very young. "Hasan, did it ever occur to you that you never knew your wife very well? You loved her for her beauty, heedless of what might lie behind it. You captured her by force and compromised her so that she had to marry you or be forever sullied and ashamed. You held her prisoner in Baghdad while you begot some sons upon her. When she had the chance, she fled from you. She never returned to Baghdad or Serendip, though she could easily have flown there in her feather-suit. What makes you think she wants to join you now, or even see your face again?"

"I know she loves me."

"You're likely to carry that touching faith with you to your execution," she said. "Tomorrow afternoon. I know the Queen; I raised her. She is crafty and cruel beyond any in the empire and her heart is a pointed stone."

"That is not my wife."

"Hasan, sometimes I wonder whether your wife exists at all. There is only one way you can save your life tomorrow. When the women parade before you, pick out the prettiest and claim her as your wife. Bring her to me and I'll beat her until she agrees to do anything you demand. That will satisfy the Queen."

"But if the Queen is my wife, she will know."

"Precisely. If she is not your wife, she won't suspect. If she *is*, she'll be satisfied to be rid of you, either by marriage or crucifixion. That's the way her mind works."

"I can't do it. I must have my wife and children."

Shawahi gave up. "Never have I seen a man so eager to die!"

In the morning Hasan stood before the palace while all the maidens of the city paraded past, a hundred at a time. The girls treated it as a festive occasion and dressed accordingly. Many of the men of the city lined up beside Hasan to help him peruse the offerings. If he didn't find a wife, some of them might.

Hasan had relinquished his original outland garments and now dressed in accordance with Wak convention. He was outfitted in a tubular length of material wound around his waist and reaching almost to the ground, surmounted by a high-collared jacket. On his head was an intricately draped flat turban which made him feel a little more at ease but whose windings were unfamiliar. Now that he was among men dressed similarly, Hasan was glad Shawahi had made him change.

Most of the women on display were dressed in two-piece costumes: a skirt of colorful cloth wound neatly over waist and hips and hanging in folds to the hem just above the bare feet; a long-sleeved blouse. A cummerbund held both in place. Black hair was brushed back and coiled attractively or tied behind.

Interspersed with this ordinary clothing were the more ornate fineries of the wealthier families: black dresses spangled with gold, set off by elegant scarves worn over the shoulders, and spectacular headdresses. Full length costumes of brightly decorated cloth, sewn with flower-patterns so thick that the color of the underlying material was a matter of conjecture. Dancing-girl costumes cut well beneath the shoulders and draped with stoles of golden thread and jeweled scarves.

Hasan was suitably impressed by the endless glitter and variety of clothing; but what amazed him most was the fact that not a single woman wore a veil. He had naturally assumed that the amazons flouted convention because of their trade, so had become accustomed to their naked countenances. Shawahi had told him the people of the Empire of Wak neither covered their faces nor called on Allah, but he had been unable to credit this completely until faced with the proof. A damsel's most intimate secret was her face—yet these girls smiled and laughed and disported themselves openly in the full sight of men, unashamed.

Once he got over the shock, he rather enjoyed this quaint naivete.

Many of the young women were fair, and not a few looked his way and smiled, knowing his mission . . . but Sana was not among them.

"Are you *sure* you can't select one to call your wife?" Shawahi whispered. "The Queen is growing impatient."

Hasan shook his head, refusing to acknowledge her meaning.

The last of the women passed. Shawahi slowly trekked into the palace.

Hasan waited, not believing that the Queen could so callously order his death. At least she would have to see him, and if she were his wife—

If she were Sana, and still could execute him, then he had no further need of life.

Palace guards emerged: grim, husky men in polished armor. Their captain approached. "Hasan of Baghdad?"

Hasan nodded. They laid hands upon him and threw him down. His face landed in the dirt so that he had to

splutter to spit it out. Guards took hold of his feet, and
hauled.

He turned his head aside and covered his face with his
hands, but even so the abrasions of dust and sand burned
into his cheek.

They *were doing it*. They were going to kill him.

At the place of execution the guards stood him up,
ripped a strip from his skirt, and bound it over his eyes.
The last thing he saw was the gleam of naked blades as
they ceremoniously flourished their weapons.

In the scant moments remaining, Hasan thought about
the circumstances that had summoned him here. Bahram
the Persian—how he would have laughed to see this scene!
Hasan was glad he had killed the evil magician. Rose—the
youngest and warmest of the princesses—how she would
cry, if ever she knew. Perhaps he should have married her;
she would certainly have made an excellent wife. But Sana
had come, the beautiful bird-maiden. . . .

No, this was the way it had to be. Sana—or death.

The blow did not strike. What were they waiting for?

"Don't get impatient, imposter," the captain said. "We
will accommodate you as soon as the Queen gives her
royal permission."

The Queen was coming here— Surely she would have
mercy, if—

Footsteps approached. He heard the soft rustle of skirts,
smelled queenly perfume.

"He is ready, Majesty," the captain said.

"Cut off his head." *Sana's voice!* "Tie his corpse over
this old crone's door, a warning to any who dare adventure
into our country under false pretenses. Proceed." *How
could she do this, seeing him?*

Rough hands grasped him again, forcing his head down.
"If you move, stranger, the cut will not be clean, and you
will die slowly," the captain warned him without emotion.
He heard the slight friction of armor as a sword was lifted
two-handed above his neck.

"O Queen!" Shawahi's voice cried out near at hand.

"O my lady, by my claim for fosterage, do not be hasty in this matter. This poor wretch is a stranger who has risked his life and traveled from the end of the earth in pursuit of his love. He has suffered what none have suffered before him, and come here only because I promised him safety; and I promised only because of my trust in your magnamimity and your sense of justice and quality of mercy. I would never have brought him here otherwise. I said to myself, 'The Queen will take pleasure in looking upon him, and in hearing him speak his verses, and in his sweet discourse and eloquence, like pearls upon a string.' And he has entered our land and eaten our food, and therefore has a claim upon our hospitality."

A pause, then Shawahi continued. "You cannot condemn him until he has seen all our women, for that was your royal word. You are the only one he has not looked upon. Will you keep your oath and show him your face?"

Sana's voice replied, but with an irony Hasan had never heard in his wife. "How can he be my husband and have had children by me, and I not know it?"

This was the point Shawahi herself had raised to Hasan, but she chose to ignore it this time. "Your word, O Queen. Can you put him to death when the terms have not been honored? Do you want the report to be spread abroad that you hate all strangers and put them to death for no reason? They will call her an evil Queen who is known for such a thing!"

"Your own stringy neck is not far from the sword," the Queen muttered. Then, to the guards: "Unbind his eyes!"

The cruel tourniquet came off. Hasan blinked at the sudden release and light, unable to focus immediately.

"Look at me, stranger, before you die," the Queen said.

Hasan shielded his eyes, squinted, and peered at the royal personage. He saw the elegant, jewel-encrusted robe, the sash of bright exotic weave, the slim lovely arms with their thick silver bracelets, the shining crown, and finally her face.

It was Sana.

Chapter 11. Sana

Shawahi was holding up his head and cleaning his face. At first he didn't realize that he had fainted; then it seemed as though a great amount of time had passed. It hadn't; the guards were still standing with blades unlimbered, and Sana had not moved or changed expression.

"If you are satisfied. . . ." she said, turning to the guards. There was no hint of recognition or compassion in her face. She was indifferent to his fate and angry at the delay; that was all.

"But Sana!" he cried, appalled.

One brow arched in a manner never characteristic of his wife. "What is this dog yowling about now?"

"Don't you know me, Sana? I'm Hasan—your husband and the father of Nasir and Mansur, your sons. How can you murder me?"

The Queen spoke to Shawahi. "This stranger is jinn-mad. He stares me in the face with wide-eyes and says I am his wife!"

Shawahi came instantly to Hasan's defense. "O Queen, do not blame him for that. There is no remedy for the lovesick. He *is* a madman, but from the force of his passion, not the jinn." Then, before Hasan could speak: "Hasan, this is Nur al-Huda, Queen of Wak—and a maid."

Hasan had been studying the Queen with growing perplexity. Her strange name—which he had translated into his own terms, as he had to do for all Wak nomenclature— was the least of his concerns. "I tell you, she is either my wife or very similar to her. She—"

"Don't you *know* what your wife looks like?" Shawahi cut in. "Are you sure you didn't see her this morning among the—"

"She looks like that," Hasan said doggedly, indicating the Queen. "But now I think this woman is *not* my—"

Nur al-Huda made a peremptory gesture. "Do you say, stranger, that I resemble your wife very closely?"

"Marvelously closely. I—"

"Exactly what is it in your wife that resembles me?"

"O my lady, you are a model of beauty and loveliness, elegance and amorous grace. Your shape is a marvel of feminine symmetry and your speech is as sweet as the songs of singing birds and your cheeks blush most becomingly and your breasts jut forward in a manner to shame all others and inflame the passions of men. In all these things you resemble her so closely that my eyes are unable to tell you apart or say which one is more comely, and your face is fair and brilliant as hers. No one in all the kingdoms of the world and of the jinn can match my wife in beauty unless it is yourself."

Nur al-Huda's mien softened somewhat, for Hasan had obviously spoken from the heart. "As lovely as that?"

"O my lady, it is impossible for me to describe your perfection, for such is beyond the tongue of a mortal."

"Not so very beyond, I think," she murmured. "And this is the beauty of your wife?"

"Yes, my lady, except—"

"Except that she has borne two children," Shawahi interposed urgently.

The Queen laughed. "Ah—then I am as fair as he *remembers* her." Hasan suddenly realized what would have happened if he had carelessly made any exception unfavorable to the Queen. Shawahi had saved him, with distaff alertness, from a fatal mistake—for Nur al-Huda did look older than Sana.

Sana's appearance, unlike that of lesser women, had in no way suffered from her motherhood. The two women were astonishingly close, but Sana retained the luster of youth. The Queen had evidently been a maid for a long time.

"Beldame," the Queen said, "take this eloquently-spoken young man back to your house and see that all his needs are attended to. I shall examine him further at another hour." She flashed an enigmatic glance at him. "It behooves us to ease the sorrow and travail of his long separation in whatever manner we may, and explore this curious affair most carefully so that we may help him win his wish."

Shawahi took Hasan's arm to lead him away, but the Queen stopped her another moment. "Deliver him into the care of your servants, mother. Return immediately to me."

"Be very careful, Hasan," the old woman murmured as they left. "The Queen is most dangerous when she smiles." But the presence of the guard prevented her from clarifying her meaning.

For ten days Hasan lived in comfort at Shawahi's house, well attended and without cares, except for uncertainty about his future and that of his mission. Shawahi was absent; the Queen had sent her on a special trip without informing him of its purpose.

Twice the Queen summoned him for an hour's dialogue in the massive stone palace.

She was perfectly polite, but asked for no further descriptions of beauty, and Hasan suffered increasing uneasiness. She *was* older than his wife, by ten years or more, and it showed more in her manner than in her appearance. Where Sana was foolish, the Queen was strong; where Sana was warm, the Queen was cold. And she had a terrible temper.

Hasan answered her questions as well as he could, not certain where they were leading but sure they had a sword-like point. He recognized, belatedly, that had it been Nur al-Huda on the palace roof in the guise of a bird-maiden, instead of Sana, he never would have conquered her. She was a warrior lass, strong as a man and adept at weaponry, and she offered neither heart nor body to any man.

He wondered why she had been so readily flattered by his descriptions the first time he saw her. This weakness of vanity did not ring true, now that he knew her better. She was vain, yes—and hot-blooded too—but in her these sentiments were given rein only when it suited her convenience. They were liabilities no more than they would have been in a man.

Meanwhile, she had promised to help him in his quest.

Hasan basked in that, and stilled his uneasiness. The Queen really wasn't as bad as Shawahi's morbid predictions.

The old woman reappeared abruptly on the tenth day. Never a pleasant sight, she was a horror now. Her skin was sallow and she was quivering as though in mortal fear. All strength of character seemed to have been drained out of her.

Twenty mamelukes of the palace guard accompanied her, their expressions businesslike. Something was wrong.

"Greetings, O venerable mother," Hasan said, hoping that bright words would dispel whatever dire news she brought.

Shawahi skipped the formalities. "Come speak with the Queen, ill-omened one! Didn't I warn you not to come to Wak? Didn't I offer you the best of my maidens for your own, if only you gave up this hapless quest before disaster? But no; you would not listen to my advice. You rejected my council and chose to bring destruction upon yourself and upon me also. Well, you have your wish. Up then, and take what you have chosen, for death is near at hand. Speak with the tyrant Queen!"

Frightened, Hasan accompanied her. And while they journeyed to the palace, the old woman told him what had happened.

After seeing that Hasan was comfortable and that the servants knew their duties, ten days ago, Shawahi returned to the Queen as directed. The latter was pacing the floor restlessly, her royal skirts whirling as she turned.

"Do you remember what he called her?" she snapped.

"O my lady—" Shawahi began, trying to comprehend what the Queen was talking about.

"The wife, crone. He called her 'Sana' . . . and he named two sons."

The old woman waited, still uncertain what this was leading to.

"It is in my mind that the stranger spoke the truth," the Queen continued. "Otherwise he surely would have se-

lected a woman of the city for his wife, whether he knew
her or not. If my thought is true, my youngest sister,
Manar al-Sana, is his wife—for the traits of surpassing
beauty and excelling grace which he described are found in
none but my sisters, and especially in her. And indeed she
has two boys which she says she adopted as foundlings
after being stranded in the wilderness. She could be the
one.''

Of course! Shawahi cursed herself for her stupidity.
Why hadn't this occurred to her when Hasan first described his wife, since she knew all the daughters of the
King well? She could so easily have enabled him to win
his wife. But now . . .

''O my mistress, what do you contemplate?'' Shawahi
inquired with a quaver. She had excellent reason to distrust
the motives of the Queen.

Nur al-Huda appraised the old woman's attitude at a
glance. One of the disconcerting things about her was the
fact that she could read Shawahi more readily than the old
woman could return the favor. ''Do not fear for his safety,
mother. I mean only to verify that my sister is his wife and
the children his, for young boys should not be isolated
from their sire. I swear by all manner of oaths that if this is
the case, I will not hinder him from taking them back to
his own country. I will send him home with wealth and
troops befitting royalty—but I must be certain, first.''

Reassured, Shawahi listened to the Queen's instructions.
She was to arm herself and travel to Manar al-Sana's
residence with a troop of horsemen and bring back the two
boys. She was to keep the mission secret, and not tell
anyone why the lads were being taken until the connection
had been verified, otherwise the test would not be valid.

Shawahi prepared herself at the palace, gathered her
escort, and made the three-day journey to the southwest
coast where the six other sisters dwelt. Each had her little
island off the main Isle, Sana's being the most distant. The
crossing was accomplished, the official request presented.

''Why of course I owe my sister a visit,'' Sana agreed.

"Only let me bid farewell to my father the King, and I will return with you now."

This was not precisely what Shawahi had intended. The trial of the boys' father-relationship had to be made without the mother present, so that no equivocation was possible. "My lady, your sister bids me also bring your two boys to her, for she has never seen them."

Sana's pleasant bearing changed. "O my mother, I cannot take them on such a journey. My vitals tremble and my heart flutters when I think of the dangers to which they might be exposed. I fear for their health even when the zephyr breathes upon them in the night."

Shawahi had been afraid of this. "What words are these, O my daughter? Surely you don't believe your sister means harm to these innocents? She is the Queen, and you dare not cross her in this matter or she will be very angry with you. It is hardly unnatural for her to want to see her nephews."

Sana bowed her head. She had never had the firmness of her sisters. "I don't know what to do. I love them so much, since they are all I have to remember their father by. How can I expose them to—" She broke off, horrified.

Shawahi caught the slip. "You did know their father, then. The boys are not foundlings."

Sana knelt and clutched the old woman's skirt. "O my mother, please, please never tell anyone that! It would mean my life."

There was more Shawahi wanted to know, but she had promised the Queen not to divulge her true purpose, and further questions would give it away. She was sure now in her own mind that Sana was Hasan's wife, and that she still loved him. But why hadn't the silly girl rejoined him in Baghdad? Or at least left word at Serendip?

"I will say nothing, my daughter," Shawahi promised, knowing that this would change nothing. How she longed to speak Hasan's name and bring the couple together again! But the given word was absolute, in Wak, and the reuniting would happen soon in any event. Once the Queen was assured of the situation, all would be well.

It gave her a warm feeling, for Shawahi had come to love Hasan as a son, and Sana, despite her softness, had been her favorite foster-daughter. The two were alike in physical beauty and warmth of personality and especially in that certain quality of naivete that was so rare in the world today.

Meanwhile there was the mission. "O my daughter, you know my affection for you and those dear to you, for indeed I raised you myself after your gracious mother died. Give your sons to my charge, so that I may take them to the Queen, and I will care for them with the same heart I cared for you. Never fear for their safety; I will dress them in two little coats of mail and protect them with my life until you join them again. You can follow me at your leisure, and all will be well."

Sana remained uncertain, but finally agreed. "Take them," she said with tears in her eyes, "and I will follow when I assemble my party in a day or so, even as you say. I know they are safe in your care."

Shawahi hoped this faith was justified. The Queen had promised, but the Queen was a law of her own.

She went next to see the King, for it would have been an act of disrespect to leave without paying homage to the nominal ruler of all the empire. She had served him loyally for all her adult life and held him in the highest esteem. He was a man who deserved more than a family of seven daughters and no son.

After the formalities, the King dismissed his retainers and associates and gave Shawahi private audience. "O faithful one," he said, "it gladdens my heart to see you again, for my mind is oppressed by a mysterious dream which I know not how to interpret."

Shawahi's days of dream interpretation were long behind her, but she was happy to help her King. "How so, O my liege and master of empires?" She had not realized how old and tired the King had become in the past few years. The spark of majesty remained, but the noble strength that had driven an empire to greatness was gone with the

color of his hair. Strong-willed Nur al-Huda would probably continue to rule, in the absence of male power. Unfor-
tunately, she had neither the wisdom nor control of her
sire; the empire was likely to suffer.

"In my dream I entered a hidden hoard, wherein was
great store of monies, of jewels, of jacinths and of other
riches. But it was as if naught could please me of all this
treasure save seven bezels, which were the finest jewels
there. I chose out one of the seven, and it was the smallest
and most lustrous of them all, and its color pleased me. So
I took it in my hand and fared forth from that treasury.
When I came outside the door I opened my hand, rejoicing
and turning over the jewel. Behold—there swooped down
on me out of the welkin a strange bird from a far land, a
creature not of our country, and snatched it from my hand
and carried it away. Whereupon sorrow and concern and
sore vexation overcame me, and I felt such exceeding
chagrin that I awoke mourning and lamenting the loss of
the jewel."

Shawahi stood silent, not daring to comment. She knew
what the King did not: that a traveler *had* entered Wak
from a distant land and was about to claim the youngest
and prettiest and most beloved of the King's seven jewels.
She knew—but was bound to silence by her promise to the
Queen.

"What interpretation do you place upon this vision?"
the King inquired. "Indeed, it sore oppresses me and
hinders my rest."

Now the burden was upon Shawahi. She could not
speak falsely to her King—but neither could she break her
oath.

He looked at her sharply. "Surely you have something
to say, O loyal mistress of my armies? Well I remember
when in all the realm there was not your peer at magic and
divination. . . ."

"That was many years ago, my master. Now I am old
and confused, and my loyalties pull me first one way and
then the other until I don't know what to do. All I can say

about your dream is that perhaps the bird took away the jewel from you because there was another who needed it more, having no treasure while you had seven. Perhaps that other will care for it and cherish it long after you—"

She had slipped as badly as had Sana, but the King only smiled. "You are right, old companion-at-arms. I shall have no need of jewels hereafter. I will not be born a king again. . . ."

Shawahi's mind was in turmoil long after that interview. The King knew he was dying. She suspected she would not see the great old monarch again, and did not want to outlive him.

She took the two boys, a fine three year old lad who seemed to resemble Hasan and his brother a year younger who favored Sana, and made the return trip swiftly between the mountains and the shore, using the special trails and pathways no one else knew. She brought the boys immediately to Queen Nur al-Huda, their aunt.

The Queen rejoiced at the sight of them. She embraced them both and pressed them to her breast. They accepted this without complaint, for she was very like their mother when she chose to be. Then she seated one upon her right thigh and the other upon her left and paid them much attention, while Shawahi marveled at this unaccustomed display of affection and thought how fine a woman the Queen might be if only she had a husband to mitigate her passions.

"Fetch me Hasan forthwith," Nur al-Huda said. So she knew him by name now! Things had certainly changed . . . possibly too much, she thought with a sudden qualm. "I have granted him my safeguard and spared him from execution. He has sought asylum in my domain and taken up abode in my city, after passing through all manner of mortal risks and enduring hardships, each more terrible than the other. . . ." She glanced meaningfully at Shawahi. "Yet he is not safe from the severance of his breath."

So the Queen still meant to kill Hasan if he was not the father of the two children. "When I bring him, will you reunite him with his sons? Or, if they are not his, will you pardon him and let him go in peace?''

The royal temper flared, frightening the children. "Fie upon you, O ill-omened old creature! How long will you try to distort my judgment in the matter of this stranger who has dared intrude himself upon us and pry into our affairs? Do you think he can come into our country uninvited and poke into our business and betray our honor, and then return safely to his own country to expose our concerns to his people and bruit them about among all the kings of the earth and send forth the report with vile merchants and others of ill repute journeying in all directions, saying, 'A mortal man has entered the Isles of Wak and traversed the Land of the Jinn and the Isles of the Birds and the Place of the Wild Beasts and the Country of Warlocks and Enchanters—and returned in safety?' This shall never be, no never; and I swear by Him who built the Heavens and spread and smoothed the earth and who created and counted all creatures that if these innocent boys are *not* his sons, I will assuredly slay him and strike off his head with my own hand! Now get out of here and *fetch me Hasan!*''

And as the old woman stumbled and fell and dragged herself away and the two boys cried in terror and the very curtains of the palace seemed to smoke with the force of her explosion, the Queen turned and added quietly to her mamelukes: "Go with this crone and fetch the fair youth who is in her house.''

Hasan was too distraught this time to pay any attention to the sturdy architecture of the palace as he entered it. In moments he would either achieve his dream, or suffer death. How he hoped the children were his!

The Queen was making merry with the two lads, who had apparently adjusted already to her mercurial moods. As Hasan approached she turned the boys to face him.

"Nasir! Mansur!" he exclaimed, recognizing them.

The older boy's eyes widened. Time had passed, and much had changed . . . but in a moment he scrambled

down from the Queen's lap and ran to his father. Seeing
this, the younger one followed. Hasan embraced both of
them.

"Merciful Buddha!" Shawahi whispered, tears of sympathy and relief streaming down her ancient face. The
servants and guards of the palace stood around with sentimental expressions.

But Nur al-Huda, strangely, was not pleased. "These,
then, are indeed your children, and their mother is your
wife?"

"Yes, O my lady!" Hasan agreed happily, unaware of
the undercurrent.

"And you are a merchant of Arabia without royal blood?"
Hasan began to get the drift. "I am, O Queen."

The Queen's eye dilated and light froth appeared at the
corners of her mouth. "You unspeakable pig!" she screamed
in his face, while he stood amazed that such beauty could
become so vile so rapidly. "Lecherous despoiler of royalty! Did you dare to lay your unclean hands upon a
princess of Wak?" She struck him in the face, a hard blow
with clenched fist in the manner of a man, and kicked him
in the chest when he tried to escape by doubling over. It
occurred to him that his motion *had* averted the blow
intended . . . "Fly for your life! If I had not sworn to do
you no evil were your story true, I would slay you this
moment!"

Shawahi tried to say something, but the Queen turned
on her. "Quiet, O ill begotten harlot! But for the fact I am
loath to break my oath, I would put you and him both to
death in the foulest fashion." The old woman retreated
and fell on the floor.

The Queen returned her attention to Hasan. "Depart,
monster, and return to your own country before I lose my
temper! I swear by my fortune and all the power of Wak
which is mine that if I ever see you again I will smite off
your head and kill anyone with you."

Then she cried to her guards. "Throw this carrion out!"
Once again the men took hold of Hasan and dragged

him on his face across the floor and thrust him out of the palace. He stumbled away, bruised and faint, his mind filled with the picture of the Queen's terrible wrath and Shawahi's horror as she realized they had been betrayed.

Chapter 12. Cap and Rod

Now Hasan understood why the old woman had mistrusted the Queen. Once again he had learned not to be naive—too late. He should have taken one of the lovely maidens of the city as a second wife, until able to search out Sana. As it was, he was virtually condemned to death, for no citizen would risk the wrath of the Queen by helping him, and he could never make his way through the lands of the Jinn and Birds and Beasts and all the rest of it alone.

What had he brought upon his wife and children? Surely the Queen would have no mercy upon them, after this.

Hasan cursed himself and wished he had never attempted this quest. He had succeeded only in bringing destruction upon everyone he loved, and he *still* had no idea where his wife was, or any power to help her. Yet he had been warned. . . .

His new Wak clothing was fouled with the dirt of the road, his face and chest smarted with the blows of the Queen and her guards, and the pebbles of the road were hard on his tender feet. He had worn sandals so long that he had no callouses on his soles.

Black-haired children ceased their play and stared at him as he passed. They knew already that he was a stranger again and an outcast.

The houses of the city diminished into primitive huts at the outskirts. Spindly rails supported leaning roofs, the thick thatch descending over the edges of the road to head-height. Bamboo and bundles of sticks lined the street, providing convenient hiding-places for the children.

Where would his own children hide?

The city ended at the river. Hasan turned and walked

beside the water, passing the crowded rickety piers reaching out from houses on stilts. Dugout boats were so common that the water beneath them was hardly visible in places. More children sat in many of them, staring passively out at him.

He passed an area of level sand where thousands of gutted fish were drying in the sun. He was hungry—but the fisherman gave such a glower when he approached that Hasan moved quickly on.

Outside the city the mountains rose inland and the short plain spread out ahead. Not far beyond this was the sea. Palms and other vegetation filled all uncultivated land.

Hasan climbed a steep hillside, remembering the hills of Serendip. Here he could overlook the city, seeing its square peaked temples and clustered residences. Tiny clouds floated above the sea, looking solid in spite of the lesson the ifrit Dahnash had taught him. A highway passed through the city, extending beyond sight in either direction, the parallel lines of its wagon-tracks threading the comparatively narrow area between the mountain range and the sea.

His attention was attracted to a caravan approaching the city from the northwest. For a moment he was tempted to descend and join it, since the merchants would not yet have heard the Queen's edict, and he knew merchant-talk; but he realized that it was traveling toward the city and would only carry him back into trouble.

Now that he had been cast out of his tranquil life of the past ten days, he envied the traveling merchants fiercely. They would enter the city and retire perhaps to all-night feasting, sitting before bowls of whipped egg and dipping tasty morsels from a common pot of boiling oil. A mushroom, a vegetable, a bit of chicken—immersed in the cooling egg froth and eaten immediately, while servants kept the pot perpetually full. The savory food alternating with warm rice wine . . . Shawahi had finally convinced him that Allah could not have meant this when He forbade intoxicants, for who could find harm in such delicious drink?

Evening was coming and Hasan was savagely hungry.

There was no one to help him, and he was foolish to dream of a banquet at such a time. He looked about, observing the richness of the land. He had foraged before, and he could do it again.

In the morning the owner politely suggested that he seek another location, and Hasan had to climb down from the elevated platform where he had spent a difficult night. He had not known what the tall structure was for; he had mounted it because the height seemed better than the richly crawling ground. Now he watched the farmer climb the hefty bamboo supports to the flat square twelve feet high and look about him at the field. Long, fine cords of fiber stretched from the platform to various parts of the field. The entire arrangement was nonsensical to Hasan—until he saw a flock of birds descend upon the growing grain and begin to feed.

The guardian grasped a cord and yanked. At the far end, near the birds, a bright grotesquely-painted banner leapt up. The birds took off in fright. The farmer let go the string and the scarecrow fell to the ground again.

Hasan smiled. Now he could see that each cord was attached to a device in a different part of the field. The birds would not raid this grain.

Farther along he came across a naked urchin squatting on a stone in a stream. The lad held a long stick with a loop at the end. A game? Hasan doubted it, for the boy was unsmiling and quite motionless. Interested, he watched, ready to learn something more while suppressing thoughts of his own predicament. The ways of these people were strange, but seemed to make good sense once understood.

The boy moved—and there, snared in the loop, was a fine fish.

Hasan came to a large leaning tree overhanging the water of a riverpool. As he rested beneath it he discovered a scroll hanging from a branch. Curious, he took it down and unrolled it. It was covered with the peculiar script of Wak that he could not read. What was it doing in such a place? If it were a message, for whom was it intended?

Probably it had nothing to do with him. Perhaps young lovers used this tree as a trysting-place, and wrote each other notes. Still, he could not avoid the feeling that it somehow concerned him, and that the matter it discussed was of extreme importance. If only he could decipher it!

He left it where it was, drawing renewed confidence from the experience in spite of his frustration. This had to be a sign, a signal of change—and his situation could hardly grow worse.

Up the river a distance two other boys were engaged in a heated debate. This was unusual, in this land, for the people were generally quite polite. They seldom spoke negatively or made a direct refusal. Buddha, it seemed, had been a passive man (not a god, as he had assumed at first), given to harmony and peace, and his followers reflected this. Only the Queen differed, though she seemed to make up for all the manners of her subjects.

Before the lads lay two objects: a rod of shining copper engraved with many talismans, and a skull-cap of fine leather, sewn from three strips and decorated with bright silver ornaments.

"It belongs to me!" exclaimed one boy. "It's mine!" returned the other. Their argument became a fight; they beat at each other with fists until one had a swollen eye and the other dripped blood from his nose.

Hasan stepped between them. "This is none of my business," he said, though the truth was that he was glad to worry about something so elementary as a boyish difference of opinion. "But it's a shame to see two such fine young men as yourselves get into such trouble. Is there some way I can help?"

The boys were quite satisfied to break it off, each having found his adversary equal to himself. "O Uncle," said one, "why don't *you* settle our dispute, since you have no personal interest."

Bright boy. "I'll be happy to, if I can. Tell me about it." Evidently these boys were not of the city, though they were well-dressed, and either hadn't heard about him or didn't care. It was nice to be involved with people again, even in so trivial a connection.

"We are twin brothers," said the second boy. "Our father was a mighty magician who lived in a cave in that mountain yonder." He pointed, as though this were an important detail, but Hasan still wasn't sure which mountain he meant. One thing, however, was now clear: sorcerer's sons would not have been trained to settle things politely.

"He died and left us this cap and this rod," put in the first boy. "And my brother tried to claim the rod, when really it was meant for me. So you tell him to take his cap and—"

"You liar!" shouted the other. "It's *my* rod!"

Hasan got them apart before any more sibling damage occurred. "Just what is the difference between these objects?" he inquired. "They look equally valuable to me, though perhaps the rod, being solid copper, is worth more. Why don't you sell them both and split the money?"

Both boys were horrified. "Sell them! You don't know their properties," the first said. Or the second; Hasan had trouble telling them apart.

He smiled benignly. "By all means tell me their properties."

"They are extraordinary," one boy said. "Our father worked on these things for a hundred and thirty-five years, until he made them perfect and equipped them with secret powers and dissolved all spells that might interfere with their action. Once he did that, he died."

How neat. "But what are their properties?"

"Each of them has a wonderful secret virtue. The rod is worth all the riches of all the Isles of Wak, and so is the cap."

"What *are* these virtues?"

The boys exchanged glances uncertainly.

"Now I can hardly settle your argument unless I know the facts," Hasan said, amused. "Either you tell me, or I'll go away and let you fight some more. Maybe you *both* can acquire bloody noses."

The boy with the nose touched it tenderly and capitulated. "We weren't supposed to tell," he said. "But the cap will make anyone who wears it invisible, and no one can see him until he takes it off."

"And the rod gives the holder authority over seven tribes of the jinn, who all are bound by its magic. When he smites it against the ground, their kings come to do him homage, and all their subjects are at his service."

Hasan subdued his laughter. "Those are very fine properties, boys. Now suppose I make a contest for you to see who deserves what. The one who wins shall have the rod, and the other will have to be satisfied with the cap. Fair enough?"

"Yes!" they exclaimed together, delighted at the simplicity of his solution.

"Good." Hasan had to remind himself that this was a perfectly serious matter to the boys. The one who won the rod would really believe he had seven tribes of jinn at his call, while the other would be certain he was invisible. He'd probably have to humor them both. At least he could make the contest real.

He picked up a stone. "I'm going to throw this stone as far as I can. Whoever reaches it and picks it up first shall have the rod, and the loser takes the cap."

"Yes, Uncle!" they said, vying with each other for a favorable position. "We're ready."

Hasan whirled around splendidly like a heathen discus-thrower and flung the stone. It sailed high through the air and disappeared behind a hill. The boys were off immediately, racing and shouldering each other aside in their separate but equal determination to win.

Now he could laugh. He let forth a bellow. Oh, for the confidence and faith of youth!

The boys topped the hill and dropped out of sight. Idly Hasan picked up the rod, resisting the temptation to tap it against the ground. He put the cap on his head. Such magic, if only it were real, would be the answer to all his problems!

He admired the fit of the cap, which seemed to have been made for him, and the balance of the rod. He felt like a king with crown and scepter. He would dispense the prizes with appropriate dignity!

The lad with the sore nose came over the hill carrying the stone, while his brother walked disconsolately behind. Hasan struck his royal pose and waited.

The boys looked around. "Where is our arbiter?" demanded the winner.

"How should I know? Maybe he flew up to heaven to join the Enlightened One, or sank down into the earth like an ifrit."

"Very funny. He's got my rod."

"Well, you can't change now. The cap is mine."

"Then where *is* your cap?"

They looked at Hasan, then at each other, in seeming alarm. "Do you think he could have—?"

"He isn't here. We'd better find him before he gets away with our stuff! You take this side of the hill, and I'll check the far side."

Hasan held his pose, playing their game. Of course they had seen him wearing the cap, and had to feign invisibility for him or ruin the contest. He could wait. They'd 'accidently' discover him soon enough.

But their search did not abate in intensity as time passed. Several times they looked directly at him, but with eyes unfocused and not even a knowing smile. This was a very serious game.

"He's taken them!" the winner said angrily. "Why did you have to blab about those properties?"

"*Me! You* were the one who—"

They were fighting again, this time with the redoubled bitterness of futility. Hasan automatically rushed up and extended his arm . . .

. . . and couldn't see it. He flexed his fingers and stared.

He *was* invisible.

*   *   *

Shawahi exclaimed in surprise as her utensils bounced on the floor. "That wicked whore of a Queen has sent a demon to torment me!" she muttered, replacing a bamboo cup on the shelf. "If only I could remember my spells—"

The cup jostled off again. Shawahi stared, then backed off. "She *did*. A demon!" She shook her head, more in frustration than fear. "What mercy can I expect, seeing how abominably she deals with her own sister!"

Hasan took off the cap and appeared before her. "Her sister?"

"Hasan! What has happened to your reason? If the Queen—"

"The Queen will never see me."

"But she has been tormenting your wife! What will she do if she lays hands upon you again?"

"My wife!"

But Shawahi insisted on learning about his acquisition of the cap of invisibility before going further into the activities of the palace. Hasan sketched the events of the past day rapidly. "It seemed to be Allah's will that I possess these things," he said, a trifle guiltily, for he did not feel easy about the manner in which he had taken them. "I certainly had better use for them than those foolish boys."

"This is the way it was destined," she said. He had been afraid that she would insist that he return the magic implements at once, yet for some reason she chose to overlook the impropriety. This did not ease his conscience.

". . . and the princess Manar al-Sana arrived yesterday afternoon with her train, sooner than I expected, and went to the palace to—"

"Sana! *Yesterday?*"

"Yes. The same day the Queen banished you. She must have been very anxious for her children, to—Hasan! What is the matter?"

He had been so close. He had assumed it was a merchant caravan. If he had gone to meet it. . . .

But even as Allah had willed that he possess the cap and

the rod, He had made him pay for them by extending the quest. Hasan had not encountered his wife, and she had gone on into the city to visit the Queen.

The two boys ran to Sana as soon as they saw her. "Our father! O our father!" Nasir cried.

She strained them to her bosom. "What! Have you seen your sire?" Her eyes closed, for she knew that their father was far away, and she could not even admit, while her sister listened, that she knew his identity.

But Shawahi was close enough to see the tears Sana tried to conceal, and overhear the murmured lament. "I wish I had never left him! If I knew any way to join him, I would take you to him now."

"But he was here!" Nasir insisted.

"Here!" Mansur echoed.

Sana embraced her boys again, half believing them. "I am the one who did this to myself and my children, and ruined my own house and the life of a fine man. I never knew how much I loved him, until I—"

Nur al-Huda had seen enough. "O whore, how did you come by these children? Did you marry secretly, or have you committed vile fornication?"

"O my sister, I never—"

"Sister, if you played the piece to a stranger, you deserve exemplary punishment. But if you married without our knowledge or permission, why did you abandon your husband and take away his children and bring them here? Why did you try to conceal their origin from us? Do you imagine we are so easily fooled?"

"Before Allah, O my sister, I—"

"Before *Allah?* What heathen mockery is this? Surely I we are fortunate to have learned your case and revealed your condition and bared your nakedness! Guards!"

And while Shawahi stood by, helpless against the wrath of her Queen, the guards seized Sana roughly and pinned back her elbows and shackled her with iron. They knotted her lovely long hair over a pole and suspended her by it. The Queen strode up and tore off her sister's dress and

beat her back so harshly with the cane that Sana screamed
in agony. Her skin rose up in great long welts.

After that the Queen cursed her and cast her into a
prison cell and sat down to write a letter to the King.
Shawahi had to bring a sheet of the valuable writing paper
made from the bark of certain trees and a vial of the
brilliant ink. This service enabled her to look over the
Queen's shoulder and read the characters as they were
printed.

Nur al-Huda had been an excellent student in her youth,
under Shawahi's tutelage, and her form was perfect. She
began carefully at the bottom left corner of the sheet and
placed symbol upon symbol in a vertical column until she
reached the top, after which she began another column at
the bottom.

The contents of the missive were quite fair: "There hath
appeared in our land a man, mortal, by name Hasan, and
our sister Manar al-Sana avoucheth that she is lawfully
married to him according to the conventions of his country
and that she bare him two sons whose origin she tried to
conceal from us and from thee; nor did she discover this to
us till there came to us this man who informed us that he
wedded her in a far domain and tarried with her three
years, after which she took her children and departed
without his knowledge, only leaving word with his mother
that he should look for her in the Isles of Wak. So we
summoned the children, and when our servant Shawahi
brought the boys before me I displayed them to this Hasan
and was certified that they were indeed his sons and she
his wife and that the story was true in every particular and
that he was blameless for his quest, and the reproach and
infamy of this matter rested with my sister. Now I feared
the rending of the veil of honor before the folk of our isles,
that it be revealed that a princess of Wak had cohabited
with a heathen commoner and borne his children; so when
this wanton, this traitress came to me I was incensed
against her and hanged her up by the hair and bastinado'd
her grievously and cast her into prison. Behold, I have

acquanted thee with her case and it is thine to command, and whatso thou orderest that will we do. Thou knowest that in this affair is dishonor and disgrace to our name, and haply the islanders will hear of it, and our shame shall become amongst them a byword; wherefore it befitteth thee to return us an answer with all speed.''

And she summoned an ifrit and instructed it to carry the message to the King and bring his reply with all haste.

Next morning the ifrit returned. ''I thought the old boy was going to die of rage and shame,'' it said, pleased. ''He wouldn't even keep your letter, but forced it back upon me. He's still got fire!''

''Begone!'' Nur al-Huda snapped, snatching the reply from the demon's hand. She had never been one to accept impertinence from the supernatural.

''But what shall I do with your original message? *I* don't want it.''

''Hang it on a tree, for all I care!''

''Yes, mistress,'' it said, and vanished.

The King's reply was brief. ''I commit her case to thee and give thee command over her life,'' it said. ''If the matter be as thou sayest, dispose of her case without consulting me.''

The Queen gave a grunt of satisfaction and sent for Manar al-Sana. They set the prisoner before her clad in haircloth, shackled and pinioned with her own hair. Sana stood abject and abashed, no longer flinching from the pain every movement brought from her welts. Shawahi knew she was calling to mind her former high estate and bemoaning her present humiliation and pain.

''Bring the ladder,'' the Queen directed her guards. Under her supervision they set it up, laid Sana upon it, and tied her supine with arms spread out and tied behind. They wound her hair about the rungs so that her head was immobile and uncomfortably tilted back. The two little boys stared uncomprehendingly.

Sana cried out, and wept, but the Queen had no pity, and no one in the palace dared offer the prisoner so much

as a kind word. Such harsh treatment was in direct viola-
tion of the principles of their religion—but they had to
obey the Queen.

"O my sister," Sana sobbed, "how can your heart be
hardened against me? Have you no mercy on me nor
concern for these little children?"

The Queen only grew angry. "O wanton! O harlot!
How shall I have compassion on you, O traitress?"

Sana tried to shake her head, but could not. "I appeal
for judgment to the Lord of the Heavens! I am innocent of
the things you revile me for. I have done no whoredom. I
am lawfully married to Hasan of Bassorah. Indeed, I
should be angry with you because of your hardheartedness
against me! How can you accuse me of harlotry without
proof?"

The Queen did not reply immediately, and for that
moment Shawahi hoped her heart had softened. But she
was only considering her next action. "How dare you
speak to me thus?"

Nur al-Huda now approached and struck Sana across the
face and breast with her hands, battering again and again
with such ferocity that the victim screamed and fainted.

"Water!" the Queen ordered, and servants dashed jars
of it across Sana's upturned face until she revived, choking. Her rough clothing was tight and disarrayed, and her
fingers twisted helplessly under the chafing bonds. The
water soaked down her hair and glistened on her face and
dripped from the sodden mass of her upper garment. Her
expression was hopeless; she was not lovely now.

But still she tried, lapsing into the mannerism she had
picked up in Baghdad.

> If I have sinned in
>   any way,
> Or done ill deed and
>   gone astray,
>   I beg—

"Dare you speak before your Queen in verse, O whore,
and seek to excuse yourself for the mortal sins you are
guilty of? I wish I could return your gigolo to you and see

how much of your wickedness and lewdness you repented then! Will you disavow the commoner?''

Sana lay still, not answering.

''The cane!'' It was presented, and Nur al-Huda bared her arms, took it up, and beat her sister along the length of her body.

''Admit your guilt!'' the Queen demanded, panting.

Sana's mouth was bruised and swollen where the hard cane had struck. Droplets of pink were spattered where the blows had cut lips against teeth and thrown the bloody spittle out. ''How can I curse the man I love?'' she cried.

''The whip!'' It was a length of plaited thongs sturdy enough to sting an elephant into full flight. The Queen brought it down across Sana's body with such force that her clothing was shredded in the narrow band it struck. More blows followed, and huge stripes showed across her hips and stomach. She was unconscious again.

Shawahi could take no more. She fled from the scene, weeping and cursing the Queen.

Nur al-Huda had not forgotten this suspect witness. ''Fetch her to me!'' she cried to the guards.

They caught Shawahi and dragged her back, then threw her on the floor and held her there. The Queen raised her whip and beat the old woman ruthlessly until she knew no more.

''Drag this ill-omened hag out on her face and dump her in the street with the rest of the garbage.''

''And indeed,'' Shawahi finished, ''the Queen repents of letting you go. She has sent men after you, promising a hundred pounds of gold and my former rank in her service to the man who brings you back. She has sworn that when she has you again she will execute you and your wife and your children together.''

Hasan realized that all this had happened while he played a foolish game with sorcerer's sons. He had laughed while his wife was being tortured!

''O my mother! I have brought dishonor and destruction upon my family and upon you. What can I do to deliver

my wife and children from this tyrannical Queen and to
restore your position to you?''

"This was not your fault, Hasan. Save yourself before
the Queen's minions capture you.''

"I must undo the damage I have done. I must save my
wife from torment.''

"How can you rescue her from the Queen? Nur al-Huda
has all the power of Wak at her command. Go and hide
yourself, O my son, and may your god grant you safe-
conduct from this cursed land.''

"No!'' But Hasan was in despair. There didn't seem to
be any avenues open to him. Sana would die, unless—

"Shawahi! The magic implements!''

She looked at him with dawning hope. "The cap and
rod! I had forgotten. Glory be to Him who quickens the
bones, though they be old and rotten as mine!''

"Do you know anything about these things?'' Hasan
still hadn't tried the rod, partly because he was afraid it
would work. How could he control seven kings of the
jinn?

Shawahi was overjoyed now. "I know the rod and I
know its maker, who was my instructor in the science of
sorcery. He was a mighty magician and spent a hundred
and thirty-five years working on this rod and this cap
before he died. And I heard him say to his two boys, 'O
my sons, these two things are not of your lot, though I
fashioned them for you, for there will come a stranger
from a far country who will take them from you by force,
and you shall not be able to prevent it.' They replied, 'O
our father, tell us in what manner he will avail to take
them,' but he said, 'I wot not, except that this stranger will
be given the signal of success by a message left in a tree in
his path by an ifrit.' And O my son, now I realize that you
are the one he spoke of, and the implements are yours by
divine will. By means of these you shall surely save your
wife and children, for even the magic of the Queen cannot
prevail against these things.''

So the rod and cap *were* his, to do with as he liked.

How intricate were the mechanisms of fate! "But how can I make my wife and children invisible, when there is only one cap? I would not trust my family to the jinn." He had not forgotten Dahnash.

Shawahi smiled. "Pay attention and I'll tell you how. I refuse to deal with the wicked Queen, after the foul fashion she has used us all. I have a mind to go to the caves of the magicians and stay there until I die. But you, O my son, have much to gain yet from this world. Don your cap and take your rod in hand and enter the place where your wife and children are. Untie Sana and smite the earth with the rod, saying 'Be ye present, O servants of these engraved!' whereupon the jinn will appear. One should present himself as one of the chiefs of the tribes, and you can command him whatever you wish."

Hasan was swayed by her certainty, but not enough. "How can I trust these jinn?"

"As long as you hold the rod, you have absolute command. There is no counterspell or evasion they can make to do you harm. It took the magician a hundred and thirty-five years to counteract everything, but he did it. Just tell the jinn to bore a hole in the wall to let you out, and to hold back the Queen's guards, if you're worried about too close a contact with the servants of the rod." She rubbed her eyes, and Hasan could see that she had bruises.

"Now let me rest my brittle bones in sleep; the beating the Queen gave me disheartens me somewhat."

"Yes, my mother," Hasan said contritely. He picked up the rod, set the cap on his head, and disappeared.

Five steps from the house he paused. Did the cap really work? Of course it did—yet new doubt assailed him. He needed one more confirmation.

He tiptoed back into the house. Shawahi had left the main room, probably seeking out a couch. He moved about, looking for her.

The rod clattered loudly against a wall. Irritated, he set it down. He couldn't have it giving him away, and it was

hard to keep it clear of obstructions when he couldn't *see* it.
He noted that it resumed visibility the moment his hand left it.

He spied Shawahi lying on a mat, her eyes closed. He
crept beside her, opened his mouth—and saw how tired
and broken she was. She had not deceived him about the
beating; black marks were on her arms and neck, and there
was dirt in her hair where it had rubbed against the ground.

Hasan backed off and left her sleeping. Of course the
cap worked!

Chapter 13. Rescue

The cap worked. He passed the guard at the outer gate of
the palace in the late afternoon sunlight, and the man stared
directly through him. Hasan accidentally scuffed a pebble,
and the guard glanced at it suspiciously and rubbed his eyes.

The great entrance-hall was empty. He almost collided
with a servant in a passage as he found his way to the
throne room. He had to be more careful; invisibility did
not mean he was secure from detection. If the Queen
suspected, she could surround him with her guards so that
he could not get away, then work some devastating
counter-spell.

After several false alarms he located the proper room.
He had to jam his hand against his mouth to stop the cry
that threatened to burst out.

Sana was there, bound to the ladder by her hair, her
clothing tattered and her face swollen and bloody. She
gave evidence of life only by the tears streaking her cheeks
and by her pained sighs. The two children sat silently
under the ladder.

Only a suggestion of the breathtaking beauty of the
bird-maiden remained. Every part of Sana's body was
bruised and red, and blood matted her shredded clothing in
several places. Her eyes were swollen almost shut, and she
was no more elegant at this moment than Shawahi.

Hasan loved her more now than he ever had in Baghdad.

The world became dark before his face and the burning tears of remorse stung his eyes. He was responsible for this! If only he had been more discreet. . . .

When he recovered himself he saw that Sana had fainted from pain. The children were playing on the floor, not understanding the terrible significance of the things that had happened.

No one was near. Hasan removed his cap.

Nasir spied him and cried out, "O our father!"

Hasan immediately became invisible again, afraid that the shout had been heard. Sana's eyes opened . . . but nobody was in sight except the children.

"O our father!" Nasir repeated.

Sana's face crumpled. "O Hasan, Hasan," she cried, "my heart breaks and my vitals are rent asunder for grief that ever I wronged you!" Then, to the boys: "What brings your father to mind at such time?"

They could not answer, except to point where there was nothing. Sana wept. "I wish I could see what you see! How I curse myself now for my foolishness and coldness to my husband. How happy I was in Baghdad with Hasan and his dear mother. If only I had never learned that he had saved my feather-suit!"

Hasan had been about to reveal himself, but now he paused.

Sana's tears ran down and wetted the floor. She had no hand free to wipe them away, and the flies buzzed and settled on her wherever they chose. "I thought I could not be happy unless I returned to Wak," she said. "And once I had my suit, the wind took my fancy and I forgot my husband and flew across the sea. Then my father the King burned my suit so that I could not stray again, and I could not return to my love, though I sorely wanted to. Would I had died on that day!"

Hasan could no longer contain himself. He took the cap from his head and stood before her.

Sana saw him and let out a scream that resounded throughout the palace. "Hasan! How did you come here?"

Her eyes overflowed again, and Hasan wept too, in sympathy.

"O my dear husband!" she said after a moment. "Fate has had its course and the pen has written what was ordained when Time began; so the blessing of Allah be upon you, go and hide wherever you came from, lest my sister discover you and murder us all!"

"O my lady and princess," Hasan returned. "I have undertaken many adventures to come here, and either I will deliver you from this torment and carry you and my children back to my country despite the nose of your wicked sister, or I shall die." He reached for her bonds.

Sana smiled, and a little of her splendor returned, but she shook her head in negation. "O my love, it is far far from the power of any except Allah Almighty to deliver me from this. Do not touch me. Save yourself and go your way and do not cast yourself into destruction, for my sister has conquering hosts none may withstand. Even if you brought me out of here and set foot beyond the city, how could we escape from the Isles and the perils of the neighboring lands? You must have seen the wonders and dangers of the road when you came here. Not even the jinn are safe. So do not add to my care by sacrificing yourself in a futile cause; save your life and leave me to my fate."

"By your life, O light of my eyes, I will not leave this place without you!" He made again to free her, but found the cords tight.

"O foolish man! You don't know what you're saying. No one can escape from these realms against the will of the Queen, though he has control over all the tribes of the jinn!"

"O lady of fair ones! I *have* control over—" He stopped. He had left the rod at Shawahi's house!

"Hasan!" But her gaze was beyond him. Someone was coming!

He jammed the cap on his head and was hidden from sight as the Queen stalked in. "O wanton, what man were you talking to?"

Sana concealed her amazement at Hasan's disappearance. "Who is with me that I could talk to, except these children?"

Angry, Nur al-Huda raised her whip and struck. Hasan lurched forward—then realized that without the rod he was powerless. One scream from the Queen would bring death upon them all, cap or not.

Helplessly he stood and watched the Queen beat Sana senseless again.

"Take her to a small cell," Nur al-Huda rapped. "I don't want to listen to her stupid self-pity any more." She strode out.

The servant-girls loosed Sana's bonds and worked her hair free of the ladder. Now that the Queen was out of sight, they were quite gentle.

"It's a shame to have this happen," one said. "She shouldn't have married a commoner, but still—"

"The Queen is jealous of her beauty and favor with the King," the other said in a conspiratorial tone.

"And that she should bear two fine sons by a handsome man, while the Queen is still a maid!"

They carried Sana to another chamber and set her down, binding her hands and feet but not putting her on the ladder again. One of them led Nasir and Mansur over, while Hasan followed quietly.

Sana revived and gazed about her blankly. "I thought I saw—" Then she remembered, and said no more. The servants, seeing her awake, made her as comfortable as they dared and departed.

Hasan removed his cap. Sana smiled, relieved that he had not been a figment of her delirium. "O my husband, none of this would have happened if I had not rebelled against you and left home without your permission. A woman never knows a man's worth until she loses him!"

"You weren't at fault," Hasan said, but he felt a warm glow. "I shouldn't have neglected you so carelessly. But now Allah has granted me the power to rescue you. Tell me—do you want to return to your father's home, in the hope he will have mercy upon you, or will you come with me to Baghdad again?''

"I have done evil, O my love—but if Allah reunites us, I will never again leave you or disagree with you. No, never!'' But as soon as she said it, she was weeping again. "Go away, Hasan. You don't know the perils of this land. You can't help me now!''

The palace girls heard her and came to the chamber, but Hasan was not in sight.

"Damn the Queen!" one exclaimed. "She shouldn't torture her own sister this way."

"There's nothing we can do," her companion replied. "If we even give her a drink of water, our heads will roll in the morning. We'll just have to leave her here for the night."

Night! Hasan's heart leapt as the girls went out. Soon it would be dark. *Then* he could lead his family out safely.

He sat beside her and told Sana of his adventures, while the shadows intensified. When the palace was dark and quiet he untied her hands and feet and kissed her between the eyes and embraced her . . . very gently.

"How long we have longed for reunion," he said, stroking her hair while she sobbed in relief. "Are we asleep or awake?" Then he set her on her feet and cautioned her to silence. He put on his cap—it seemed to make no difference, in the dark—and picked up Nasir while she carried Mansur.

The throne room was empty. They moved through it in silence, still afraid of discovery, though the entire palace seemed to be unattended. A single guard stood in the entrance hall, leaning against a stone column, and that was all.

Hasan whispered another word of caution and squared his cap. One guard was sufficient to ruin everything, if he could not be efficiently subdued. Hasan had no weapon, but did have a length of the cord used to bind Sana. A loop of that around the guard's neck—

A lamp flickered in the alcove beside the sentry. Hasan

was pleased to observe no shadow behind himself. He was still invisible. He approached the guard, raised the cord between his two hands—

The guard emitted a great snort. Hasan backed off, afraid the man had discovered him. He waited, poised. The guard snorted again, but did not move. His head rested against the column and his hands fell slackly. Hasan studied him with suspicion.

A minute passed.

The guard was asleep! Fully armed and standing—but snorting fitfully against the wall! Hasan hastened back to Sana and gave instructions. Then, while he stood alertly beside the unalert guard, glad that no violence was necessary after all, she and the boys tiptoed past.

No guard stood at the front gate. The one assigned to this post had retired, apparently, and locked up for the night.

Hasan came up short. "There is no majesty and there is no might except in Allah, the Glorious, the Great!" he swore. He beat one hand against the other in frustration. "O dispeller of hopes! I thought of everything but this! now none of us can escape the palace!"

Sana wept with disappointment. "Now there is nothing we can do but kill ourselves and thus escape this awful trap. Otherwise we will all be terribly tortured tomorrow."

But as they stood before the gate exclaiming in distress, a voice called from the other side.

"Hasan of Bassorah!"

Amazed, he did not dare to answer. Had the Queen discovered them already?

"I will not open to you or your wife unless you promise to obey my command!" the voice continued.

Sana clutched him, speechless with terror, and Hasan himself was tempted to run back into the palace. Someone or *something* certainly had found them out.

"What's the matter with you?" the voice persisted querulously. "Do you lack the courtesy to answer a poor old woman?"

"Shawahi!" Hasan cried, weak with relief. "O mistress

of Calamities, we promise to do whatever you bid. Only hurry and open the door before the guard wakes and comes upon us.''

A dry laugh. ''Who do you think cast the spell of sleep over that guard and all the servants too?''

The gate clanked and swung open. Shawahi was there, riding astride an enormous jar of red crockery with a rope of palm-fiber about its neck. It was suspended in mid-air and quivered like a colt.

Shawahi cackled at their astonishment. ''O my children, I know forty modes of magic, by the least of which I could make this city into a dashing sea, swollen with clashing billows, and ensorcel each damsel within to a fish and each man to a crab, and all before dawn!''

''But why didn't you do that before?'' Hasan asked her.

The old woman looked abashed. ''The Queen has counterspells, and I'm long out of practice.''

Hasan did not pursue the issue. He realized that few illusions were permitted the aged. Perhaps Shawahi had been a potent sorceress in the flush of her youth—but only minor spells were available to her today.

''What is the promise you demanded for opening the gate?'' he inquired, closing it carefully behind them.

''You must swear to take me with you, and not leave me to the vengeance of that whorish harlot the Queen. Whatever happens to you shall happen to me; if you do not escape, I shall perish with you. I would never survive the torments of that abominable woman, that tribadist, that—''

Sana embraced her. ''O yes, my mother. You shall come with us. We know how wonderful you are.''

''Follow me!'' Shawahi shouted, giving her magical steed a slap with the rein.

The jar bucked and dropped to the ground, depositing her in a heap. She cursed and kicked at it, but her mount was lifeless.

''That spell was guaranteed for a full day's normal use!'' she complained.

Hasan suppressed a smile and helped her to her feet. ''It

may have spoiled, in all the years you stored it," he said.
"Let me get my rod and we'll have all the magic we need."

Shawahi scrambled to the jar and reached inside. "Why do you think I came after you?" She drew out the rod. "Take off that cap so I can give it to you!"

He kept forgetting that he was invisible. He rectified the matter and accepted the rod. "Let's remove ourselves a space before we experiment."

In the morning, weary but far from the city, they camped at the foot of a mighty chasm. Sheer rock rose vertically two hundred feet or more, and the walls curved in and out so that it was impossible to sight along the length of the path.

"The Queen won't find us here!" Shawahi announced with satisfaction.

"Bring out your rod, Hasan."

He obliged, wishing she had phrased that request a little differently. He held it in his hands for a moment, studying the intricate workmanship and the seven complex patterns engraved along its length. Now that the time had come, he was distinctly nervous. What were the words he was supposed to say?

"Come *on*, lad. We have very little time."

Shamed by Shawahi's rebuke, Hasan lifted the rod and struck it against the earth. "Ho, you servants of these names, appear to me and acquaint me with your conditions!"

The earth shook and cracked open, and sulphurous billows of smoke roiled up. Had he said the proper words?

The air cleared. Seven enormous ifrits stood before him, their feet as big as Shawahi's jar and their heads reaching high into the air. As one, they dropped to their knees and kissed the ground. "Here we are at your service, O our lord and ruler. What is your command? One word from you, and we will dry up the seas and remove mountains from their places!"

Hasan clutched the rod tightly and somehow held his

ground. "Who are you and what are your races and tribes
and clans?"

They kissed the earth again and spoke with one voice,
so that the echoes reverberated throughout the canyon.
"We are seven kings, each ruling over seven tribes of the
jinn of all types, and numerous lesser orders, flyers, and
divers, dwellers in mountains and wastes and valleys and
haunters of the seas. So bid us do whatever you will, for we
are your servants and slaves, and whoever possesses this
rod has dominion over all our necks, and we owe him
obedience."

Much of this passed Hasan by, though he got its import,
largely because the rolling echoes confused the multiple
sound of their speech and left him struggling for the
meaning.

"How about showing me your tribes and hosts?"

"O our lord, if we did that, we would be afraid for your
safety, for the name of our hosts is legion and they come in
divers forms and fashions and figures. Some are without
heads and others without bodies, while still others are in
the likeness of ravening beasts. There is no room here for
them all, and—"

They spoke in septuple unison, and he still could hardly
understand them. He had a bright idea. "Do any of you
have in your tribe a firedrake named Dahnash?"

"Be he ifrit, jinn or demon?"

"Ifrit. A flying one."

They consulted reverberantly. "O master, we have seven
hundred and fifteen flying firedrakes named Dahnash."

"Seven hun—!" Hasan tried again. "The one I want
did service for the Shaykh Abu al-Ruwaysh several months
ago."

They consulted again. "Master, only six flying ifrits
named Dahnash have done service for the Black Shaykh in
the past year."

"This one has an abominable sense of humor—"

One king struck his head with his fist—a blow that
would have pulverized a mortal. "You desire *that* Dahnash?"

"Well, I know him," Hasan said, wondering whether it was such a good idea after all. "If you could turn him over to me for the duration, so I wouldn't have to bother you with little things . . . Well, you could go home, or whatever it is you do in your off hours, until—"

"Fair enough, Master!"

A clap of thunder deafened his ears. The seven enormous kings were gone, and in their place:

"Dahnash bin Faktash reporting as directed," the single ifrit said. Then it looked again. "O *brother!*"

Hasan smiled. This was his ifrit, all right.

Shawahi took Sana's arm. "Come, my daughter. I know some ancient medicines that will heal your injuries in no time. Leave this business to Hasan." They departed with the children, although Nasir looked as though he would rather have stayed to talk with the ifrit. Hasan dreaded to think what mannerisms the boy might pick up from such exposure.

He got down to business. "I am now the owner of this rod of power over the jinn," he said.

"Let me see that, mortal," Dahnash said respectfully.

Hasan handed it over, then abruptly wondered what he had done. The ifrit smiled. "Alas, the power of such command is not granted to such as me," he said. "This rod is marvelously well counterspelled. Anyway, it would lead to a paradox, because I'm already under the indirect command of the rod."

"Paradox?"

"You wouldn't understand. What other information do you require from me?"

Hasan took back the rod and studied its design. "I'm having a little trouble discovering the extent of this talisman's usefulness. When I asked to see all the tribes it commanded, they gave me some—"

"That is easily explained, mortal. The rod is designed most carefully to give the owner absolute power over the jinn, and to protect him from the consequences of its use.

Believe me, mortal, you *need* such protection! So the kings couldn't show you their legions.''

"I don't understand."

"It figures." Dahnash tried again. "Let's say you gave the order and they obeyed. Then you took one look at the horrendous shapes of their minions and went mad from the vision. What use would the rod be to you then?"

Hasan got the point. No wonder it had taken so long to fashion the implement. It had to guard against human stupidity and inhuman ingenuity. But for that, he would already have blundered twice: once in looking upon the mind-destroying jinn, and once by giving the rod to Dahnash. "Then I can never look upon them all?"

"You could direct them to appear in alternate shapes, such as dancing girls, or eunuchs, depending upon your taste."

"Suppose I just tell the kings to carry us all back to Baghdad?"

"Null program, mortal."

"Why not? They're strong enough, aren't they?"

"Certainly—but they happen to be bound by the covenant of Solomon, son of David, which prohibits them from bearing the sons of Adam upon their backs. It's all part of the rod's defensive configuration."

"But you carried me on your back."

"I was operating as an independent agent. Now you have my services through the command of the rod, which means the covenant applies. Matter of Demonical Precedent, bin-Bishr vs. al-Khawwas, Pleistocene period."

Hasan shook his head in bewilderment. "This all seems very complicated."

"Naturally—to *you*."

"Well, what *can* these ifrits do for me?"

"O mortal, they can do many things. They can advise, they can fight, they can bring you all manner of riches and banquets, they can foretell the future. There is a variety of ifrit for every purpose."

Hasan brightened. "Well suppose I ask them to predict how I'm going to get back to Baghdad?"

"Negative, mortal."

"But you said—"

"Law of exclusion of self applies."

"What are you talking about?"

Dahnash laughed in his most insulting manner. "Haven't you heard the one about the barber? He bleeds every citizen in the village who doesn't bleed himself. So does the barber bleed himself or doesn't he?"

Hasan stared at him. The ifrit sighed. "Take my word for it, mortal—an ifrit can't predict the future when he is himself to be the agent of that future."

The more he talked with this insolent spirit, the more confused he became. "All right. Can you give me any advice on how to get home?"

"Certainly. What made you think I couldn't?"

"Do it, then."

"Make the kings harness you horses of the jinn, that can carry you and your company to your own country."

Now he was getting somewhere. He avoided inquiring why jinn-horses could carry people when the jinn themselves couldn't. "How long will that take?"

"Well, it's a seven year journey by foot, but the horses can make it in less than a year. You'll have to endure terrible perils and hardships and horrors and all the usual, and traverse thirsty valleys and frightful wastes and horrible mountains without number—"

This was beginning to sound familiar. "Can we get safely off Wak, at least?"

"We cannot promise you that, mortal."

"Are you telling me the jinn have no power against common mortals?"

Dahnash looked nettled. "It isn't as though we operate in a vacuum, you know. We—"

"Vacuum?"

"Never mind, mortal. The point is, the rulers of Wak have powerful counteracting magic. For one thing, when one of their weapons strikes one of us, that ifrit is permanently put out of commission in his present form. Those amazon armies are the worst of all. They—''

Now Hasan understood why Shawahi had not been concerned about their journey through the Land of the Jinn, when the amazons were marching. But now, of course, it was a different matter, since their party was on the side of the jinn and the amazons were the enemy.

"Can you bring us the horses, or do I have to summon the kings again?"

"I can handle it, mortal." And Dahnash struck the ground with his foot and dropped into the gulf that opened under him. "Classy exit, no?" His voice said as the ground closed. In a little while he reappeared leading a fine black horse, saddled and bridled.

Hasan checked the animal while the ifrit went for another. A pair of saddle bags hung from the bow, with a leathern bottle of water in one pocket and an ample supply of human food in the other. Good—it was tempting to order the ifrit to bring them a sumptuous repast complete with servants, right here in the canyon, but it was essential to get as far away from the Queen as possible. He realized that the rod was not an automatic solution to all his problems; it was merely a tool that gave him a fighting chance against the might of Wak.

Dahnash returned with a second horse, similarly provisioned, and Hasan rounded up his party. Sana looked much better; the old woman had done a fine job of restoration and medication. He wondered whether the ifrits could recommend additional remedies, but decided to leave well enough alone.

The third horse arrived. Hasan mounted the first, taking Nasir before him, while Sana took Mansur on the second. Shawahi brought up the rear.

"Dahnash," Hasan said, "You can go now—but come as soon as I call you, in case I need you again."

"I can hardly wait," the ifrit replied sourly, and whirled into nothing.

Chapter 14. Battle

Hasan urged his steed, and it began to run with a strong, easy stride. The others followed, faster and faster, until the wind sang past their ears and tore at their clothing.

They were on their way.

All day they fared on the tireless horses, riding through the steep mountains and misty valleys, past leaning palms and giant flowers and jungle-thick vegetation. This was the richest country he had ever seen. The horses seemed to know the way, and their only delay was the need to give Sana periodic rests.

Just before evening a black object appeared far ahead, like a tremendous column of smoke twisting skyward. Hasan's muscles tensed. He recited portions of the Koran and Holy Writ and prayed to Allah for safety from the malice of the Queen. But the thing was *ahead* of them, and he did not dare delay their escape by turning aside.

It grew plainer as they approached. It was an ifrit of monstrous size, with a head like a huge dome and tusks like grapnels and jaws like a city street and nostrils like ewers and ears like leather bags and a mouth like a cave and teeth like pillars of stone and hands like giant forks and legs like masts. Its head was in the high clouds and its feet plowed the bowels of the earth.

Hasan held up the rod, ready to summon the seven kings, for he was certain this creature was not of their number. If the Queen had conjured it to head him off—

But the giant bowed and kissed the ground before him. "O Hasan of Bassorah, have no fear of me. I am the chief of the dwellers in this land of the jinn. I am a Moslem, and not many here are of my faith. I have heard of you and of your coming; when I learned how disgracefully the Queen of the mortals of Wak had treated you, I became distressed at this place of magic and terror, and I decided to leave it forever and dwell in some other region, far from man and jinni and void of inhabitants, so that I might live there alone and worship Allah in peace until my fate ran out. Let me accompany you and be your guide until you depart from Wak. I will not appear except at night, and in this manner you can cover much greater distance and insure your safety."

When Hasan heard this he rejoiced. "Allah reward you well, O noble ifrit! Lead on."

And the towering spirit flew ahead and guided them, a glowing pillar of smoke in the night, so that they accomplished a full day's journey when they would otherwise have had to stop for the night. They talked and laughed among themselves, no longer weary, pleased at their deliverance and sure of success.

In the morning they stopped and took food and water from the saddlebags and refreshed themselves. The world looked very good, and Hasan was especially pleased to see how well Sana was doing.

Ahead thrust the mighty conic mountain of the marid that had so alarmed Hasan during the approach to the Queen's city. This time he saw it from the south side, and the landscape amazed him.

They were on the slant of a verdant mountain pass. Close at hand the green jungle vegetation was solid and teeming with life—but it soon fell away to a wasteland of black ash and jagged rock. Ridges of dark material were formed into roughly circular patterns, concave within, as though the land were an ocean caught in the act of splashing. There was no life at all in this area, and somber wisps of smoke hung over the cauldrons and gulleys. Beyond, the land ascended into the slope of the major cone, a monstrous and sinister mass.

To one side, miles away but made close by the scope of this calamitous landscape, stood the temple Shawahi had spoken of. It was a terraced mound of stone, built tier upon tier to form a wide low pyramid with elaborate arches and decorations lining every level. In the center rose a pointed dome not unlike that of the Caliph's palace in Baghdad. But if the dome were of similar size—and while distance made certainty impossible, Hasan thought it was—the temple itself was many times the size of any structure in Harun al-Rashid's empire. It dwarfed the dome completely.

How many centuries had it taken to fashion this temple? Or had the labor been done by the jinn? He started to ask Shawahi, but her attention was elsewhere.

Behind them appeared an ugly dust cloud that walled the horizon along the ridge of the hill as far as the eye could see and darkened the day. When Hasan saw this he turned pale, not even having to conjecture what kind of host could raise a cloud of dust even in the moist jungle.

A frightful crying and clamor struck their ears. "O my son," Shawahi said, "this is the army of Wak, that has overtaken us in spite of our haste. The Queen will soon lay violent hands upon us."

"What can we do, O my mother?"

"Summon the kings of the jinn. This time they will have to fight, and we must pray that their power can prevail against that of the Queen."

Hasan struck the earth with the rod. The ground broke open and the seven kings rose up to stand before him again.

"Can you stop the army of Wak?" Hasan asked them.

Giant heads turned to contemplate the pursuing clouds. "Master, we can try. But the forces of Wak are the most powerful array on earth, and our magic is as nothing against this. The Queen has potent counterspells. We shall have to fight them hand-to-hand."

"Is there any way we can escape without doing battle?"

"No, master."

Hasan sighed. "Meet them, then. Turn them back if you can, but kill them if you must. I commit the matter to your hands."

"Master we shall have to summon our entire horde. You must go far up the mountain, so that the sight of our minions does not harm you and you are safe from the carnage of battle. We know you are right and the Queen is wrong, and this gives us strength—but the conflict will be cruel."

"I understand. We'll go to the temple there."

"No!" cried Shawahi. "All the records of the empire are there, and the priests are loyal to the Queen. The moment we set foot in it, we'll be in her power."

Hasan turned his eyes dubiously toward the cone. "There?"

The giant ifrit who had guided them appeared. "O mortal, do not go near that mountain. I am the chief of all the jinn of this land, excepting only those of the seven kings," he paused to nod at the standing royalty, who returned the gesture with aloof courtesy, "but I have no power *there*."

"I don't understand," Hasan said. He wished he didn't have to repeat himself so frequently.

"The kings govern forty-nine jinnish tribes of the world," Shawahi explained, "while the chief has authority over the local spirits. But the mountain is the home of Magma the Marid."

"I think you told me that before." Hasan didn't see why that should be so significant.

"A single marid has more power than all the creatures of the Land of the Jinn," the chief said.

"And all our kingdoms too," the kings added.

"*And* the forces of Wak," Shawahi said.

Hasan looked at the cone with dubious respect. "All that in one little mountain?"

They nodded gravely.

"Well then. Why don't we ask Magma for help?"

The kings stood around and shuffled their feet like small boys, and the chief averted his face. Even Shawahi seemed to be at a loss for words.

Hasan had a suspicion he was being stupid again, and it made him angry. "All right! Kings, go set up for your battle. I'll have Dahnash bring me progress reports." They vanished. "Chief, if you want to help, you can set up a personal guard for the women and children so they don't get hurt in case there's a breakthrough." The chief vanished. "Dahnash!" The ifrit appeared.

"A regular little Caesar," Dahnash remarked.

Hasan drew him to one side. "What's the situation with the marid of the mountain?"

Dahnash looked at the cone and edged away. "Well—"

"You were the one who told me all about marids. How they sink ships in the sea and blow away cities with a single breath. Now tell me about this Magma."

"Mortal, maybe we'd better move away a space while I explain. No sense asking for trouble."

Hasan restrained his impatience and got his party moving toward a mountain overlooking both the temple and the cone, and commanding a good view of the black plain between them where the kings were already conjuring legions into existence. He was at a loss to comprehend this reluctance on the part of the ifrits, who should have little to fear from one of their own number.

"I told you about the five orders of—" Dahnash began.

"Yes, I'm sure I did. Well, the power of the groups varies exponentially, not arithmetically, and—"

"I wish you'd speak intelligibly."

"Yes, mortal," Dahnash said, frustrated. "Every group has its specialized members, and likewise the marids, but they're not so limited. Most of them used to be gods, you know. In modern times they've been demoted—but they still pack plenty of power.

"Now take Magma. He's mostly a fire spirit, now—but he can tear up the air and shake the ground something awful, too. If he were closer to the ocean, he could make a wave that would swamp every city on the coast. I mean, he's got *power*, straight, raw elemental force. He doesn't have to pussyfoot with inertia and centrifugal dynamics the way ifrits do. He—"

"Get to the point," Hasan snapped, still unwilling to admit that he couldn't follow many of the ifrit's terms. "Why can't we ask him to help us stop the Queen?"

Dahnash stared. "Ask him to—mortal, are you out of your mind?"

Hasan waited in stony silence.

"Mortal, I've been trying to tell you. Magma is a *marid*. That's no ordinary spook. He doesn't *help* people."

"Well, what *does* he do?"

"He sleeps."

Hasan took a deep breath. "I mean, when he isn't sleeping?"

"He destroys."

He was getting nowhere. "You're telling me we'd better leave Magma strictly alone?"

"I'm telling you."

"Then I'd better appoint someone to see that he remains undisturbed. The battle may get a little noisy, and it's right on his flank." He looked at Dahnash.

The ifrit retreated. "Now hold on, mortal. I wouldn't dare go near—why, he'd abolish me like so much imagination if—"

The chief appeared. "I will watch him, Hasan. Magma knows me. I can probably look down his chimney every so often without bothering him."

"Good. You keep me informed on Magma, and Dahnash will keep track of the progress of the battle." Hasan had discovered that he rather liked the feeling of generalship.

By noon Queen Nur al-Huda's troops were ranked upon the plain. They were, Hasan noted with surprise, largely male; only the Queen's elite personal guard was amazon. Columns marched over the hill in seemingly endless array and spread like flowing water across the field, armor and weapons glittering. But once in place, the battle array opened in a monstrous flower, the bright shields countless petals, spears like—

A flower! Hasan had marveled more than once at the circular rafflesias, like bowls three feet or more in diameter, containing a central cluster of stamens. They were beautiful from a distance—but perfumed like offal.

One of these was growing on the plain. Five circular phalanxes, each massed with hundreds of footmen, clustered around the outside: enormous leaves. A circular column represented the outer rim of the blossom, and a smaller circle was the inner disk. In the center stood clusters of men with spears held high, the stamens: twenty-five groups in the largest circle, fifteen more in the medium circle, five in the smallest.

The amazons stood in the very center, protecting the Queen.

The army of the seven kings, in contrast, was a motley horde. From this distance it was impossible to distinguish individual features, but Hasan could tell that the majority of the creatures was grotesquely unhuman. Some were small, like warty toads and hairy spiders; others were enormous like warty rhinoceroses and hairy ghouls; the remainder was similarly repulsive but less describable.

The ifrit organization had no beauty. There seemed to be no discipline, no unifying pattern.

It seemed so wrong to be on the ugly side. Hasan felt guilty, and he knew that Sana, standing beside him in silence, felt it too, for she turned away and entered the tent the ifrits had provided. Mansur, the younger boy, went with her, but Nasir stayed outside to gaze round-eyed at the preparations.

"We'll tear up that stinking flower soon enough," Shawahi said with grim anticipation, and Nasir clapped his little hands and grinned.

Dahnash appeared. "They are sounding the charge!" He vanished.

There in the ravaged landscape the ravage of battle began. The clotted mobs of the ifrit army charged upon the living flower. Hasan saw the outer leaves sway as though ruffled by a cosmic breeze, then bend and dissolve into individual contests. He heard the clash of weapon upon claw and spear upon shell.

Dahnash appeared. "Enemy units engaged," he announced. "Aggressor casualties heavy; ours moderate."

"Wait!" Hasan yelled before the ifrit left again. "I can't follow all that. Isn't there some way I can see the battle for myself?"

"Mortal, it isn't safe. One of our own dogfaces might snap you up accidentally."

"Couldn't I wear the cap and ride the back of one of the chief's ifrits? No one would know I was near, and the covenant doesn't apply to his subjects, does it?"

Dahnash remained doubtful. "The flak is pretty heavy . . ."

"Let me do it!" Shawahi said. "I haven't got so long to live anyway, and I'm an expert military observer. Give me the cap."

Hasan agreed reluctantly. He wanted to see the action himself, but Shawahi was right. She could learn a lot more in a short time than he could. He handed her the cap.

She selected a flying ifrit and was off. Hasan noticed that all of the ifrit remained in sight, though the old woman was totally invisible. Apparently there were limits to what contact with the cap-wearer would do. A small object disappeared, but not a second individual.

Another thought came. He had missed the obvious again! Why not—

"It wouldn't work," Dahnash said, "The chief's ifrits are bound to their homeland. They couldn't carry you home."

The outer leaves of the flower pattern were locked in turmoil. It was impossible to tell from here who was winning or even what was happening. Was war always as confused as this?

The chief appeared. "Magma is sleeping restlessly," he reported. "I'm afraid the noise of the battle is irritating him."

"Can't be helped. We can't withdraw now." Secretly, Hasan hoped the marid would wake. He wanted to see what would happen. But he also knew that this was a foolish desire. He was getting blasé about magic, and that could be a fatal attitude.

Shawahi's ifrit came in for a landing. "What carnage!" the old woman exclaimed when she appeared, not at all put out. "Our champions are locked in deadly combat with theirs. Heads are flying from shoulders, trunks are falling, blood is flowing in rills, and arms and legs are floating about disconnected. Beautiful!''

''I want to see!'' Nasir cried.

''But who is winning?''

She thought for a moment. She evidently hadn't considered the matter. ''I think we have the advantage,'' she said uncertainly. ''It's rather confused in the melee. . . .'' Then her face lighted. ''But you should see those jinn spout flames from their nostrils! That engagement is a—''

''A real scorcher,'' Dahnash said as he appeared. He was gone again.

Nasir jumped up and down. ''I want to see! I want to see!'' Hasan decided the boy would never have made a Buddhist.

All afternoon the conflict raged. Gradually the lovely flower on the battlefield broke down, as first the leaves withered and then the outer circles of the blossom dissolved. But the ranks of the jinn were thinning also, and Hasan knew the issue wasn't settled yet.

At dusk the two hosts drew apart, and at either end of the field the flickering campfires blazed. It was beautiful— but the night breeze also brought the stench of gore. Dim light flickered as well from the smoke above the mountain. Magma was rolling about, perhaps annoyed by the odor.

The more distant mountains ringed the entire scene in somber evening splendor. How could such an ugly situation be so beautiful!

The seven kings reported to Hasan. ''They will not withstand us more than three days, for we had the better of them today. We took two thousand prisoners and slew numbers beyond counting.''

''How many did we lose?'' Hasan inquired.

The kings looked embarrassed. ''About the same number—but our army is larger than theirs.''

Hasan was reassured, but Shawahi shook her head and said nothing.

The kings returned to their troops. The chief's guard set

up sentries, while the majority slept on the ground. This surprised Hasan; he hadn't realized that ifrits had to sleep too, though it made sense when he thought about it. He retired to the tent and spent a night in Sana's arms like none he remembered.

The lovely flower bloomed again in the morning. Once more the ifrit horde engulfed it like a savage carnivore—anomalous as the concept might be—and drenched the plain with blood. Again Magma the Marid tumbled fretfully in his sleep, puffs of steam and ash signaling his displeasure as surely as the chief's steady reports. But Dahnash brought indications of a favorable outcome, and Hasan, rested and vigorous for the first time in days, was happy to agree.

Only Shawahi was worried. "The amazons have not yet fought," was all she would say when pressed.

By afternoon the melee on the plain was subsiding. Scattered battles now showed where before there had been a continuous press, and corpses, human and bestial, were piled in grotesque mounds. The sides appeared to be evenly matched. It looked as though there would be few survivors of either army on the plain tomorrow.

But the chief's warriors had not even tasted battle. Many of them were disappointed, but this was where Hasan saw their real advantage. If any of the Queen's troops survived, he could wipe them out with a single foray from these reserves. There had been no need to worry.

Sana came out to watch the finish, smiling. "I'm glad it's over," she said. "I don't like fighting—and Huda *is* my sister. She'll go home now."

"After everything she's done to you, you can say that?"

"Well, she's Queen, and has to do what she feels is right."

Hasan looked at the bruises that still showed on Sana's face. Yet he knew that forgiveness was in her nature. How could she have married him, otherwise, after the way he kidnapped her?

Something else occurred to him. "You say she'll go home now? Surely she is dead."

"No, my husband. See—her circle is not on the field tonight, yet it was unbroken today."

She was right. Where had the Queen gone? Had she fled to her city before the battle ended, to escape capture?

The seven kings reported again at dusk. "Master, the field is ours," they said. "We have routed the army of Wak, though its mistress escaped us."

"So I noticed. Well," Hasan said, thinking of his wife's sentiments, "she can't do us much harm by herself. All we want is to be left in peace to finish our journey. Tomorrow we'll—"

He was interrupted by an outcry from the defensive perimeter. Helmets and shields were advancing upon their camp in a compact mass.

"The amazons," Shawahi said. "She held them in reserve."

Suddenly the hillside was lighted with the flame from the mouths of fighting jinn. Hasan saw the enemy: armored ranks of women, the same troops he had accompanied to Wak. Now they were fighting, not traveling—and he was on the other side.

More ifrits appeared as the chief rallied his reserves. There were many of them—great animal shapes and creatures never seen by man. But though their rush seemed irresistible, the surging helmets of the amazon task force swept steadily closer.

Hasan hastily ordered sword and armor and put them on. Shawahi, veteran that she was, had never removed hers. Sana donned a tunic of finely woven metal, and even the two little boys were happily outfitted for defense. Hasan summoned Dahnash and set him to guard Sana and the children.

"But my love—where are you going?" Sana cried, holding him.

"I have to fight."

"Fight here. We shall all be lost if you die out there in battle."

Hasan was not afraid. He had always thought he would be terrified to face professional troops in combat, but the violence of the past few days and his present responsibilities as commander of the jinn and protector of his family inured him to the qualms he might once have had. He was ready to fight, to overcome, to kill—and if need be, to die in defense of those he loved.

Assured of this, he found he had the courage to stay back from the thick of the fray and stand guard over his family. There was nothing he had to prove.

The clamor and carnage pushed closer. Peering out into the night, he could see the potent arm of the enemy line reaching toward the center of the camp, cutting down everything that sought to block its advance. Shawahi was right: the amazons were a different breed from ordinary troops. The Queen had neatly engaged and neutralized the forces available through the rod before making her serious attack. Just when he had thought the battle was over, the real encounter had begun.

He saw a single amazon, pert and agile in her armor, attack a ponderous animal-ifrit twice her height. Its gleaming dagger-teeth clashed together like steel striking stone. The ifrit rose upon two muscular hind legs, balancing against its mighty tail, small front legs almost hidden beneath its monstrous head. Red eyes flared, mottled gray jaws gaped. It roared with the sound of fifty wounded tigers and brought its open mouth down upon the woman, an orifice big enough to engulf half her body at a single bite.

Her sword flashed. The tip of the creature's tongue dropped meatily to the ground. Her spear flew out and buried itself in the ifrit's distended belly. She leapt upon it as it toppled and kicked with metal-pointed toes at its eyes. One of its awful hind feet came up to rake her body. Her armor tore free as though it were paper, and blood flowed

richly down her side, but she slit its throat and went
without pause on to the next opponent.

No man Hasan had seen could have done it—yet this
was just a single encounter among hundreds. And he was
on the other side.

One after the other, the ifrits came and died. Some were
like outsized rhinoceroses, carrying curved wraparound
bone-armor on their heads many feet across, with three
devastating horns rising from the center. Others were low
and flat, armored all over but with sharp spikes sticking
out in rows and with crushing maces on their tails. Still
others were giant birds, with stubby wings and beaks that
crunched off arms and feet with every peck. But terrible as
these forms were, most of the quivering bodies mounding
the area immediately before the tent were ifrit bodies, and
most of the agonized dying screams gurgled from ifrit
throats.

They screamed a long time, for though the ifrits could
be destroyed, they could not die completely.

Breakthrough! And the battle had come to Hasan. He
clapped the cap upon his head so that the enemy could not
see him and laid about him with the sword. Shawahi took
her place beside him on the left, adroitly keeping her
sword away from the seemingly empty space he occupied,
and Dahnash took the right. Now there were no sour
comments from the former and no smart remarks from the
latter. The moment of decision was upon them all, and
the odds, truly revealed at last, were against them.

Shawahi was old, but she had trained these amazons for
many years. She was still a match for any one of the
savage women. Dahnash, for all his impertinence, turned
out to know how to use a sword when he had to. He was
not a firebreather—smoke rings were all he could muster—
but he was sharp-eyed and agile and he loved his present
shape well.

Hasan had had good training under the tutelage of Eldest, back on Serendip. He knew how to cover his vulnerable spots and wait for proper opportunity before wasting a

stroke. With the enormous advantage of invisibility, he should have had easy success.

It was not to be. The amazon facing him was tall, strong and skillful. Though her helmet covered most of her hair and part of her face, her features were as delicate and fair as those of a girl just blossoming into womanhood. Though her shield and armor covered all of her torso, Hasan could tell by the necessary shaping of it and the movements of her body that she had a figure to drive a rutting sultan out of his mind.

It was very difficult to strike such a woman with malicious intent.

Hasan hesitated, but she did not. She blinked once, prettily, when he put the cap on; then she whirled her sword in a dazzling arc before her, trying to cut him down before he could move. He parried with his shield, almost thrown off balance by the genuine force of the blow—but immediately she was slashing from the opposite side, forcing him to parry again and thus reveal his position. These girls must have been warned about the cap, and the uncertain nature of the illumination evened the odds considerably. Hasan could see her only vaguely when the torches of ifrit breath subsided, and her movements were so quick and her attack so swift and sure that he had no opportunity to avoid her blows and thus hide himself effectively.

Her sword clanged against his helmet, knocking it askew and smashing the metal against one ear. He was unhurt, and the cap, by a miracle, remained in position, but this forced him to realize the danger he was in. The next swing might contact with his neck instead, and sever his invisible head. She knew his size and defensive posture, and could and would destroy him by aiming her slashes where his vulnerable parts ought to be.

"Hurry, Hasan!" Shawahi cried. She knew what was holding him back, and how fatal this hesitancy could be. The gap was widening; more amazons were filling in behind the first three. A giant corpse was in view: Hasan recognized it as the immortal remains of one of the kings, honoring his commitment to the rod to the end—defunct at the hands of these same feminine warriors. This was no game he was playing, no polite demurral of the fairer sex; this was his life and the lives of his loved ones, and the figure before him was not a damsel but his enemy.

Hasan threw himself flat on the ground, knowing that what would be suicidal when visible was a winning tactic now. The amazon almost lost her footing as her sword whistled through empty space. He caught her shapely toe and yanked. The metal slipper came off and she fell. He kneeled, took his sword in both hands, and smashed the edge across her exposed ankles.

He was sick when her foot flew off—but she gave him no time to think about it. Her body flexed and she was on her knees, her blade slicing into his shoulder. The fine ifrit armor halted it, but not before she gouged a painful chunk from the muscle next to his neck. His shield dropped for an instant as his arm was paralyzed, and the point of her sword jammed into his breastplate. Too low—but had she been able to see him, that blow would have skewered his neck. She was rapidly bleeding to death, but she meant to kill him yet.

Hasan aimed carefully and plunged his sword point through her face.

She fell back, blood spouting horribly as his blade came free—but even then she made no sound, and her two hands came up not to clutch at her own face, but to claw at his. One razor nail ripped into the corner of his mouth; then, at last she died.

Three more amazons were descending upon him. Their expressions showed both berserk fury and alert awareness of his position and advantage. Only death would stop them.

He fought barbarously, using his invisibility in whatever manner it could be used. He knew that he was no match for an amazon in fair combat, and that they gave no quarter and outnumbered him. He bashed against them with his shield and kicked at their feet, and when one fell against him he flattened her face with a mailed fist, and when one fell away from him he rammed his spear up under her metal skirt.

Still they came. Hasan fell to the ground, weary and smarting from numerous injuries. Beautiful warriors trod over him, thinking his unseen body a corpse. The tents burst into flame, and he heard the screams of his children.

He scrambled up, finding new strength. Shawahi and Dahnash were still fighting a rearguard action, limned against the flames, but they were beset by crowding amazons. A second scream soared from the flame.

It was Hasan's turn to go berserk. He was never able to remember what he did, nor did he care to try, but two amazons writhed on the ground in agony behind him while he charged through the sheets of flame.

The heat blinded him. "Sana! Nasir! Mansur!"

There was no answer. He stumbled over a body, dropped to the earth beside it, and found that there was still air to breathe next to the ground though the flames raged over his head. He touched the prone figure and felt blood and a female shape. "Sana!"

But it was an amazon, slashed and burned. His own head was burning, and he pawed at it until the blazing cloth fell away. Now he could see that this woman's face was lovely even in the pyre. He recognized the royally born damsel Shawahi had offered him that day the army bathed in the ocean, so long ago. Never again would she charm men with her splendor or laugh amid friendly waves.

Perhaps he had been the one to kill her.

Hard hands grasped him from behind. An animal sound came from his throat as he struggled to free himself, but the grip was huge and tight. "I'm on your side, Hasan," a voice grunted in his ear. "Had you not lost your cap, I would not have found you in time."

It was the chief. They leapt into the air, leaving the flames and the horrors they enveloped below.

"My wife! My children!"

"I carried them to safety," the chief said. "They

screamed when I picked them up, just as you did, but there was no time to reason with them.''

Limp relief washed over him. His family was safe!

''Put me down and fetch Shawahi!'' he said, surprising himself.

''I have already assigned a minion,'' the chief reassured him.

They gathered in a dark gully near the conic mountain. ''This is not safe,'' the chief said, ''but there was very little time. The Queen has won the day.''

Not even Dahnash cared to point out that it was night.

''But what of the seven kings?'' Hasan said.

Four shapes appeared. ''Our brothers are gone,'' the remaining kings said sadly. ''Our troops are vanquished, our magic abolished.''

''I have only what you see here,'' the chief added. No more than a dozen bedraggled ifrits remained.

Hasan made a formal head count. Beside the five mortals, there were the chief, the four kings, Dahnash and the chief's remnant. Hardly more than a score of the thousands who had gone to battle so proudly two days before. But if the Queen's forces had been similarly ravaged—

Torches glimmered in the distance, and there came the sound of marching feet. Dahnash flew into the night.

He was back in a moment. ''She's got a full division left,'' he said. ''I'm glad they don't make female ifrits like that!''

''Take us away from here!'' Hasan said to the chief.

The chief shook his head. ''Hasan, my last flyer broke his wing transporting the old woman, and the kings are forbidden by covenant to carry the sons of Adam. I am the only one who can do it—and though I can take you anywhere, I can carry only one of you at a time, or the two children.''

Hasan exchanged glances with the two women. ''Take the children to my mother in Baghdad. The rest of us will stay and fight.''

''But that will take me many hours, even days if I keep

low enough to maintain their warmth. You cannot hope to withstand the force of Wak and the magic of the Queen without my help.''

"Take them!" Sana cried, tears streaming down her face. She gave each boy a final hug and kiss. Hasan did the same, and so did Shawahi. The chief looked at them sadly, then took a boy under each arm. They screamed and cried, not wanting to go, but Hasan signaled the ifrit away and put his arms around each woman.

Sana sobbed openly as the chief disappeared into the sky and the cries of Nasir and Mansur dwindled in the distance. Even Shawahi shed a tear. "Is your mother a gentle woman?" Shawahi inquired.

"She is very like yourself," Hasan said.

Chapter 15. Magma

The marching torches descended the hillside and spread out below. The gully was some distance around the cone, so that the amazons had to cross the plain to reach it. Their torches circled and formed once more into the terrible flower pattern, glowing and swaying in the night, a signal to the world that the Queen had won and would have her revenge. How could he ever have thought it beautiful!

"Why does she pursue us?" Hasan murmured, unable to take his gaze from the menace. "Doesn't she know she would never see us again, if she let us go?"

"You are a handsome man," Shawahi said. "Did you not know?"

Hasan mulled that over in his mind, but could not make sense of it. "How long will it take them to reach us?" he asked Dahnash.

"An hour, mortal—no more."

"How long can we hold them off?"

"A minute," Shawahi said. "I trained those troops. Nor can we flee or hide from the Queen's magic."

"It is in the hands of Allah, then." But somehow he felt that Allah's will was far removed from Wak. It would take a miracle to vanquish the Queen, and Hasan's life deserved no miracle.

If only Uncle Ab or the Black Shaykh were here to advise him! There must be some avenue of escape.

The Shaykh! Hasan still had a pouch of incense to summon him!

"You!" he called to one of the waiting ifrits. "Can you make a fire?"

"Yes, master," the creature said. He shuffled forward—a six-foot lizard with tusks.

"Good boy!" Hasan patted the scaly head. "I am going to sprinkle some powder and say a few words, and I want you to burn it up."

"Yes, master," the ifrit said. This one didn't seem overly bright. Probably it was actually one of the lower orders, a jinn perhaps. But he needed fire, not brains.

He took the perfumed leather pouch and shook a little of the powder into his palm. He flung it away from him—not entirely trusting the firedrake's aim—and sang out "Burn!"

A jet of fire shot from the lizard's mouth, igniting the powder in midair. "Abu al—Ruwaysh!" Hasan shouted.

The Black Shaykh stood before him. "Wake Magma," he said, and vanished.

"But—" But Hasan protested to emptiness.

"Wak is out of his territory," Shawahi said. "I have heard of him. He can't violate his covenant with the old King of the Isles."

Hasan was disappointed. He had hoped the Shaykh could help them. "All I wanted was advice how to save our lives. Just a few words." He paused, nursing his hurt. "Wake Magma?"

Shawahi looked at the smoldering cone, then down to the advancing flower of torches. "Even against her, I hesitate," she said. "But there is no other way. If the Black Shaykh advises it—"

This development did not dismay Hasan unduly. His curiosity about the marid might be satisfied after all. He hoped there would be a spectacular display. "How can we wake him, if all the sounds of battle couldn't?"

"Magma isn't very sound asleep now," Dahnash said. "That battle irritated him so much that any little thing might jog him alert."

"Like a rock down his chimney?" Hasan inquired softly.

"Ho mortal! You said it!"

There was a silence. Dahnash began to look nervous. "Now just a moment—"

"Who else can do it? You're the only flying ifrit left."

Dahnash paced about uncomfortably. "But Magma is a *marid*. If he caught me fooling around his—"

Sana and Shawahi added their stares.

Dahnash was distinctly unhappy. "I suppose I'm under orders."

Sana reached up and kissed him. The days of hope since their escape had done much to restore her beauty. "Too bad they don't make female ifrits like that," Dahnash said, mollified.

Shawahi had already located a sizable stone. "I'll put a noxious spell on this so that it will explode with the foulest of stinks," she said. "That should make him rumble."

"When Magma rumbles, that's a *rumble!*" Dahnash said, recovering some slight enthusiasm. He hefted the stone. "In case I don't. . . ." He shook his head. "Forget it. I don't seem to have any classic final utterance."

He leapt into the air, steadied his burden, and sailed heavily into the night.

Shawahi turned away. "When a mortal dies, his soul lives on unhampered, until he is reborn," she said. "An ifrit has no such escape."

"Is there really any danger?" Hasan asked her, surprised at her tone.

"Magma is a marid, just as Dahnash pointed out."

Hasan had no reply. He watched the great cone and wondered what would develop. They were all so *serious* about it! They seemed to be more concerned with Magma's sleep than their own impending murder at the hands of the Queen. Dahnash had told him about fire and redhot

rock and quivering ground, and he had seen some of the
smoke himself, but this didn't seem sufficient to do more
than annoy the amazon army. What was to prevent them
from shielding their eyes from the fire and walking around
the hot rock? Even if some of them were burned, more than
enough would remain to wipe out the fugitives.

Of course, a large-scale distraction might enable his
party to escape on foot. That must be it.

A tiny speck appeared in the light above the cone. A mote
dropped down. Hasan almost thought he heard a faint
"Ho ho!"

They waited. Nothing happened.

In a few minutes Dahnash reappeared. "I got away!" he
exclaimed, jubilant. "Magma never saw me!"

"Maybe you didn't wake him," Hasan said. Had all the
buildup been for this? "We saw you drop the stone, but
nothing happened."

"I woke him, mortal. His chimney's clogged, so it'll
take him a little while to get going, but I felt him stir when
the pebble hit! What a stench! Any moment now—"

The ground shuddered. "See what I mean? You can tell
he's alive now, if you just listen. When a marid gets mad,
he broadcasts his mad all over the cosmos. Listen."

Hasan listened. He heard nothing. Even the single earth-
shudder had subsided, and there seemed to be no wind or
animal noise of any kind. "I mean with your mind,"
Dahnash said. "You can feel him in your head."

Another pause. "O Hasan!" Sana exclaimed. "I can
hear it!"

Then Hasan began to pick it up. There *was* something—
distant, marginal, almost beyond the range of whatever
sense applied, but immensely powerful. It came clearer as
he concentrated.

A surging liquid reservoir under enormous pressure . . .
churning gases bubbling through liquid rock . . . a long
nasal tunnel reaching up . . . a massive stone plug holding
back the building pressure.

Hasan shook his head. This was ridiculous! Rock was
solid, not liquid, and gas was just another kind of air.

It could not even *move* rock, let alone bubble through it.

"Magma doesn't follow *your* feeble conceptions," Dahnash said. "If he chooses to bubble steam through stone, he bubbles it. If he wants to set brown earth on fire, he sets it. He's got magic no one else can touch. Listen. . . ."

Hasan listened.

Magma seethed and bubbled in molten fury. For centuries he had slept, puffing out his ashy breath during fragmentary dreams, bracing against the warm sides of his liquid burrow as he flopped over for another nap. But recently there had been cacophony beside his mountain, and rivering blood smirched his sacred domicile. His dreams were disturbed, his temper strained. But for the fact that it was a lot of trouble to rouse himself, he would have blasted away the irritation.

Fortunately the disturbance stopped, and he drifted with lesser anger back to sleep. There was no need for—

A deliberate pebble pinked his nostril. Well, it was a minor matter. Then an odor filtered in. . . .

Essence of rafflesia. Magma hesitated sleepily, deciding how much rage he could spare. The mortals of Wak weren't supposed to bother him. He sent up a current to investigate—and discovered that his nose was largely clogged.

If there was anything the marid of the mountain couldn't abide, it was confinement. The pebble was forgotten as he generated pressure. One sneeze would—

The obstruction held. Magma's sneeze reverberated the length of the chimney and bubbled uncomfortably back through his main chamber. Now his stomach was upset—and he still couldn't breathe.

He belched. The stupendous volume of gas shot upward, blasting against the confining plug . . . and turned aside to bathe him in its nausea again. He choked.

Magma was fully awake at last. His rage was towering. That a god should suffer such indignity! He prepared to tear loose on the orgy of the millennium.

The gases, under control now, surged and mounted the chimney, carrying volatile metals before them. They pressed against the unyielding plug. Magma gradually increased the force, ramming more and more substance into the chimney. There was nothing on the earth or in it that would resist the marid's concentrated push for long.

Fingers of gas and liquid bored into the plug. Spirals of Magma's deeper substances animated it, searching, probing, drilling, twisting.

He had hold of it now. Magma threw all his titanic primeval energies, the power of which had fashioned the world itself in the old days when he ruled everything, behind the plug.

It blew.

"Cover your eyes!" Shawahi screamed. The ground bucked beneath them.

Hasan clapped his hands to his face, but the blast of light seemed to cut right through them and outline the top of the cone in fire, shooting brilliant fury high into the air.

From Magma's throat came a thunderous roar of triumph. A thick column of incandescent debris shot up, spreading into boiling clouds which flashed now white, now black. The mass of smoke took the shape of the most monstrous ifrit Hasan had ever seen.

No ifrit, that. It was the marid.

Magma roared again, a deafening detonation. Hasan covered his ears, but the sound could no more be stopped than the light, and his ears continued to ring. How could there be more sound from the mountain when the marid had already escaped?

Another roar. They came every few minutes now, and Hasan realized that Magma had only begun to show his strength.

Morning came. Hours had passed, seeming like minutes while they cowered in the gully listening to Magma's wrath. There was no sign of the Queen's army.

Even as the day brightened, the air filled with choking sulphurous fumes. A dense cloud of smoke rolled over,

turning the day to night again. The blasts came louder, and
the ground shook steadily.

Then there was a stillness.

"Is it over?" Hasan inquired hopefully.

Shawahi and Dahnash stared at him. "Over? Magma is
a *marid*."

As though that explained everything. "Well maybe we'd
better move on before the Queen finds us."

"Don't worry about the Queen. She'll be busy enough
with Magma," Shawahi said, smiling to herself.

They began their trek, however, away from the mountain. The rumbles began again as they did so. "He's
spotted them," Dahnash said.

"But why should he go after them, when *we* did it?"

"I framed them," Shawahi said.

An impenetrable swirl of smoke obscured the cone, and
lightning flashed from that cloud into the surrounding air.
Hot ash rained down upon them, making immediate cover
necessary. Hasan was surprised to discover that the parti-
cles, though white with heat, could be brushed off quickly
from the skin without extreme effect. The party was able
to proceed through the strange storm by holding bundles of
large leaves overhead.

A wind came up, gentle at first, but rapidly increasing
to violence. Dust blew into the eyes, nose and mouth. The
world tasted of whirling ashes.

They were in the jungle now, blindly charging through
trees and trailing vines. Wild beasts swarmed about them,
but paid no attention to the human party. Even tigers and
pythons were intent only upon escape. Hasan would have
marveled at this unusual camaraderie of living things if he
hadn't had other problems to take his attention.

The explosions resumed, louder than ever. Larger fragments fell from the sky, some the size of human heads.

They traveled desperate miles, but neither noise nor
smoke seemed to diminish. The sound of Magma became
a sustained roar, deafening the world with its power. Light

ash covered every leaf of the jungle trees and carpeted the ground.

At last they could travel no more. Sana was sobbing and gasping for breath, her face grimed with dust, and Shawahi wasn't much better off. Even the ifrits seemed morose and tired.

Magma's cloud had formed into a pine tree many miles high, the last time Hasan had glimpsed it. He hoped the tree would not come crashing in their direction. All they could do was wait, tired and hungry and afraid.

"I *think* we're far enough away," Shawahi said.

All night Magma vented his fury into the sky. The trees of the forest shriveled and burned, and when the morning came the sun appeared only as a distant bloody ball behind a curtain of sickly yellow.

They ate what they could stomach, drank from the water bags the ifrits were still able to provide, and slept. There was nothing else to do, though the roiling dreams of the marid clothed their slumber in nightmare. Would they ever see a normal world again?

On the third day the earth jumped again with a cataclysmic blast. Hasan was thrown to the ground, head spinning again with the violence of both external and internal rage. He tried to cover Sana, waiting for the hot fragments to smash into the ground, killing whom they would. Magma had multiplied his power manyfold . . .

Nothing happened.

A stiff wind lifted the smoke and haze to reveal the devastated jungle. Ash was inches deep over everything, and not a creature moved.

But Hasan's mind was empty. Magma was gone.

By mutual consent they traveled back to the mountain. The distance which had seemed interminable through the raining stone now became short. In hours they were back.

Hasan looked upon the scene, hardly crediting it. The cone was gone; the neighboring temple was gone; even the plain upon which the ifrits had battled the Queen's army

was gone, and the protective gully. All that remained was
a giant circular valley, a cauldron more than two thousand
paces across, wisps of fog hovering above it. Waves of
heat still emanated. "Magma did—*this?*"

Shawahi nodded. "He sleeps again—but he isn't gone.
A marid is never gone." She stared wistfully at the place
the temple had occupied. "All the records and artifacts of
the Wak empire were there," she murmured. "Magma
destroyed everything. I wonder if it was not too great a
price to pay for the safety of three fugitives."

Hasan didn't know what to say. He felt painfully guilty
about his overeager, ignorant desire to see the marid
wake. True, the Queen had been a terror—but she was
undoubtedly a capable ruler. How could he equate the
success of his quest with the destruction of an empire?

They turned away and began to organize for the journey
to Arabia. The four kings provided food and horses and a
magnificent tent for the party to relax in before undertaking the hardships of travel.

But others had survived the holocaust. The scouting
ifrits brought in no less a person than Queen Nur al-Huda
and several of her chief officers. They were dizzy and
bemused, but her magic had saved them from death. They
were all that was left of the magnificent amazon army.

The kings brought Hasan a throne of alabaster inlaid
with jewels and pearls so that he could sit in judgment.
They brought another of ivory plaited with glittering gold
threads for the princess Manar al-Sana, and a third for
Shawahi Zat al-Dawahi. There, near the brink of the disaster wrought by the marid of the mountain, the three awaited
the prisoners.

The Queen was pinioned at the elbows and fettered at
the feet, but her imperious beauty had not deserted her.
She wore a flexible jacket of python skin, and did not
look at all ashamed for the damage resulting from her
intractable attitude.

Shawahi was overcome by rage. Hasan had thought she
was mellowing toward the Queen, now that the battle was

over, but he had underestimated the wrath of a woman who had been betrayed.

"O harlot, O tyrant," Shawahi screeched from her throne. "Your recompense for your despicable deeds which have demolished the accomplishment of an empire shall be to be bound to the tails of two mares who have been denied water until their thirst is burning and who are released in sight of water; and two bitches starved for a week shall be released to follow you and rend your skin. After that your flesh shall be cut off and fed to them piece by piece. How could you treat your own sister with such infamy, O strumpet, knowing that she was lawfully married in the sight of Allah, which these two worship? Women were not created except for men and to give them pleasure!"

Hasan looked at Sana, but her eyes were tightly closed. "Put these captives to the sword," he said.

Shawahi agreed vehemently. "Slay them all! Do not spare a single one!" She seemed to have forgotten her earlier laments about the demise of an empire. Slaying the Queen would hardly bring it back.

Sana opened her eyes and spoke to the Queen. "O my sister, what has come upon us? How can you be conquered and captive in your own country?"

"This is a mighty matter, sister," Nur al-Huda replied, while Hasan listened in wonder. "But it is true: this merchantman has gotten the mastery of us and all our realm. His army defeated ours." The Queen was making no apologies for her defeat.

"But he did it only by means of his cap and rod," Sana protested.

"True—but it was a fair encounter. I am in his power now and will accept his decision. My only regret is that there was ever misunderstanding between princesses of Wak."

Sana turned on Hasan. "What are you doing to my sister? What has she done to you to deserve punishment at your hands?"

"She tortured you. For that a thousand deaths are too little."

"But she had reason for everything she did. Wak does not recognize pagan marriage, nor is a princess allowed to take up with a commoner. But you—you have set my father's heart on fire for the loss of me. What will happen to him if he loses my sister also?"

Hasan looked at Shawahi in bewilderment. "She is young; she has a foolishly soft heart," the old woman said. "Isn't that the way you like her?"

"But the Queen—"

"What does it matter to you? If you want sternness of character, marry the Queen. You can do that now, you know, for you are the first to have conquered her. On the other hand, if you want Sana—"

Hasan bowed to the inevitable. It was easier to get along with women of any age if he didn't try too hard to make them fit man's logic. "It's your decision," he told his wife. "Do whatever you will."

She clapped her hands happily. "Release my sister and the other captives."

The ifrit kings looked as frustrated as Hasan felt, and Dahnash turned his back. But Sana jumped off her throne, ran to Nur al-Huda and embraced her tearfully.

"O my sister," said the Queen, "forgive me for the malice with which I treated you."

Hasan was reminded uncomfortably of his own early encounter with Bahram the Persian. Bahram had beaten him and treated him miserably, but pleaded for forgiveness when the situation had altered. He had trusted the man . . . and thereby learned a terrible lesson.

Yet this decision had also led to his discovery of the palace at Serendip, his meeting with the delightful sisters there, and his marriage to Sana herself. He would not change it now if it were in his power to do so.

Was it possible that Sana's foolish forgiveness of her treacherous and calculating sister would also lead to better things? Whatever was fated, Shawahi was right: Sana's beauty had won him, but it was her innocence that held

him. Even the princesses of Serendip knew the meaning of
vengeance—but not Sana.

Hasan stood, walked to the brink of Magma's chasm,
and drew out the magic rod. Fate could no longer justify his
possession of it. He broke it across his knee and threw the
pieces into the chasm.

"You have given us our freedom," the four kings said.
Then each in turn bowed formally to him and disappeared.
The horses and supplies remained, and he knew he had
done the right thing. It was the time for generosity.

He dismissed the ifrits of the chief, and trod wearily to
the main tent. He was suddenly lonely.

But not for long. Sana joined him presently, and all the
ravages of Magma's wrath faded to insignificance amid the
delight she brought.

Next morning Queen Nur al-Huda came to him and
kissed him with all the distant warmth she could muster.
"My sister has told me all about you, Hasan. I know now
that whatever your birth, you are an honorable man and a
worthy husband to her. I'm sorry that I ever stood between
you or caused you trouble in any way." And much as he
had thought he hated this woman, he felt reluctant tears of
gratitude come to his eyes. Sana was not the only soft-
hearted one.

What was it Shawahi had said about the Queen? That
she would not let them go in peace . . . because he was a
handsome man? Was it possible that she was not so different from her younger sister, after all? Her strange acceptance of defeat. . . .

Shawahi came. Nur al-Huda turned to her. "O my
venerable mother, I am deprived of all my troops, and no
one can train new ones as well as you. Will you return
with me and govern my armies again?"

The old woman huffed herself up angrily. "Return with
you? I—" Then she paused, looked at Hasan, looked at
the Queen, and seemed indefinably to regain the stature
Hasan had observed the first time he met her. Shawahi had

been powerful then, but had somehow become ineffective when deprived of her position. All that fell away now. "I think I'd better."

Make that three softhearts, Hasan thought. The Queen was really stronger than all of them, and had prevailed.

The Queen embraced Sana once more while Hasan felt strange sorrow at this parting of the two loveliest women in the world. Too bad it was forbidden to marry sisters. . . .

Then the Queen and her party rode south, and it was over. Never again would he have adventures to match these.

But Sana was beside him, radiant and enchanting, and it was all worthwhile. There were so many dear friends to meet again, and they would visit them all on the return: the King of the Land of Camphor, the Black Shaykh and his four elderly disciples, Uncle Ab, and of course the seven princesses of Serendip. His heart cheered as he thought of Rose, and he was eager to proceed.

"One minute, mortal."

It was Dahnash. "I'm on my own time now, mortal, so you know it means something," the ifrit said. "I just wanted you to know I've had a change of heart." He paused.

"One man *is* worth a thousand jinn," Dahnash said seriously. "Provided it is the right man." He smiled, saluted, and faded from view.

As the whirling dustcloud formed, Hasan was sure he heard a distinct "Ho ho!"

Author's Note

My thesis for my B.A. in Creative Writing from God-dard College in 1956 was the longest in the history of the college: 95,000 words. It was in fact my first novel, *The Unstilled World*. That novel was never published, though I later reworked a portion of it and that portion became *Sos the Rope*. Nine years later, in 1965, I completed my second, *Chthon*, which was my first to be published. In 1966 I completed the collaborative *Pretender*, though that did not see mass-market publication until 1985. My fourth novel, completed in January 1967, was *Hasan*. I think that of all the novels I have written, this one has the most remarkable history. So let's go back to the beginning.

My father read to me when I was young, and it is a tradition I carried on, reading to my daughter Penny. One of the things he introduced me to in that manner was *The Arabian Nights*—the tales of a Thousand Nights and a Night. Today few people seem to be conversant with these fabulous stories, and that's too bad. So I sought a way to bring them to the attention of contemporary readers. I obtained three translations of the *Nights*, one of them running to sixteen volumes, and read as much of them as I could, seeking the ideal Tale to adapt. I decided on "Hasan and the Bird Maiden," a phenomenal story that I had in all three versions. There were differences between them, of course; for example, the Mardrus & Mathers translation, which was rendered from Arabic to French, and from French to English, contains a scene wherein a giant breaks wind so forcefully as to blow Hasan across the landscape, but it also abridges the tale, ending it at the point Hasan finds the Bird Maiden again and borrows a flying suit for himself and flies home with her and the children. The most complete version is that presented in the Richard Burton translation, while those who prefer "family reading" should go to the Lane translation. All versions of all the Tales are well worth reading by those who like this sort of thing, as I do; I merely chose the particular Tale I deemed best for my purpose.

But I also operated on another level. I recognized in this tale a historic basis. The pattern of some genuine exploration was there, masked by the magic explanations provided by those who did not understand or did not believe the truth. What was the truth? I researched to discover it—and believe I succeeded. Hasan traveled to Ceylon—now called Sri Lanka, but which I called Serendip, because of the story of the Three Princes of Serendip, who always found what they weren't looking for. In the 18th century Horace Walpole used this story to coin the word "serendipity." Serendip was the original name for Ceylon. The descriptions in the Tale of Hasan align with this interpretation. Hasan later traveled through India to Tibet, where a wise man sent him along to China (Cathay), then down the coast to Indo-China, Malay, and finally Sumatra. Thus the map of Hasan's travels is the map of Asia, and the differing cultures he encountered are those of that continent. I had to do quite a bit of research and adjustment, for if the distances described in the original Tale are taken literally, the Isle of Wak would be fifty thousand miles from Asia

Minor (twice the circumference of the Earth) yet would
speak the same language. Now the medieval Arab empire
was large, but not *that* large. In the year 800 A.D. it
extended all the way from southern France to western
India, embracing more territory than the Roman empire at
its height. But Asia is larger than that, and more diversi-
fied. I compromised on a journey of about twelve thousand
miles, and tried to present the real languages and cultures
he would have encountered.

I found an interesting sidelight when I researched the
Arab empire. The conquest of the region was explosive
and generally gentle by historic standards. By that I mean
that the conquerors did not practice genocide or leave
mountains of severed heads in their wake, though there
was plenty of blood shed. They did not impose their
culture on their subjects; instead they avidly absorbed all
that their civilized subjects had to offer. They became
civilized, and made a kind of golden age that put to shame
the relatively barbaric domain of Charlemagne in the west.
The "Dark Age" was dark only in Europe. The subject
peoples of the Arab world saw the advantage in conform-
ing to the ways of the conquerors, and adopted them by
stages. This is where I see the lesson of history: what is
truly most important to people—their politics, their religion, or their language? The subject peoples of Asia,
Africa and Europe gave up first their politics, so that must
have been least important. Then they yielded their reli-
gions, adopting Allah. Finally they let go their several
languages in favor of the language of Arabia. I suspect that
they, like most of the world's people, had invested most
effort in their language, and least in their political structures. People value what they have worked for. Yet today
we are in an arms race that has the potential to destroy the
world, in the name of politics, while our language and
literacy decline.

And so, in the course of my research, I became immersed in the world of Harun al-Rashid of 800 A.D. I
discovered the joys of vicarious travel, and indeed it seemed

that I had been there. I had researched the Babylonian
Empire of 539 B.C. for *Pretender*, and found it fascinating;
this was even more so. Such experiences were gradually
leading me from fantasy to archaeology. Certainly I am
interested in the future—but the future is guesswork, while
the past is available via research. In many cases my novels
have impact on my outlook, and *Hasan* had more than
most. I remain glad I did it, even though it really isn't my
novel; it's merely a retelling of a tale more than a thousand
years old. I hope that my readers have shared some mea-
sure of my enthusiasm for it.

So how did *Hasan* fare on the market? I couldn't even
find a publisher for it! Larry Ashmead at Doubleday heard
of the project and asked to see it, but rejected it on the
basis of a sample as inadequate. (The sample was the
beginning up to Hasan's first encounter with Rose.)
Ballantine rejected it as not fitting within its ambience. I
kept trying, through 1967 and 1968: Ace, Lancer, Avon,
Fawcett, McGraw Hill, Harper & Row, Viking, F&SF
(sample chapters), Dell. Hardcovers, paperbacks, maga-
zines—all rejects. Avon responded in a fast three weeks,
while Lancer took almost five months and only returned
the manuscript after two queries.

Seeing that I was making no headway the conventional
way, I tried an unconventional approach. I believed in my
novel, and felt that the assorted editors were demonstrating
bad judgment. I'm not partial to the judgment of review-
ers, either, who sometimes strike me as failed writers
looking for failures in what others manage to get published. But if the one type didn't appreciate my novel,
maybe the other type would. I wrote to the fan reviewer,
Richard Delap, and asked whether he would be willing to
review my novel unpublished. Flattered, he agreed, and I
sent him the carbon. He did publish his review, in a
fanzine, and the review was favorable. Delap found fault
with several of my published novels, but *Hasan* he really
liked, and I don't think this was because of the circum-
stance. It was just his kind of novel. Meanwhile, Walker

was in the process of rejecting it, giving a progress report in two months but returning it in four. That made twelve bounces.

Came a letter from Ted White. Now my relations with White had been mixed, and I feared something I had said somewhere was setting him off. But no, he had seen the review and wanted to see the novel. The top copy wasn't back from Walker yet, so I sent him the carbon May 10, 1969. May 29 came his phone call: he was buying it for *Fantastic Stories*. He could only pay a penny a word, and by his estimate that 87,000 word novel was only 70,000 words long, so that meant $700. No, he wasn't trying to cheat me; Ted White was on a tight budget and honestly didn't know how to calculate wordage. When he ran the novel, in two installments, its full length manifested, and squeezed out part of his own editorial. I was so glad to get the sale, after a dozen rejections, that I wasn't about to quibble about wordage. The novel was well received by the readers, and I remember the entire matter with pleasure. My persistence and innovative marketing, combined with Richard Delap's willingness to give fair coverage to an unpublished manuscript, and Ted White's acumen in seeking material combined to put this novel in print and make a special kind of history, and I don't believe that any of us ever regretted this. I don't think any other novel has been sold that way, before or since. Though I have my differences with Ted White, I regard him as a better writer than credited, and an excellent editor. I speak as one who has had some terrible editing on occasion. As for Richard Delap, I still take issue with many of his reviews, but somehow I don't bear him the malice I reserve for other reviewers.

Meanwhile I continued to try the book market, and picked up rejections from Pocket Books' new Trident imprint and Macmillan. Then I had word from my collaborator on two other novels, Robert Margroff, that he had been to a convention and met the editor at Berkely, who was eager for material. So I sent *Hasan* there—and in just seventeen days had an acceptance. Berkely paid an advance of $1500 against six percent royalties. That money, coming as it did at the time some others were instituting a blacklist against me and when I had assumed the expense of moving to a larger house to accommodate our expanding family, in late 1969, was a godsend; it eased a financial bind. Thus *Hasan* helped my finances as well as my mind. So now I had fourteen rejections and two sales. Then Berkely changed editors, and the new editor, in the manner of that kind, wouldn't publish what the old one had bought. *Hasan* was written off—that is, they simply never published it. I kept the money, but had no book publication.

Enter fandom again. Both Richard Delap and Ted White had been basically creatures of fandom, though of course Ted had become professional. Another fan, Robert Reginald, wrote to ask me for biographical and bibliographical information, as he was compiling a book about genre authors. I obliged, not expecting much; these projects come and go and few amount to anything spectacular. But this one *was* spectacular; in 1970 he published *Stella Nova* under the imprint "Unicorn & Son" and it was a phenomenal production, with information on several hundred genre writers. Later he set up his own publishing house, Borgo Press, devoted mainly to a series of critical booklets on genre authors. He expressed interest in *Hasan*, which he had read in the magazine version. So I signed a contract with him, and the novel had its third sale, and was published in a nice small-press edition in 1977.

An editor at Dell read that edition and bought it for mass-market publication. That publisher had rejected it, a decade before, but the change of editors can blow fair as well as foul. Fourth sale. It was published in December 1979. Its success was not spectacular, and it was allowed to go out of print. Then in 1984 Tor picked up most of my out-of-print novels, *Hasan* included, for republication under its imprint. Fifth sale. Which I think concludes the most remarkable of my marketing histories: fourteen bounces, five sales, and the first sale the result of a fanzine review of the unsold manuscript. The lesson here, I believe, is never to give up hope. My success, in this and in general, owes as much to determination as to talent.

There is a contemporary Bird Maiden. She is one of my fantasy fans—I happen to have a number of these—who also works with raptors. These are birds of prey: hawks and such. No, no rocs; there don't seem to be many of those around these days. She cares for the injured ones, and when they recover, sends them back to the wild. Naturally I dubbed her the Bird Maiden, and now she even answers to that appelation. And, naturally, at the time I was shaping up this edition of *Hasan*, the Bird Maiden phoned. She was on her way from the American Midwest to Europe, where birds really *are* maidens, to study fantasy there. She didn't know I was working on this novel, and I forgot to mention it; it really was coincidence, if you believe in that phenomenon. Well, I hope she finds her Hasan, too. Or maybe a roc.

Do I plan to do more Arabian Nights Tales adaptations? Originally I was open to that notion, but somewhere in the course of the struggle to get *Hasan* into print my eagerness flagged. I believe I put just as much effort into this novel as I do into those I generate from scratch, and its success has been less than those others. But those who like this type of story need not be concerned; go to the library and check out one of the major translations mentioned here (don't bother with the children's versions) and start reading. It's good stuff.

PIERS ANTHONY

- [ ] 53114-0 ANTHONOLOGY
      53115-9 $3.50
                                    Canada $3.95

- [ ] 53112-4 HASAN
      53113-2 $2.95
                                    Canada $3.50

- [ ] 53108-6 PRETENDER (with Francis Hall) $3.50
      53109-4   Canada $3.95

- [ ] 53116-7 PROSTHO PLUS
      53117-5 $2.95
                                    Canada $3.75

- [ ] 53110-8 RACE AGAINST TIME $2.95
      53111-6   Canada $3.50

- [ ] 53118-3 THE RING (with Robert E. Margroff) $2.95
      53119-1   Canada $3.75

- [ ] 93724-5 SHADE OF THE TREE (Hardcover) $15.95

- [ ] 53120-5 STEPPE $3.50
      53121-3   Canada $4.50

Buy them at your local bookstore or use this handy coupon:
Clip and mail this page with your order

TOR BOOKS—Reader Service Dept.
49 West 24 Street, 9th Floor, New York, N.Y. 10010

Please send me the book(s) I have checked above. I am enclosing
$_____ (please add $1.00 to cover postage and handling).
Send check or money order only—no cash or C.O.D.'s.

Mr./Mrs./Miss _____

Address _____

City _____ State/Zip _____

Please allow six weeks for delivery. Prices subject to change without
notice.

FRED SABERHAGEN

- [ ] 55316-0 BERSERKER BASE (with Anderson, Bryant, Donaldson, Nivens, Willis and Zelazny) (Trade) $6.95
- [ ] 55317-9 Canada $7.95

- [ ] 55320-9 THE BERSERKER WARS $2.95
- [ ] 55321-7 Canada $3.50

- [ ] 48568-9 A CENTURY OF PROGRESS $2.95

- [ ] 48539-5 COILS (with Roger Zelazny) $2.95

- [ ] 48564-6 THE EARTH DESCENDED $2.95

- [ ] 55298-9 THE FIRST BOOK OF SWORDS $2.95
- [ ] 55299-7 Canada $3.50

- [ ] 55305-5 THE SECOND BOOK OF SWORDS $2.95
- [ ] 55306-3 Canada $3.50

- [ ] 55307-1 THE THIRD BOOK OF SWORDS $2.95
- [ ] 55308-X Canada $3.50

Buy them at your local bookstore or use this handy coupon:
Clip and mail this page with your order

TOR BOOKS—Reader Service Dept.
49 W. 24 Street, 9th Floor, New York, NY 10010

Please send me the book(s) I have checked above. I am enclosing
$_____ (please add $1.00 to cover postage and handling).
Send check or money order only—no cash or C.O.D.'s.

Mr./Mrs./Miss _____

Address _____

City _____ State/Zip _____

Please allow six weeks for delivery. Prices subject to change without
notice.

GORDON R. DICKSON

☐	53068-3 53069-1	Hoka! (with Poul Anderson)	$2.95 Canada $3.50
☐	53556-1 53557-X	Sleepwalkers' World	$2.95 Canada $3.50
☐	53564-2 53565-0	The Outposter	$2.95 Canada $3.50
☐	48525-5	Planet Run *with Keith Laumer*	$2.75
☐	48556-5	The Pritcher Mass	$2.75
☐	48576-X	The Man From Earth	$2.95
☐	53562-6 53563-4	The Last Master	$2.95 Canada $3.50
☐	53550-2 53551-0	BEYOND THE DAR AL-HARB	$2.95 Canada $3.50
☐	53558-8 53559-6	SPACE WINNERS	$2.95 Canada $3.50
☐	53552-9 53553-7	STEEL BROTHER	$2.95 Canada $3.50

Buy them at your local bookstore or use this handy coupon:
Clip and mail this page with your order

TOR BOOKS—Reader Service Dept.
49 W. 24 Street, 9th Floor, New York, NY 10010

Please send me the book(s) I have checked above. I am enclosing
$_____ (please add $1.00 to cover postage and handling).
Send check or money order only—no cash or C.O.D.'s.

Mr./Mrs./Miss _____

Address _____

City _____ State/Zip _____

Please allow six weeks for delivery. Prices subject to change without
notice.

CONAN

- [ ] 54238-X   CONAN THE DESTROYER $2.95
  54239-8   Canada $3.50

- [ ] 54228-2   CONAN THE DEFENDER $2.95
  54229-0   Canada $3.50

- [ ] 54225-8   CONAN THE INVINCIBLE $2.95
  54226-6   Canada $3.50

- [ ] 54236-3   CONAN THE MAGNIFICENT $2.95
  54237-1   Canada $3.50

- [ ] 54231-2   CONAN THE UNCONQUERED $2.95
  54232-0   Canada $3.50

- [ ] 54246-0   CONAN THE VICTORIOUS $2.95
  54247-9   Canada $3.50

- [ ] 54248-7   CONAN THE FEARLESS (trade) $6.95
  54249-5   Canada $7.95

- [ ] 54242-8   CONAN THE TRIUMPHANT $2.95
  54243-6   Canada $3.50

- [ ] 54244-4   CONAN THE VALOROUS (trade) $6.95
  54245-2   Canada $7.95

Buy them at your local bookstore or use this handy coupon:
Clip and mail this page with your order

TOR BOOKS—Reader Service Dept.
49 W. 24 Street, 9th Floor, New York, NY 10010

Please send me the book(s) I have checked above. I am enclosing
$_____ (please add $1.00 to cover postage and handling).
Send check or money order only—no cash or C.O.D.'s.

Mr./Mrs./Miss _____

Address _____

City _____ State/Zip _____

Please allow six weeks for delivery. Prices subject to change without
notice.

KEITH LAUMER

☐	54369-6	*The Monitors*	$2.75
	54370-X		Canada $3.25
☐	54373-4	*A Trace of Memory*	$2.95
	54374-2		Canada $3.50
☐	48503-4	*The Breaking Earth*	$2.50
☐	48509-3	*The House in November* and *The Other Sky*	$2.50
☐	54375-0	*Worlds of the Imperium*	$2.75
	54376-1		Canada $3.25
☐	48551-4	*Knight of Delusions*	$2.75
☐	48559-X	*The Infinite Cage*	$2.75
☐	54366-1	*The Glory Game*	$2.75
	54367-X		Canada $3.25
☐	48525-5	*Planet Run*	$2.50
☐	54371-8	*Once There Was a Giant*	$2.50
	54372-6		Canada $2.95

Buy them at your local bookstore or use this handy coupon:
Clip and mail this page with your order

TOR BOOKS—Reader Service Dept.
49 W. 24 Street, 9th Floor, New York, NY 10010

Please send me the book(s) I have checked above. I am enclosing
$_____ (please add $1.00 to cover postage and handling).
Send check or money order only—no cash or C.O.D.'s.

Mr./Mrs./Miss _____

Address _____

City _____ State/Zip _____

Please allow six weeks for delivery. Prices subject to change without notice.

HARRY HARRISON

☐	48505-0	A Transatlantic Tunnel, Hurrah!	$2.50
☐	48540-9	The Jupiter Plague	$2.95
☐	48565-4	Planet of the Damned	$2.95
☐	48557-3	Planet of No Return	$2.75
☐	48031-8	The QE2 Is Missing	$2.95
☐	48554-9	A Rebel in Time	$3.50

Buy them at your local bookstore or use this handy coupon:
Clip and mail this page with your order

TOR BOOKS—Reader Service Dept.
49 W. 24 Street, 9th Floor, New York, NY 10010

Please send me the book(s) I have checked above. I am enclosing
$_____ (please add $1.00 to cover postage and handling).
Send check or money order only—no cash or C.O.D.'s.

Mr./Mrs./Miss _____
Address _____
City _____ State/Zip _____
Please allow six weeks for delivery. Prices subject to change without
notice.